EARLY PRAISE

"Dark and captivating. A fresh and addicting take on the horror genre."

— CANDACE ROBINSON, AUTHOR OF THE *WICKED SOULS* DUOLOGY

"[Braun] writes phenomenal characters who have to deal with dark scenarios as best as they can and she does it so very well. This was a great collection and a perfect place for those who've not read her work to dive in."

— STEVE STRED, AUTHOR OF *MASTODON*

"Theresa Braun brings a fresh, emotive, and genuinely terrifying approach to the horror genre, one which sets her apart as a unique new voice in modern gothic fiction."

— READER'S FAVORITE REVIEW

"The unique combination of seemingly unrelated individual tales forms an eerie and unsettling menagerie of terror sure to entice horror fans."

— BOOK LIFE FOR *PUBLISHERS WEEKLY*

THE BROKEN DARKNESS

THERESA BRAUN

CONTENTS

DEAD OVER HEELS

None of this is his fault, but here we sit at the police station. The cold, white walls are scuffed and dirty. Scrolling mug shots of wanted criminals flash by on a mounted monitor. My hand is clutching Sebastian's, although I'm not sure he's even aware of it after all we've been through.

His eyes are glazed over, his sandy-colored hair both matted and cowlick-y. He wears the circumstantial evidence: a scratched face and a split lower lip. Not to mention, his gray shirt is caked with blood and soaked in sweat.

It's all rather fuzzy, but there's dried blood under my fingernails. I'm pretty sure I'm to blame for everything.

My eyes are already swollen, but all I want to do is cry even more. I rest my head on Sebastian's shoulder and pray he can forgive me. I'm here now. That should count for something.

I guess you could say he's my boyfriend. Early on he told me he didn't want to see anyone else. I didn't either. Even though it's been only about a month, I have to admit I've never felt this way. We're in love. I'd like to think it's even stronger now.

The problem is, I never knew finding the one would be such a double-edged sword.

"Make another candle," my friend Liz, who worked at the Wiccan shop, advised.

"I've already made a shitload of them," I complained.

"One more. Put your all into it."

Maybe it was worth another shot. Magic isn't really an exact science. So, that's what I did. I had nothing to lose, except a few dollars.

I purchased yet another glass tower of wax, this time red, and sprinkled a smattering of herbs and oils onto that bad boy. This time I didn't use *Cunningham's Encyclopedia of Magical Herbs*, but went on good old-fashioned instinct. The scents of dragon's blood and sweet amber mixed with what smelled like dried grass. My hands encircled the concoction, and I offered up a pure intention for true love to finally find me. I'd tried dozens of strategies over the years, everything short of frolicking naked in the forest, raising supplication to the ancient gods.

After I ignited the wick, the thing flared up like a Roman candle. I'm no witch, but considered I might have gotten this one right as the flames jumped to heaven with my desires. It flickered and flamed in my bathtub until it wore itself out.

Sometimes things are out of our control or beyond our understanding. I just needed it to work once. How could that have been too much to ask?

A couple of weeks later, there I was, getting out of my car, feeling hopeful. I had no pretense this date was my soulmate, but his profile and our chats had been promising.

The River House Restaurant, where I'd agreed to meet Sebastian, was near the old Discovery Center: a former schoolhouse and inn renovated as an interactive natural history and science museum. My very first job had been working there in the gift store. I recalled the countless mornings I'd climbed the front porch steps of the large, colonial building—back before the River-walk became so built up and full of bars and restaurants—usually doing my best to shake off the effects of yet another all-night scream fest between my parents. I'd always pass the room with the tarantulas as fast as I could, praying they would never escape and find me down the hall while I was in the middle of struggling to make change. Funny how it all seemed so recent, even though it was over fifteen years ago.

After almost tripping up the creaky stairs to the front door of *The River House*, I took a second to catch my breath. I never could walk like a normal person in heels. If only my mother had given me lessons. Are there lessons for such things?

When I grasped the doorknob, it seemed to be opening at the hands of someone on the other side, but there wasn't anyone there. The teenage hostess, wearing a black pullover and miniskirt, grinned at me as I sat in the waiting area.

Usually the guy arrived before me, wherever we met for the date. However, it was going on fifteen minutes after our sched-uled meeting time. Any number of things could've delayed him, or maybe he'd spied my bumbling in heels and bailed. Some men want the natural vixen, after all. I banished the insecurities, feeling silly.

It was strange to be sitting there in the first place. The hours of online scrolling, skimming through awful profiles, then making small talk and wondering if there would be enough of a connection, had been torture. When the guy wasn't a weirdo, it became a whole different problem. The anxiousness would set in: would he call or text? Would we go out again? It was almost better if I didn't care.

Daring the powers that be to grant my prayers for love had become my mission, at least before Sebastian came along. After a frustrating bout of fruitless interactions, I had actually deleted all of my profiles when he sent me a message… or so I thought.

It seemed easy enough to deactivate both the free and paid subscription sites. I've never been a computer genius, but I could definitely navigate a few clicks. I suppose it could've been human error. My intuition told me 'no' on that score. There must have been a bug in the system. I mean, computer programs have glitches all the time, right? It could have been the candle, but I doubted that. None of the other candles had worked. Why this one?

When I read what he wrote—something like "Hi, you seem like a woman of substance. Noticed you're into spiritual things. This reiki master would like to get to know you."—I was intrigued. Most guys had no idea what reiki was and, if I told them about it, they acted as if they'd rather clean their toilets than hear about healing energy.

I mulled over his message. The fact that there wasn't a pic of him in a dog collar or a lame line that said, "I'll be your prince until you find your king" was so refreshing. I couldn't pass Sebastian up, especially after checking out his mysterious, yet boyish online vibe. We agreed on many of the dating site's personality or preference questions, but there were still some open for discussion, like why he wouldn't choose to kill all the mosquitos on the planet. Was that because he'd never been bitten, or because he thought about the viability of the world's ecosystem?

Snapshots of him were sans an alcoholic drink in hand. He was with sober-looking friends at concerts or festivals. There were no 'hilarious' pics of him next to a blowup doll—actually, not even any shirtless pics—and no grammatical mistakes.

That really turned me on.

We messaged for a few days. It came up in passing that we had both lost parents. His dad had died many years ago, and both my parents were gone. I wasn't ready to share that story yet, but I wondered what other big things we might have in common.

So, there I was, but Sebastian was now almost thirty minutes late. The insecurities poked at me once again.

Several couples had already been seated. I examined my phone for any messages. Nothing. My stomach bottomed out. I was being stood up. My urge to take a break from dating had been justified.

I canvassed the premises, searching for *The River House*'s bar, but when I found the tiny area none of the stools were empty. Thankfully, I remembered I had wine at home. As I looped my purse over my arm and made for the exit, the door swung open, and I recognized Sebastian right away. He wasn't as tall as I thought he'd be, but his angled features looked better in person. He wore crisp, pressed-looking blue jeans and a white button down shirt, rolled at the sleeves.

"You must be Veronica." He slipped his phone into his back pocket and offered his hand.

"That I am."

Why didn't he use that phone to call or text?

I gave his hand a steady grip, but wished it was a crushing

one. My anger and disappointment were making my cheeks warm.

"Sorry I'm late."

He gave me a wink; one that told me he wasn't an expert winker. His slight awkwardness was endearing, although only a minor save in light of his tardiness.

I waited for some explanation, my eyebrows slightly raised.

"Crazy day. Got stuck at work. Then traffic. My phone's almost dead."

Sounds like bullshit if you have to lay it on that thick.

I wasn't going to dignify his excuses with a response. He was lucky I hadn't left yet, and those few extra seconds had apparently made all the difference in trapping me for the moment.

Lucky me.

"Two?" The hostess already clutched a pair of menus.

Sebastian's light brown eyes were outlined by thick lashes and, as he turned to nod and smile at the girl, I found I missed his gaze. I sensed a kind heart in him; that was one of the reasons I decided to go through with the date. A kind heart is hard to find… and, if I'm honest, I'd say I sensed some chemistry, too.

We followed the hostess for only a few steps and were seated at a table in front of the window, overlooking the patrons on the porch, and with the Intracoastal Waterway in the distance. The musty perfume of worn wood paneling and antique furniture blended with the aroma of savory meat and spices escaping from the kitchen.

As soon as we settled into the chairs, the server came for our drink order. He had light eyes, a strong jaw line, and a serious expression. "For the lady?"

"Dirty martini, please."

I'd heard my share of 'dirty' jokes and braced myself.

However, Sebastian just scratched his chin. He was either repressing an innuendo, or had expected me to get a glass of wine.

"How dirty?" The waiter, still serious, put his hands behind his back.

I tried not to laugh. Regular dirty was fine, but that wasn't fun to say. "Extra dirty, please."

Sebastian looked to the server with an approving eye and a sly grin. The waiter kept a straight face, despite the probable fact that this wasn't the first or last time he'd heard the line.

"Do you have Crystal Head vodka?" Sebastian asked.

I'd always thought the skull bottle looked so cool, but had never tasted it. I'd never heard anyone ask for it, either.

"No, sir, I don't believe so," the waiter said.

"Have you had it?"

"Can't say that I have." The response was deadpan.

Sebastian's expression went limp, probably because he'd expected to have better banter with the restaurant staff. "Then Ketel One on the rocks for me, please."

While scanning through the menu and sipping our drinks upon their speedy delivery, we discussed the standard first meeting fare: more details about what we did for a living, where we grew up, and a little bit of what we were looking for in life.

His gaze lowered to my cleavage.

If he's really interested in just a hook up, he could at least be more discreet about it.

Then his eyes lifted, stopping near my neck.

"I *also* like your silver triquetra," Sebastian said, closing the menu.

So you admit you were looking?

I bit the inside of my cheek to stifle a laugh at his ridiculousness. For the moment, he had saved himself by actually recognizing my pendant. Not only did he know what it was called, but he didn't make some obvious reference to the television show *Charmed*, which had made the emblem famous, but somehow cheapened its profound significance.

"Thanks." I grasped the Celtic trinity design with my left hand. "It's my favorite symbol."

"Mine, too. It's ancient and represents so many things."

My heartbeat quickened. "Like protection and magic."

"Exactly. I have a version of it tattooed on my upper arm. Obviously, I can't show it to you right now. You'll just have to take my word for it."

Sebastian's cheeks had long indentations, like extended dimples, when he smiled. I found myself hoping that, if things went well, then one day I'd get a closer look at that tattoo…and the rest of him.

Now I'm the one with impure thoughts. I'm such a hypocrite sometimes.

"I don't have any reason to doubt you," I said.

Actually, I really didn't believe he had the tattoo, but I tried to focus more on flirting than on my cynicism.

The waiter approached, taking a pad from his waist. "What can I get for you?"

"I'll have the lamb stew." I pushed the menu to the edge of the table and stared at Sebastian.

"Prime rib. Medium rare."

"Will that be all?" The server picked up the leather bound folders from the table and from Sebastian's hand.

"Yes, thank you," Sebastian said, looking to me for confirmation which I gave in the form of a smile.

When we were alone again, he continued our conversation. "Your profile indicated something like 'girl-next-door with an edge.' I'm counting on that."

An exact quote. Nice going.

I raised my glass and batted my lashes at him. "Here's to you having an edge as well. Weird is always more interesting."

As long as you don't expect me to go to swing clubs, like that guy with the dog collar. There are *lines to be drawn.*

"Exactly."

We both took a drink.

"I was hoping you'd like to take the Fort Lauderdale ghost tour after dinner. This restaurant's actually on it," he said.

"Oh, yeah?"

My profile indicated I had an interest in the supernatural. Clearly Sebastian was capitalizing on that, but he wasn't aware that I already knew a lot of the neighborhood lore. Back in the day, my Discovery Center co-workers were always spinning new and old yarns.

"What's the story behind this place?" I asked, curious to see if his details matched any of the ones I'd heard.

"I don't really remember exactly—just that the guy who first lived here died young and was a bit of a prankster. He's always turning lights on and off and making the ceiling fan move when it's not on."

"Is that right?" The stories I heard were more ominous, involving poker games gone wrong and jilted lovers, but I didn't want to one-up him on our first date. Being a know-it-all usually killed romance. *Men have fragile egos*, my mom always used to tell me before I knew what that even meant. Missing her was a dull pain that never went away.

"Apparently some of his kids and his wife are ghosts, too: a loving family even in the afterlife." Sebastian put his hands under the table to shake it.

I couldn't help but laugh. "Very funny. I think we can debunk that haunting."

"Ghost hunting lingo. Impressive."

"That's how I suck you in. It's all about the verbiage." I grinned, crossing my arms and resting them on the white tablecloth.

"You've a few other things going for you." His hand inched toward mine, and I tried not to flinch.

My face flushed. "Why, thank you. You're not so bad yourself."

He pulled away and sat up, taking a swig of his vodka.

My attention veered next to us, a forty-something couple holding hands over the table. Their touch lingered, a sign this wasn't their first encounter. She smiled softly at him, her eyes sparkling. I guessed he did the same, since all I saw was the back of his sun-bleached hair. She wore a simple white dress with a sweater draped over her shoulders, and her reddish hair was swept up.

The woman seemed familiar. Had I seen her in an old magazine? Did I come across that hairstyle once while sitting at the salon and thumbing through a lookbook? The more I stared, something about her made me think of my mother. I thought I'd stopped searching for my mom in stranger's faces, hoping she might be out there somewhere.

As I studied the couple, their palpable passion reminded me of the feeling I wanted to finally experience. When I was younger, my dad had chased away all of the boys who were ever interested in me. They had never been good enough for one reason or another, and it didn't seem like my luck had improved much since then.

"You okay?" Sebastian's honey-colored eyes locked with mine.

"I'm sorry. It's just that the woman at the table over there reminds me of my mother."

He followed my gaze and smiled. "She's pretty."

"Isn't she?"

"I don't know what I would've done without my mother," Sebastian said, looking back at me and shaking his head slowly. "She ended up raising me herself. Fortunately, she finally found the right doctor and medications, thanks to the insurance money. She used all the energy she had left to fight to get it. The court gave her a hard time, since she couldn't prove my dad was dead. It took years. He never showed up anywhere, despite the insurance company's investigation. When the payout finally came through, she put some of it aside to send me to law school."

"That's awesome. What happened to your father?" I knew his father was dead, but none of the details.

"I don't know." He shrugged and the corners of his mouth turned downward. "I knew my parents were having tough times. My mom was always sick—she sometimes had seizures—and my dad was exhausted trying to take care of her, even though I helped. But I never thought he'd just not come home one night, especially on Christmas Eve. I was at that age when Santa was such a big deal, and I still… believed. I guess that was the year my childhood died." He swallowed. "I didn't want to open presents. All I wanted was my father."

He's gone through this, too?

My surprise melded into sympathy, then sorrow. This seemed so hard to believe and, glancing away and up at the ceiling, I willed away the welling tears.

"I'm so sorry," I managed.

I didn't want to look like a fool in front of him, but recalling my mother's leaving us was like my very own fresh avalanche of heartbreak. It was hard enough to watch Sebastian talk about his, even though the circumstances were a little different.

Sebastian and his mom seemed to have embraced the possibility that his dad had been killed—maybe hit by a car, or struck down by illness somehow—and I supposed that, even if his body had never been found, accepting he was dead was easier than just never knowing. Of course, I couldn't say I wished my mother had died, but sometimes I wished I'd had that kind of closure, even as much as I hated thinking those things. Was it better to believe the worst, or to give in to the fear that she really was able to abandon me?

She only meant to go out for awhile to check on my grandmother. I watched her pull away in the yellow cab. Later, my father said that wasn't true. He said she hadn't loved us enough. I always speculated about why he'd said that, even though I'd thought it, too. I couldn't understand why she was gone. But the other part of me knew how controlling and self-centered my dad always was. I was too intimidated by him to ever ask questions. Eventually, I guess I just accepted what he said *was* true.

Sebastian was looking at me curiously, and his eyes were glassy. He waved to the waiter for another round of drinks.

I sniffed, cleared my throat, and tried to sound matter-of-fact. "Oddly, my mother didn't come home one Christmas Eve either. My father was an asshole, so I couldn't blame her for leaving. Still, it didn't make things any easier."

"I know what you mean." He wiped his face with the napkin. "Such a strange coincidence."

Maybe it was our shared trauma, or maybe it was a combination of things, but I felt warmth emanate from my heart and spread throughout my chest.

For once, I didn't feel so alone.

"I'm not sure there's such a thing as coincidence," I said. "I know it sounds crazy, and it's kind of a cliché, but I feel like we've always known each other."

I immediately regretted saying that. Being too open on first dates was a recipe for not making it to a second…but I also contemplated the candle for true love and whether or not it had finally delivered. It was way too early to tell, of course. And I was still way too skeptical.

"Yeah, it does feel that way. I don't talk too much about my mother, especially with someone I don't know very well." He flashed his shining white and slightly crooked teeth.

"Well, I go around revealing my deepest psychological issues with everyone who will listen." I flipped my hair as I became distracted again by the couple, still holding hands and hypnotized by each other. "You know, I've been watching that table over there and it seems they've been here a long while."

"I hadn't noticed." Sebastian turned to them. "They don't even have any drinks yet."

"Nope."

A food runner appeared with our meals, placing them before us. Our server appeared, setting down another martini glass and another rocks glass.

"Thanks," Sebastian said.

"How's everything?" the waiter asked.

"Great. Hey, could you send a couple of drinks to that table over there?" Sebastian shot me a wink as he spoke.

"Aw, that's so nice," I said.

The server's mouth fell open. "Sir, who do you mean?"

"The two over there." Sebastian nodded at the couple.

Just then, the pair released their hand-holding, got up, and started toward the door. She adjusted the sweater over her shoulders. He cradled the small of her back, kissed her temple, and they were gone.

"Sir, no one's been sitting there all night."

I could feel my eyes widen.

Sebastian's brow furrowed while he threw back his drink in one gulp. "Um, okay," he mumbled. "Never mind."

Apparently he didn't want to argue with the server, especially since our rapport with him hadn't been all that smooth thus far. I was grateful Sebastian hadn't tempted the guy to add an unordered side of spit to our meal.

There was a long silent pause as the waiter whisked away, then we simultaneously picked up our silverware to attack the food on our plates. I'd had experiences I couldn't explain before, but wasn't sure yet if this was one of them.

"He won't be working here too long." Sebastian chewed a bite.

"You think he's just unobservant?"

"There are a few empty tables in here. It's not like he's over-whelmed. Then again, I didn't even notice the couple come in. Did you?"

I retraced the evening in my mind. "No, I didn't."

Perhaps we were so focused on each other to be aware of anything else. Of course, if I said that out loud, I'd be giving away too many of my feelings.

I need to get a grip on myself.

I had to lighten the mood, since it was swiftly nose diving. Since we had discussed it earlier, the possibility of paranormal phenomenon seemed to hover over my head.

"I think we might already be on the ghost tour," I said.

He chuckled. "Could be. That was freaking crazy."

"Maybe they were the original owners—although it kinda seemed like they were on a date or something."

"Yeah, who the hell knows?"

I tasted the stew, the lamb's marinated juices, with the slightest hint of Worcester sauce, was heavy on my tongue. We needed a change of subject. My attempt was feeble, but well-meaning: "So, do you like scary movies?"

"Who needs scary movies when you can live them?" Sebastian forked a piece of bloody meat into his mouth. He chewed carefully and swallowed. "Maybe I've seen my share of them already."

We managed to recap the run of '80s horror flicks we watched as kids, from Freddy Krueger to Michael Myers to Pinhead. Night had crept upon us and the half-moon shone through the far window.

Sebastian paid the check, and we strolled along the Riverwalk, having missed the nightly ghost tour, not that we needed it anyway. I carried my shoes, after giving up on wobbling in them. We shared our favorite things to do in our free time, and other light topics.

My yawns got more frequent. Eventually, he walked me to my car, which had a white envelope under the wiper.

"Damn, I guess I should've extended my time on the meter," I said.

He yanked the ticket from the windshield. "Let me take care of it."

I thought about whether or not to put my personal information and license plate number into his hands. "You don't have to do that."

"I insist." Sebastian folded it and put it in his pocket. "I was late. It's the least I can do."

Well, he had a point. I allowed myself to trust him.

Then, he stepped closer to me. Since I was on the curb and he was standing in the street, our faces were level. He leaned in to kiss me, as if he had already tasted my lips so many times before. I closed my eyes and relished the meeting of our mouths. When he pulled away, I swayed.

"Goodnight," I said.

"Goodnight."

He watched me key into my vehicle and start the engine.

Because he didn't invite himself over to my place, or try to lure me to his, I knew he thought we had real potential for a relation-ship. I also knew better than to be completely gung-ho about him, though. There was always the chance that he was just playing me… although it didn't feel like it.

The night had ended, but where we were going as a couple had possibilities.

Sebastian and I had been seeing each other for a little over a month when he asked me where I wanted to go to dinner on Christmas Eve, the day that marked thirty days of exclusivity. That spot on the calendar held additional meaning for both of us, each having lost a parent on that date, but now we could celebrate the day as an indication of new beginnings.

We hadn't spoken much about what happened at *The River House* the night we first met, but it had always been in the back of my mind. Eager to know more, I had gone back there on my own a couple of times, but never saw anything. The need to understand dulled a little, but had never left me. It was that—and my romantic sensibilities—that prompted me to tell Sebastian I wanted to return to the scene of our first date. He agreed.

Christmas Eve arrived. We held hands while strolling along the sidewalk. The late December air felt refreshingly crisp, and I hugged Sebastian's arm for warmth. He beamed as we stepped onto the path leading to the restaurant's stairs.

Evergreen branches and white lights wound around the pillars of the porch and the railing leading to the door decked with a Christmas wreath. The scent of pine filled me with unease. If Sebastian had holiday anxiety like I did, he hid it well. I focused on how I always looked forward to receiving his silly text messages or seeing him on our date nights.

Sebastian held the door for me. He hadn't ditched his best behaviors yet, and had even been consistently on time—knock on wood.

He scanned the restaurant before speaking with the hostess, a different teenage girl wearing a black pullover and miniskirt.

"Could we please have *that* table?" Sebastian indicated the same one we had shared a month ago. Apparently he was also a sentimental romantic.

"Sure, no problem." She lifted the menus from their slot and led us to our destination.

"I like your dress," she said, smiling at me.

It was pale blue with a tattoo-like design of hearts and angel wings; I was glad I'd felt brave enough to wear it, even though it was a little outside my normal color palette.

"Thanks," I said, slipping off my red sweater.

Sebastian pulled out the chair for me.

"Thanks, sweetie."

He grinned briefly before sitting down and unfurling the napkin into his lap. "So, here we are again."

"And so we are. Wonder if anything unusual will happen, or if that was a one time thing." I unrolled the silverware and made a ghost with my hand and napkin, flying it over the tablecloth.

He chuckled. "Halloween's over, baby."

"Every day should be Halloween!" That was what I really wanted, but then it wouldn't have been special. "Next year we need to dress up."

"That all depends on what costumes you have in mind."

"Oh, I don't know. Pirates?" I wetted my lips. "You'd make a sexy pirate."

Actually, any period costume would have done. Heck, he'd

even be an adorable vampire, as overdone as that was. It was my personal fallback, but I sure as hell wasn't going to bring that up. I couldn't stand the thought of him mocking my gothic tendencies. There was already enough fodder with my almost all-black wardrobe and dark eyeshadow.

"We'll have to duke it out, since I might want to see you in a zombie nurse getup." He sneered playfully before perusing the menu.

The waitress, clutching someone else's bill, put a finger in the air to signal she'd be back in a minute.

As she passed by, turning away, the lights seemed to dim and the empty table next to us illuminated. It felt like we were on stage and other characters were about to make their entrance for their most significant lines.

The couple we had witnessed weeks prior materialized gradually like the fade in of a movie scene. I couldn't have been sure, but the people sitting in the dining room didn't seem to be the same ones I recalled noticing when we were seated. Their clothing seemed dated: pastels and patterned shirts and dresses. Only tacky tourists would wear anything like it, and we were in a hip part of town. I looked to Sebastian, but he was staring fixedly at the scene. At least that meant he could see it too.

My attention returned to the couple. A candle burned between them. A glass of red wine sat in front of the woman—her auburn hair spilling over her shoulders in waves—and a glass of white in front of her blond companion. He gave her hand a kiss and leaned in to whisper something in her ear. She giggled and touched her nose to his.

Outside, a car squealed on the pavement. Looking out of the window, I spotted a red Mustang. A tall, stocky man burst from the car door, not even bothering to close it. He stomped up the front steps and shoved the door open, flinging it back on its hinges. The restaurant chatter ceased and a few patrons gasped.

"You lying bitch!" he yelled.

I glanced at Sebastian, his mouth open and his expression paralyzed.

"Jack, please," the woman at the table beside ours begged. Her lover moved to stand, and she tugged at his arm. "Don't, Ryan. It'll only make things worse."

It wasn't until she said the name Jack that I realized the man was a younger version of my father. And the woman didn't just resemble my mother—she *was* my mother. I inhaled deeply as I realized my breathing was shallow, almost non-existent. My mind had refused to identify them in order to avoid reliving the pain of losing her. That much was finally sinking in, even though I still didn't know what was going on. How could I be seeing her, and what was my dad doing here? My mind froze for a moment as if time stood still.

Sebastian reached for my hand, his face ashen as he looked at the blond man, whose face was finally turned toward us.

"That's my dad!" he whispered, staring wide-eyed at me.

His dad and my mom knew each other?

I met Sebastian's strained gaze, and my heart pounded, my throat tight. I couldn't speak.

"Let's go." My father's voice was level and firm through gritted teeth.

"I'll come with you, Jack. Just calm down." My mom turned to Ryan and put her hand on his cheek as if she might never feel the warmth of his face against her skin again. "It's okay. It'll all sort itself out. You'll see."

Ryan grabbed her hand as she stood to depart. She glanced back at him with forlorn eyes. "You have to let me go."

Clearly, he was willing to do almost anything to hold on.

"Today, Cheryl." My father's posture stiffened even more, and he clenched his fists at his sides. "*Today*!"

My mother's white dress made her look like an angel as she took flight from her lover's side and faced her husband. He gripped her arm and dragged her from the restaurant and down the stairs. The only other sound was the slamming of the car doors and the tires screeching along the asphalt.

Ryan, appearing absolutely dejected, consumed the rest of his wine. The waiter brought the bill, probably hoping the troubled patron would make an immediate exit. As he paid the check, a flash of what looked like lightning revealed an x-ray of Ryan's face: just the briefest glimmer of his skull.

I tried to process what I'd seen, but the spotlight was already fading on the now vacant table. The ambiance in the dining room resumed its original brightness.

Sebastian caught the server's attention, and she came over to us with a smile.

"A dirty martini and Ketel One on the rocks, please," he said with a slight shake in his voice.

"Certainly, sir."

"And some water, please," I said right as the server turned away.

She nodded, smiled, and left us.

"Did you see that?" he asked.

"What, your drink order?" I sniggered, covering my mouth. It was just like me to resort to humor in the worst of times.

"You know what I mean." He gazed intently into my eyes.

I knew exactly what he meant. "Yeah. Pretty sure that was my dad dragging my mom out of here… but how the hell—?"

Feeling jittery, I squeezed my napkin with one hand. Sebastian still clasped my other. His hand was remarkably firm and steady, a sense that helped tether me to the real world. My sweaty palms began to cool as my body's trembling lessened.

His gaze darted around the room, as if he was trying to find answers hidden between the tables, and he rubbed his forehead with his free hand.

"That means my father and your mother must've had an affair? What are the chances of that?"

It was then I noticed the resemblance between Sebastian and his dad. His hair was darker, but those light brown eyes were alike, and the structure of their faces—those pronounced dimples —were just the same.

"When did they die? I mean, we know when they left us—but when the hell did they *die*?"

My brain started exercising like it had never done before. The Rubik's Cube, the GRE, and my Master's thesis on Jungian psychoanalysis all seemed like simple level capacity in comparison to the riddle at hand.

"I don't have any answers." I squeezed his hand. "Let's just let this sink in."

Sebastian didn't seem to hear me or, if he did, he was ignoring my suggestion. "Did they run away together *that* night?"

"But then why would my mom get in the car?"

"I don't know. Maybe she got out at some point?"

"Maybe." I bit my lip. "All I know is that she didn't come home again."

I distinctly remembered only falling half-asleep, one ear listening for her coming through the front door. As it got later and later, or earlier and earlier, panic and worry set in. It was the night we always celebrated Christmas, yet the presents were still unopened under the tree. The balance of my childhood universe had been destroyed. Where had she gone?

I cleared my throat, trying to push the bitter memory away. "What about your dad?"

"He didn't come home." He wiped his forehead with the napkin. "I don't want to talk about this anymore. Let's order and eat. We can sort it out later."

The thought of eating made my stomach queasy. "Let's eat somewhere else. I need to get outta here."

"Okay." He gulped his Ketel One.

I downed the last sip of my martini and held the glass of ice water in my hand. The chill against my skin had a calming effect.

Sebastian motioned to the waitress for the check. As soon as it came, he inserted his credit card into the folder, and we waited in impatient, awkward silence. His foot tapped under the table, and he watched me with a concerned expression. It wasn't like me to be so quiet.

"Baby, are you okay?"

I wrung the napkin in my lap. "I will be when we get outta here."

The bill came, and I'd never seen Sebastian sign his name so rapidly before slamming the pen back inside the folder. "Let's go."

He held out his hand, waiting for me. As soon as his fingers clasped mine, he turned to go, and charged out of the dining room, pulling me along behind him like the railroad cars tagging after a runaway train. I was so dazed I was grateful he took the wheel, so to speak.

Once we made it outside, Sebastian's shoulders relaxed and his breathing steadied. My heartbeat drummed. We stood there for a few minutes as he put his arm around me. The wind had died down, and I snuggled into the warmth of his chest.

"This is all so insane," he muttered.

The air of unreality hadn't yet cleared around me. All I could do was nod slowly.

We ambled aimlessly along the winding sidewalk, now arm in arm. The serpentine twists of the path under our feet provided me with a welcome hypnotic meditation. Sebastian's stride was a little quicker, though he was trying not to rush me. Was he anxious to put distance between us and *The River House*?

A piercing shriek split the air. We picked up our pace through the trees and shrubs that lined the sidewalk. Veering in a straight line toward the sound had us cutting across the paved walkway. My heels teetered in the grass.

A red Mustang was parked in the street.

It can't be.

I broke into a sweat, wondering what would unfold. I had trouble standing, confused by whether or not I was in the reality of the present or had slipped into the past. I was a kid again, feeling a parental altercation brewing. Here I was, crouching on the metaphorical stairs while waiting to hang onto their every word. Except this time, I wasn't a child and there were no stairs to hide behind.

"No, Jack!" my mom screamed from the car.

Even after all these years, I recognized her voice at once. The car door opened, and my father's broad figure emerged. I could see her try to grab the back of his polo shirt, but he ripped himself free.

Sebastian and I crept closer to the scene as if a vortex of emotional turmoil sucked us in. The tension stiffened my body once my feet stopped. We were a two person audience standing right in front of an invisible stage.

Ryan wandered unaware on the path along the Riverwalk, his head hanging and his body hunched. He clutched his stomach.

"You son of a bitch!" my father yelled, rushing at Ryan like a linebacker.

Ryan looked up, stunned. "Just leave me alone. You've won."

My father's eyes narrowed and his evil expression immobilized me. I had never seen such fury and hatred in anyone before. The smell of his Brut aftershave made his presence so uncomfortably familiar.

He balled up a fist and hit Ryan squarely in the mouth, sending a gout of blood spewing into the air. Droplets fell to the concrete as Ryan staggered, wilting from the blow. He started to raise his hands, feebly trying to fend off the attack, but my father hit him again, fist smashing into Ryan's temple hard enough to send him reeling.

Red streamed from Ryan's mouth, then his nose…and I could do nothing but watch as he crumpled to the ground, becoming less and less recognizable beneath the onslaught of my father's wrath.

Ryan lay completely limp in the grass. Bile rose to my throat, and I gripped Sebastian's arm tightly. Had my dad really killed someone with his bare hands? I surveyed the area, spotting the train tracks in the distance behind me. The Intracoastal lay beyond the expanse of the walkway. Several trees shrouded *The River House* and the other buildings on either side of the turnabout where the car was parked. Even though we were in public view, there was an eerie air of privacy.

My mother had fallen to her knees, her hand clamped over her mouth. She must have had the desperate urge to help Ryan, but knew my father's hostility would be unleashed upon her if she dared. She slowly rose to her feet, her eyes coming into sharp focus as if she had been sobered by the violence.

"No!" my mother shouted as she dashed to where her husband pummeled her lover. "What are you doing, you asshole?"

She walloped my dad with her sable-colored hobo purse,

whipping the leather along his back and at his head. Her hands had shortened the length of the long strap, and the massive silver buckles jangled upon impact.

I remembered waiting in an eternal checkout line with her at JCPenney to purchase that bag. She told me her version of the three little pigs, how they all lived in a brick house and invited the wolf over for a BBQ where he'd be taught a lesson.

The purse must have contained a ton of contents, since it thumped audibly. My father tried to ignore the blows thudding around his shoulders as he hunched over Ryan's prone, bloody body. I saw the white shine of loose teeth, knocked out in the grass. Realizing his mission was complete, my dad turned to my mother with a satisfied smirk. Her eyes grew wide and sad, her mouth bowed in horror…and then she swung the bag back and hit him as hard as she could in the face.

He staggered, but only briefly. Then he seized the purse from her and flung the strap around her neck, yanking it tight. She gurgled and moaned as the air squeezed from her throat. Her hands fumbled for the strap, scrabbling to pull it loose. Her eyelids fluttered. She lost foothold, and it appeared the leather around her neck suspended her in the air.

My breathing shallowed, and I grew woozy. It was as if I was dying with her.

I buried my head in Sebastian's shirt, tears flooding my eyes. There was no way I could watch what I knew must have been my mother's last breaths. We were bonded—emotionally, and by blood—and I was sure I felt something of her pain inside me. My instinct was to run to her, to try and do something, but I knew that the opportunity was long past, and my heart broke all over again. This time the hurt wrenched even deeper. She never really left me. God, how could I have ever thought that? It was my murderous, lying father who ripped her away from my life.

When I looked back to see what was happening, my father had lifted Ryan and lugged him to the Mustang. He fumbled for his keys and managed to open the trunk, then flopped the lifeless body into it. The lid of the trunk banged. As my dad returned to scoop up my mother, one of her white heels fell from her foot, landing on the road.

I recalled seeing her hide those pumps deep in her closet years before. She'd shushed me to secrecy. The first time she had put them on was for my ballet performance when I was seven. My father raged at her. Who did she think she was and who was she trying to look sexy for? Even though she swore he was the only one, he made her vow to throw the heels away. He never wanted to see them again. She said she would. It was the first lie I remember her telling him. I knew those shoes were her silent rebellion, the one thing that made her feel beautiful. She couldn't throw that away.

In the scene playing out before my eyes, my dad carried her limp form into the passenger seat and slammed the door. In his frantic scramble to leave, he spotted my mother's shoe. He snatched it up, scowled at it in disdain, and threw it into the backseat. Then he climbed into the driver's side, locking himself in. The car squealed away, the burning rubber leaving smoke in its wake.

Rage boiled inside me. He had taken her from me. He had no right—and to lie about it all those years!

Whatever my dad did with the bodies, I now knew why he'd gotten rid of his beloved Mustang. He said it was because he couldn't afford it anymore, because mom had left and she wasn't helping with the bills. *Left? You bastard!* He'd played it off like he was a broken man after mom had gone. He was heartbroken she betrayed us, didn't love us anymore. Now I knew the truth and couldn't do a damn thing about it. There was no confronting him about his crimes or the chance for justice. It left me feeling so powerless.

Suddenly I realized my feet hurt. Somehow I had managed to weather all of this while standing in my black patent leather heels. I kicked them up into my hands as if they had wronged me for the last time.

Sebastian took me by the arm, and we tottered back to his car. We must both have been too stunned to talk.

The ride was a blur until I noticed he wasn't taking me back to his house. We were en route to my place. I shot him a sidelong glance while he kept his focus on the road.

My insides twisted and the onrush of rejection swam within me. Maybe we'd never see each other again. Or maybe I was being dramatic. All I knew was that being abandoned was a sensation as familiar as putting on a worn pair of jeans. If only I could trash them for good.

We pulled into the parking lot in front of my building. After a few moments, I turned to Sebastian, his eyes and mouth all droopy.

"Veronica, I really care about you. I just don't know if I can keep seeing you."

If he didn't want to be with me anymore, I wouldn't chase him or beg, but I craved some kind of lucid closure. And that wasn't happening tonight.

"We're too confused right now. Call me tomorrow," I said.

"I don't know what there is to talk about." His eyes glistened. "Your dad killed mine."

"He killed my mom, too," I protested. "We both lost someone we loved that night."

Sebastian shook his head slowly, and I tried to hide my fury. It felt as if my father was still managing to ruin my life from beyond the grave…like he was driving Sebastian away from me, just as he had with all the others. I remembered, years ago, when he intercepted one of my phone calls. I heard him telling one of my teenage boyfriends: *"Don't even think about asking her to the damn prom. She's not going,"* before plunking the receiver down. When prom night eventually came, I was sprawled on my bed, crying over what could've been.

"There has to be a reason we met," I said. "This is just too damn crazy. We can't give up now!"

"I just don't know how I can look at you without thinking about it."

He might as well have punched my gut. I didn't want Sebastian to hurt every time he saw or thought of me. Even stronger was the idea of not having him in my life. I reached for a silver lining, or at least a tinge of silver.

"It's over. My father's dead. He suffered through pancreatic cancer."

I peered out of the window, listening to the frogs croaking in the canal. My thoughts turned to witnessing my dad's eyes and skin gradually yellow, his dramatic weight loss, and his frequent visits to the bathroom to vomit. He had grown even more irritable and nasty, especially after refusing chemo. His determination to die as soon as possible frightened me. I'd known I'd be losing another parent and it forced me to contemplate my own mortality, and to fixate even more on my mother's disappearance.

Now, I felt guilty that I was glad karma had seemed to punish my father for what he'd done.

"But it's not over," Sebastian said, wrapping his fingers around the steering wheel and closing them like coiling snakes. "Somehow we relived it tonight. We'll never be the same… and to think they're stuck in some kind of replay of what they went through. It's horrific."

"It *is* horrific. But now we know that they didn't abandon us.

We didn't do anything wrong. *I* didn't do anything wrong. It was my father—not me."

"And what if they hadn't cheated?" Sebastian asked hotly. "What about that? I know that doesn't justify murder… but it's a lot to deal with."

"I know. There's a lot of blame to go around." I chewed one of my hangnails before stuffing my hands under my thighs. I didn't want to join Sebastian in vilifying the cheating. Obviously I had no idea what it was like to stand in his shoes but, from my own pair, I could understand why my mother had strayed. "Look, I care about you, too. Let's talk tomorrow."

The conviction rang out in my voice as if I spoke on a mountain to a bunch of apostles. Sebastian leaned in, grabbed the sides of my head and pulled me to his lips. It was a reassurance that we might not be over after all. This whole thing had us cemented together.

Another Christmas. There was no tree in my condo. My excuse was always that the cats would only climb it and shatter the ornaments. The truth was I had no interest in putting one up. If I ever got an ornament as a present, I would always re-gift it, unless it was personalized. Then I'd have to toss it in the garbage. Part of me would always mourn the loss of the cute sparkly snowman or candy cane with googly eyes, but sending it to the dump was my way of telling God what I thought of the holiday.

I fixed my ordinary organic oatmeal with almond milk and watched the coffee steam in my "New Orleans Voodoo" mug. I smiled at its design: a skull and crossbones wearing a top hat embossed with a fleur de lis. There had always been a chance that a form of magic would one day manifest in my life. Not the Disney kind, but the spooky, take-your-breath-away kind. I'd say that was what I'd been waiting for. That was the vague hope I'd always had while flirting with the occult from time to time. However, instead of seeking a priestess to teach me the ways of slaughtering animals to get what I wanted, I merely stuck to burning the occasional candle. It felt safe. Then I could wait around patiently for the outcome.

Last night had been freaky, and my breath had been taken away, but was it really magic? Maybe the vague intention of my candle ritual *had* come to fruition…after all, Sebastian had come into my life, and I knew now that my mom hadn't abandoned me. She really had loved me. She hadn't *meant* to leave me, which made my heart hurt when I thought of the years together that she and I had missed out on…years my father had stolen from us.

My faith in magic—if this was what it was—couldn't help but be tainted by what seemed to be the price that had to be paid in order to balance the scales. If it had brought me and Sebastian together, the ghosts of our parents were robbing us of a carefree honeymoon phase. I wasn't against getting some closure for our suffering, but still…it sucked.

After eating the last spoonful of cereal, I rinsed the bowl in the sink. Then, after taking some quick gulps of coffee, I dialed Sebastian. I'd told him to call me, but I didn't think that really mattered. We were beyond all of the beginning-of-relationship games, as if I really cared about any of that stupid crap anyway. If we were meant to be together, my calling him first or sitting by the phone waiting for him wouldn't make a damned difference. In fact, the waiting would have been more excruciating.

"Hey," I said when he answered. "Merry Christmas." My voice was hesitant, more like a question than a statement.

"You, too." There was a pause as if he didn't know what to say. "I'm sorry about last night, I—"

"Don't worry about it. It was crazy all around. I get it."

"I'd like to see you later. I told my mom I'd stop by—thought maybe you'd come with me. I know it's weird under the circumstances, but I don't want to go alone."

"Sure. It would be nice to meet her."

He was right about it being weird. The beloved specters had taken up residence in my head, and I would want to ask his mom what she knew. Would she have some missing pieces for my inquisitive mind?

"I was hoping we could do something first," I said, pacing in my living room.

I'd been concocting a rather bold plan, but I didn't want to tell him about it over the phone.

"Yeah? What?"

"I'll come get you around six. Tell you about it then."

"All right," he said, though he didn't sound too sure.

"See you soon."

Sebastian, in a charcoal jersey and jeans, got into my black Mazda.

"Hey," he said, and leaned in to kiss me. "What are you up to?"

After stashing his keys into his pocket, he buckled his seat belt. Scrutinizing the car's interior, he turned to study the back seat. There might have been some empty water bottles lying next to my purse on the floor. He sniffed the air, apparently noticing the fragrance of rose, lavender, and rosemary coming from back there. I had become desensitized to it while driving around.

I turned down the radio. "So the two times we've been at *The River House*, it's been around seven, right?"

"Yeah, thereabouts."

"There's gotta be something to that. That's when we've been seeing things."

"What're you getting at?"

I put the car in reverse and backed out of his driveway. "I'm hoping we see them again tonight."

Sebastian's face tensed. "Haven't we seen enough?"

"I think we need to try to release them. You know, send them to the light. You said they're trapped in this loop of reliving their nightmare over and over. Maybe we can end it."

"Wh—?" Sebastian massaged his forehead. "What about your dad?"

"What about him? We can send him off to wherever he belongs. Then, maybe we can heal, once we've helped them move on."

"What makes you think we can do this?"

"Haven't you seen *Poltergeist*?"

He winced, and I knew I should have thought this conversation through more thoroughly. Using Hollywood wasn't going to strengthen my case. "Yeah, but she was a medium and that was a movie."

The fast food signs blurred by as we drove. For a moment, I said nothing. I knew I had to do this…and I knew he had to be involved. I couldn't explain it better than that. "I know, but we're more suited to the job. Who better than their own kids?"

"You do realize how crazy this sounds, right?" His attention was somewhere beyond the windshield.

"I have a good feeling about it," I assured him, wishing I could convey the adrenaline high I felt.

Sebastian still stared ahead of him, as if he was talking to the glass. "Look, I have a confession to make."

"What?"

"I'm not really into all this paranormal stuff. I went along with it because I was into you. Going on a ghost tour isn't my thing, but I knew you'd like it. And then we actually saw ghosts—something I didn't even believe in before I met you. It's really messed me up."

"What about your New Age interests? Was that a lie?"

"No, I didn't lie about that…but I mainly got into it because it made my mom feel better. We meditated together. I took her to reiki circles. It gave her something to believe in. And *I* wanted to believe in something, too. Now, the supernatural is all up in my face. It's a reminder that there wasn't any superpower that could keep her alive. But these ghosts, or whatever they are, won't let me just live an ordinary life."

"I know, baby," I said quietly. After all, what else was there to say? He was right.

I parked on the street, just steps away from where we saw our parents attacked. Sebastian hopped out of the car and tended to the parking meter. He handed the time stamped slip to me, and I tossed it onto the dash. Considering he was so befuddled, I was happy he hadn't demanded to leave. An aspect of him must have been curious.

Sebastian and I stood in the place we had the night before outside *The River House*. I sank onto a bench, a semi-circular hedge enclosing it, making it a private cove. He sat next to me. In the space between us, I set a short white candle I'd pulled from my purse.

Sebastian raised an eyebrow.

The scent of lavender oil permeated the air as I lit the wick. The fire bobbed and wavered. I mentally called in all of our angels and guides for help, including Archangel Azrael, who is supposed to specialize in transitioning spirits to the afterlife. He appeared in one of the angel books I'd rummaged through that morning.

"I think we should think of our parents, send them our love… and hope they appear," I said.

Sebastian half-smiled and shook his head. "This is so cheesy."

"I know, but you're here, aren't you? And don't worry. I'm not going to tell anyone about this."

I put my hand on my heart and closed my eyes. *Maybe this is cheesy. Maybe it is a long shot.* However, if it was such a waste of time and energy, I questioned why I'd had such a strong impulse to bring him here.

We sat in silence. The evening air swirled around us at a brisk seventy degrees: warm for a Florida Christmas. Birds squawked overhead. A pale moth spiraled by before flitting on its way. I eventually checked to see if Sebastian was awake. His eyes were in fact open, and he was studying the blades of grass.

Glancing at my cell, I noticed it was after seven o'clock. Perhaps the time wasn't so magical after all. I sighed. Sebastian must have heard me because he reached for my hand. His skin was warm, and I sensed an exchange of prickly electricity. I wondered if it was this connection that my mother and Sebastian's father risked everything for—the notion that no one else in the world could make you feel so safe or so thrilled to be alive.

It was then that my mother and Ryan came into focus like two people stepping out of a mist. They held hands, swinging their interlinked fingers like little kids. My eyes filled with tears as they seemed to recognize Sebastian and me. My mother met my gaze, and she shone brighter than a light bulb getting a surge of power. Ryan glowed just as brilliantly as he focused on Sebastian.

Not caring who might be outside in this public space with us, I spoke the words as they came to me. "We love you, Mom, Ryan. It's 2020 now, and you have been dead for several years. You must find eternal peace on the other side. Release the hold you have here. It's time to go."

Sebastian squeezed my hand lightly. The candle's flame fluctuated in the glass.

Still hand in hand, my mom and Ryan continued promenading toward us, their faces relaxed and pleasant as if a constant stream of bliss coursed through them. For a moment I pretended they were alive instead of ethereal—that later I'd see my mother and it'd be like one of our happiest days.

I missed her giggling with me while we sang old Elton John songs and made cookies in the kitchen. We would lick the mixing spoon, taking turns, like sisters. She would dab my nose with flour and tightly enfold me in her arms. Sometimes I thought I might suffocate in her love.

Burgeoning warmth flooded my chest. I had been so caught up in the sensations gushing through me that I hadn't realized my mother and Sebastian's father were still floating toward our bench.

They advanced at a more rapid pace now, moving like a time warp as their spirits passed through us. A wind sent my hair flapping around my face. My bones chilled. All the hairs on the nape of my neck stood to attention, and I let go of Sebastian's hand so I could wrap my arms around myself to generate some heat.

Sebastian and I spun around to examine what might be at our backs. I half-expected to catch a snapshot of the couple still stepping along the lawn, after having walked right through us. However, they had vanished.

The night appeared darker. I felt devastatingly abandoned once again, just like when I was huddled in my childhood closet, the accordion door pulled shut. I used to pray it was a portal to another dimension where my mother was…where she would hug me like she used to, tickling my back with her fingertips and tracing circles through my T-shirt. But that dream never came true.

An echoing snarl became an animalistic roar, snatching me from my childhood memory. Once my eyes met the source of the sound, I saw my father barreling straight at us.

"You can't leave me!"

Was it his spirit that had trapped them here?

His eyes turned completely white and his arms reached out in front of him, anxious to grab hold of something. Before Sebastian or I could move, my dad seemed to ride an airstream. His form became transparent, then vaporous, until it merged with Sebastian, dissolving into him. The impact pushed him against the bench, shoving his head backward. Slowly, he sat erect once again.

Sebastian's head rotated in my direction, his eyes white from being rolled all the way back, eyelids twitching. The person I had grown to know and love had been replaced. Sebastian wasn't there anymore. Vile loathing radiated from his body, triggering a sharp fear that took root in my core and made me shaky.

"Sebastian, can you hear me?" I asked unsteadily.

He glowered at the ground.

When I looked down, following his gaze, he seemed fixated on my feet. "You're such a lying bitch! I told you to get rid of those!"

He lunged at my heels, which were classic pumps like my mother's, only mine were black. I jerked my leg away, but not before he caught hold of my jeans. Struggling to yank myself free,

I toppled to the grass. His grip was firm, his eyes like pools of milk. He growled, trying to yank the shoes off my feet.

"I always knew you were screwing around on me, you whore!" The voice was my father's: the exact same tone he used when berating me so many years before.

My chest tightened. I had to do something. My mind searched through a warehouse of files. "Daddy, it's me, Veronica. Mom's gone, remember?"

He gathered a lock of my auburn hair in his fingers and appraised it. "Cheryl, stop your games! I'm so tired of all your fucking games!"

The hollowness in his voice was now inhuman, like an automated recording.

I covered my face with my arms as Sebastian kneeled on my thighs, his weight pinning my lower body. He pushed down on my chest with one hand, and I felt the firmness of the earth at my back. I tried to roll away, but couldn't. My arms went back to their defensive position, shielding me from the pointed heel of my shoe as he tried to bring it crashing down onto my face.

It was then that I screamed. The sound sliced through the night, and my vocal cords felt as if they were shredding my throat.

"You better shut up!" the voice coming from Sebastian warned. He grappled with my arms, moving them enough to slap his free hand over my mouth. He inched up my torso, resting his knees on one of my arms. I kicked my legs, but it was no use.

I wasn't going anywhere, and my muffled screams were purposeless.

Before I could do anything else, the heel came down again. I turned my head, but that only meant that it stabbed my cheek instead of my eye. The force had driven it through and into my mouth. I felt the grit of the heel's tip as it drilled into my tongue.

The metallic taste of pooling blood made me gag. I moaned at the stinging pain, wanting to plead for my life.

Daddy, no! Please, don't hurt me, Daddy!

He pulled the heel out. It slipped along my ripped flesh. I didn't know what else to do but keep my eyes closed and resign myself to the attack. As I did, the heel drilled the skull above my eye and then seconds later it punctured my neck. Blood ebbed from the wounds. Each time the pain of the old point of entry lessened to make way for the unbearable sensation of the new. My heart pumped overtime, and I choked on the fluid in my throat.

Where are the people in the park? Why isn't someone helping me?

He must have known I was past the point of crying out for help because he lifted his hand from my mouth. I opened my eyes only to see the heel coming right down into one of them.

All I saw was darkness as my senses dulled. It was like falling into the deepest part of the ocean, knowing I'd never rise back to the surface. Had he penetrated my brain? His hands were on my neck, squeezing until I felt, heard, and tasted the darkness. The entire world went black. The last thing I heard was the muted screech of a stranger's voice.

"What the hell are you doing?"

It was too late.

The interrogation is over. We sat for hours in the closet of a room, going over it again and again. Sebastian really didn't know exactly what happened. How could he?

All I can do now is spoon him here in his cell bed. It really feels like a plank of plywood covered in sandpaper bedding. The thread count on the sheets is pretty terrible. My mother would be appalled. I'm not ready to go wherever she is.

Our breathing is in sync, and I lightly kiss Sebastian's back. I think he's started to sob. His heaving has me holding him even tighter. If only he would turn to me and look into my eyes again. That would make me feel so much better.

Who knows when the trial will be. Things aren't looking so good. There are witnesses. His prints are on my shoe, and then there's the blood spatter evidence. It probably looks like some lover's quarrel gone horrifically wrong. We never really had the chance to have a real fight. We never had the chance for much at all.

My heart bleeds for him. By now I hope my father is finally damned in hell… or maybe just damned to roam the yard outside *The River House* forever, alone at last.

Sebastian will be damned to a life in prison.

It's not the way I wanted to spend eternity with the man I love, but it will have to do. At least we're together. If only he could see and hear me. I won't ever give up trying, though.

I'll never leave him.

COLLECTING EMPTIES

Ahand shook me awake. My head felt like it had been hit by a sledge hammer. My mouth was cotton dry. Some guy in a white T-shirt with a sweaty face stared squarely at me. I gathered the sheet to cover up my bra and panties.

Another guy put the nearly empty vodka bottle on the floor so he could carry away the nightstand.

"Get up." The same dude who woke me waved his hands up. He looked at his bare wrist, miming that time ticked by.

Wearing the sheet like a toga, I tumbled from the mattress just as someone pulled it from under me and dragged it away. Not another stick of furniture in sight.

Where were my clothes—my shoes? My cellphone?

Shit, my car was still at the bar.

Mister Blue Eyes from the night before crystalized in my memory. They were like the Bahamian cobalt ocean from my honeymoon cruise. My husband and I suddenly hadn't had anything to say as a married couple. The chemistry had waned away as I watched him ogle other bikinis, breasts both fake and real, and not even in his peripheral vision.

His expression whenever I'd been on top was a lament that there wasn't enough to hold onto. That's liquid diets for you. When I shoved him over the rail, that was my commentary on not having enough 'cushion for the pushin'' for him. In terms of his compliments, I had always come up with nothing—and so did the search and rescue crew.

Whenever I'd been drinking, I ignored my husband's smirk that said he was a nobler drunk. His skin and eyes never reddened, never bloated or puffed. He never slurred his words, but his brain cells always collided as he sputtered his disapproving, self-righteous words. Meanwhile, I'd see myself floating out of my body, leaving any decisions to the intoxicated shell of me. I taunted that shell to do something shameful, to pass out at Thanksgiving dinner, to pee in the closet in the middle of the night. She was more than happy to oblige.

He'd only said he loved me when he was sober, which made me believe it couldn't be true. Kissing her after the shots of Patron—was that a dream, or had I *really* seen them? Maybe it was my thoughts I couldn't hold onto.

There was a hefty life insurance policy, so I decided to tie one on *again* to celebrate. I took that me with no filter, no morals, and no limits to the bar. After four straight up martinis, Mr. Blue Eyes insisted I have another drink. I vomited forth scraps of life with my late husband, but wished it had been the acid and chips and salsa from my stomach, all soaked with liquor. That might've been less humiliating, easier to clean up. Blue Eyes hung onto my every word, like I was some sort of gorgeous model with the mind of whoever the most intelligent woman on the planet is. Ha! Sadly there's no female Einstein.

Blue Eyes insisted I was too hammered to drive—my pretty

face shouldn't get splattered on a windshield somewhere. Part of me wanted that though. A suicide pact with the me that can never drink enough. I'll have only a glass, two glasses…a bottle. The hard stuff was most efficient.

I remember making a pitch outside the bar for sleeping it off in my car. I was okay. I'd done it before. With a gleam in his eyes of seeing me naked, he claimed the cops circled this particular bar. Once someone got arrested for getting a jacket out of the passenger seat before having a DD drive him home. Can't be in the vehicle drunk. It's the law—and just another one I don't follow.

Those blue eyes seemed nice enough. And if he was a Ted Bundy, I was ready to kiss my life goodbye. I didn't remember all of it anyway, since I was in a constant liquor induced haze. Everyone loved me there. And hated me. I didn't care which.

I remember thinking what a good decision it was to go home with Blue Eyes. Before we entered his immense house, spotless, sparsely furnished, he parked his Lexus in the spacious garage. Like a gentleman, he opened the car door and helped me inside. Then I helped myself out of my little black dress, throwing it over my shoulder, stumbling for the bedroom in my black lace unmentionables. He watched me while pushing away the panting Yorkie with the side of his loafer.

Blue Eyes touched me all over, rushed and sloppy. Either I complied with his every whim, or I passed out. He wouldn't have been the first man I blacked out on, nor the last.

So I guess that's what I get for my list of sins, as long as my legs. I've tried baring my soul to a therapist, but my escapades only got more shameful as I verbalized them, breathing them back to life. And I still kept drinking, programmed to get to any happy hour, whether already buzzed or not.

I grabbed my black dress—oddly smelling like blood—from

the middle of the room, completely trampled by the movers as they got the last of the lamps and rolled up the area rug. I drained the last drops from the deserted vodka bottle.

Thinking of how Blue Eyes turned out to be such an asshole, I spied a heap beyond the cracked open closet door. That's right. Blue Eyes nudged me early, saying I'd have to leave. He was supposedly moving in a couple of hours. Thinking it was another man's chauvinistic effort to send me on my walk of shame, I clawed him bloody with my acrylic nails. As he yelped, I'd strangled him with my little black dress. That much came back to me. I must've gotten him into the closet. As I pulled the accordion door completely closed, I glimpsed a motionless paw. Didn't remember doing that. What a shame. I really love animals.

Strapping on my heels, I passed an abandoned dog dish and empty water bowl. I couldn't eye it directly. Grabbing his car keys from the kitchen counter, I exited the vacant house and sped away in the Lexus.

THE CELESTIAL ASSIGNMENT

You know that meme of the angel statue, its face in its hands, with the caption: "This is probably what my guardian angel looks like"? Well, that's the only thing on the wall in this stark room meant for some 12-step spiritual garbage.

I was mystified as fuck the first time I sat here. The last thing I'd remembered was having a beer with one of my side pieces before witnessing her chuck my body into an unmarked grave. The bitch walked right through me as I grilled her about what she'd done.

Next thing I know, I transported into this very chair. Looking around the circle, I noted everyone's arms tattooed with wings in shades matching their clothing.

"What am I doing here?" I asked, studying the new gray markings growing iridescent on my skin.

"You're getting a new assignment," said someone with platinum hair. His wings were the real deal, tucked at his back, and he wore a white T-shirt and white jeans.

"As opposed to what?"

"Going back to earth. That hasn't been working." He stared at me with his unnaturally light blue eyes. "Don't worry, there's a manual under your seat."

That's when I zoned out. The rest of them yammered on as I frantically retraced my memory for clues to why I was here. What kind of demented lunatic would make me an angel, if that's what I was? I hadn't even stepped one foot in a church, at least in my most recent life. That's when it hit me I'd had more than one incarnation on earth. The mere vocabulary of it made me shiver.

With a jolt, my feet landed on slick linoleum, the burning odor of disinfectant and stale medicine in the air. A woman screamed in a hospital bed, her legs pried open with a sheet over them. Ugh. I'd never liked babies and had zero fatherly instincts. As the infant cried and was handed to the mother, the dad busy snapping Polaroids, I heard a whisper: "She's your responsibility now."

As my questions flooded in, that damned manual appeared in my hand. Annoyed the heavenly head honchos hadn't downloaded the content into my brain, I held onto it, lest I be struck by lightning.

"Hello, Celeste," the mother cooed to the baby.

I tapped my foot.

The irony of the name irked the shit out of me.

As a reluctant guardian angel, I figured my job involved keeping this pipsqueak's hand off the hot stove, and her mouth away from poisons in the cabinets. Most of the time, I yawned in the periphery, especially since I was trapped in this fucking hick town somewhere in the middle of Wisconsin. Countless Crayon doodles and finger paintings were the extent of my excitement. Eventually, I rejoiced when of a few close calls at the wheel of her parents' car gave me something to do. But then there was her painfully awkward discovery of boys. Once she inadvertently brushed this dude's junk at a dance. Her first kiss was lame as shit. It was like being tuned into the Nickelodeon Channel. Her interactions with a new boy made me gag—they'd finish each other's sentences and giggle like idiots. What did I do to deserve this?

Another bloody meeting.

Shifting in my plastic chair, I dared an inquiry. "So, how common is it for them to feel that whole 'soul mate' thing? That's what Celeste calls it." I noted my use of 'them' like I was never human. Ever.

Some of the 12-steppers acted like I was tripping on acid. Eye rolls. Deep sighs. Shaking of heads. One humored me, reporting he'd noticed something like it, but it didn't last. Another angel mentioned his guy had been married fifty years to the same woman but wasn't sure if that counted. Just thinking about seeing the same face for that long made me die a little more inside.

As I listened to their pathetic drivel I searched my mind for someone memorable. The only thing surfacing was a mental nudie magazine of smoking hot war prizes, pent-up chambermaids, scantily clad harem girls, or the barely legal chicks next to me at the bar. They liked me and I liked it—the chase, me fucking them. Oh, the endless taste of their wet pussies, the sensation of their nails pressing into my back, and the smell of perfume mixing with sweat.

Horrified, I touched my crotch. I wasn't hard. My guy hadn't even twitched, a depressing fact eclipsing the conclusive evidence that soul mates didn't exist, a detail that no longer interested me.

I missed boozing, Sports Center, and Skinamax. Instead, I was forcibly glued to Celeste's rom-com channel. She and this boy wrote each other daily notes on paper, which tells you how far this story goes back. He didn't know it, but she saved every correspondence. I read that shoebox of adorable shit in her closet once when she slept, just for something to do. It likely broke one of the manual's codes, which I'd skimmed over for show. I'd suspected I had a wingman (funny now, isn't it?) always tailing my ass. So far, no one's struck me with lightning. Good times.

One day, while hovering over the lovebirds at school, I noticed how average looking this chump was. When he told his lame jokes and issued his cheap compliments, Celeste's eyes twinkled as she blushed. In the next couple of weeks, he started writing notes to other girls on the sly. I didn't have enough fingers or toes to count how many times I'd kept a girl on a string, while already sweet talking her best friend or sister. The old me would've applauded the dude. This new me, not so much. It was like Celeste and me were still the offense, but this guy suddenly switched to defense. My competitive switch flipped. And I don't play nice. Too bad I'm stuck warming the bench.

This little princess's face was like an explosion of fireworks every time her guy strutted down the hallway, but his eyes steeled. She'd slump her shoulders, failing to understand why the notes and phone calls had dwindled. I wondered what her next move was, since I'd seen her devious side. You see, the other night her brother ratted her out for talking on the phone too late, inciting an inquiry from their parents about who the caller was. Little bro later rapped on her bedroom window way past his curfew. She'd pretended to be asleep, suffering zero guilt the next day when it turned out their parents had heard him use the noisy front door. As a result, he got an hour lecture about the significance of rules. Since then, I expected her to get all badass with this boy saga. Nope. All she wanted to do was roll over like a puppy itching for a belly rub.

The prom was coming up, and he didn't ask her. But the girl clung to those notes, rereading them. Whenever another schoolgirl squealed before or after class, having just gotten her precious invite, Celeste's jealousy pinged. Waiting for the phone to ring, she listened to her mountain of mixed grunge tapes. God almighty —obsessive much?

My angel influence remained hit or miss, but I encouraged the poor sap to ask him to the prom, just to pull the Band-Aid off the situation. Monday morning came and he told her he didn't have the money. I patted her teary self on the back so we could skedaddle, but she said she'd spring for the tickets. I yelled at her to save her breath, but she kept at it. He said there were the tux and the flowers, and he couldn't let her pay. Truth was, he'd an easier conquest on his horizon, one who'd already given him a hand job in his car. Good for him, I thought, after I'd seen that memory flash in his eyes. For a minute, I longed for some of his X-rated entertainment.

The week of the prom, Celeste spotted him with the other girl. Consequently, up until graduation, she moped in her dark bedroom, alternative riffs and refrains of "love hurts" pumping into her ears, and mine. If this one stupid guy hadn't given her a second thought, why'd she give a rat's ass about him? Ah, the agony.

Back at training headquarters a few months later, I suffered an interrogated about how things were going.

The platinum-haired douchebag piped up. "No revelations yet?"

"Yeah, she's taking this all too seriously." I crossed my arms.

"No, I mean about yourself."

"Not really."

"Nothing over the past few centuries comes to mind?"

"Why should it? Aren't I just a bodyguard?" That's when I felt something slap onto my chest. I glanced at the sticky nametag reading "Hello, I'm Will" with "and I'm a sociopath" in tiny letters underneath. "Very funny," I said with a smirk.

"The truth hurts, doesn't it?"

"Hurts?"

"That's your problem. You don't self-reflect. Your whole existence is about gratification." His eyes narrowed as he propped his chin on his hand. "Your homework is to meditate on that. And on what love is."

Repressing a laugh, I half-expected another manual to appear under my chair—the love edition. Jumpstarting my heart was infinitely more useless now than it had ever been. I could've told them I wasn't cut out to be some fucking radiant being of light.

After the meeting, I geared up for more unbearable Nickelodeon re-runs. Staying out of Celeste's thoughts helped me avoid thinking about love and wanting to puke.

At some point, she ran into the guy from high school at the college library. If only I'd seen that coming, I would've knocked a book off the shelf or something. It was dumbfounding when her face illuminated and she resolved to let bygones be bygones, like she'd been lobotomized or something.

I sighed when he offered to drive her to school. Oh, here we go. And there began a year of sharing their trivial hopes and dreams, singing off tune to the radio, and stealing googly glances at each other in the car. Then came the sickening season finale. I'm not shitting you. It was raining so hard the umbrella they shared was pointless. That's when the horndog kissed her, and she kissed him back. Instead of fast-forwarding to some long-awaited fucking, like I'd hoped, I envisioned kids, trips to Europe, the two of them holding hands in old age—stuff I gave zero shits about. Was I seeing their future together? This asshole? Come on.

The next season involved romantic picnics and walks on the beach, and other such drivel. He even constructed an easel for her birthday surprise. She gifted him her first finished painting of an ethereal figure enveloped in tongues of fire. The back dedication: 'You'll always be the flame.' My eyes rolled so far back into my head I caught a migraine, Cheap Trick's "The Flame" playing in my mind. Where was the rip cord to make this all stop?

He helped her transport all her other art-class assignments on the top of his car. After many attempts to get into her pants, he never got past her matching sets of lace bra and panties. I didn't blame him for hanging in for the lay as long as he did. However, instead of giving him her body, she wrote him a poem. Almost choking, he read it with a grimace, pocketing it. Afterwards, their classes conflicted. They didn't carpool. He never called again.

A few drive-bys, another gawk at the stash of notes, and a shitload of tears later, she sucked it up while finishing her degree. She wouldn't be alone for long. There was something special about her, even though I couldn't put my finger on it. Whenever she flipped her long, blonde hair when no one was looking, or when she winked at herself in her rearview mirror, it made me smile. I'd never spent this much time with a girl before, and I had no idea why I was so damn relieved her romantic nemesis had ditched her.

In all of Celeste's college courses, I sat in a nearby desk. Not my idea of fun. Still no breakthroughs concerning love, but I sure did absorb a lot of art history, inspired by the promise of sex. I fantasized about those classic works coming to life, all those luscious lips worshipping my cock. The day Celeste had her first class with her former flame's (see what I did there?) fiancé interrupted my titillating escapades. They had mutual acquaintances, or Celeste would never have been the wiser. Not this shit again. Not him. Seeing her cry so much had started to make me feel sorry for her. That, and those Garbage lyrics drove me mad.

At the next meeting, I asked if there was some magic dust or something to cure Celeste. Nah. Apparently I had to coast until this girl kicked the bucket, and I met my new ward who I hoped would be more like a porn star.

Years went by. During the thousandth group session or so, I discovered the guardian angel of Celeste's old boyfriend had been in my circle this whole time. Classic.

"So, what's your assignment been up to?" I asked her after the meeting.

She pushed her pink glasses up with her middle finger, looking me up and down and crossing her arms. "Why do you care?"

"Just curious."

"Let's see if any of this is familiar to you." She put a finger to her pink lips. "He's been married three times, for starters. According to him, that college girl turned into a bitch. With his talent for neglect, he drove another spouse to cheat. It takes more than sex and material objects to keep a woman's heart—oh, yeah, like you'd know," she said with a caustic sneer.

Where'd she get off judging me? I held my tongue to hear more.

"The next wife died out of the blue. At the last second, he'd spouted the old, 'You're the only woman I've ever loved. Don't leave me' kind of crap. He simply didn't want to lose his head-turning trophy who'd also made coffee and packed his lunch every morning. All that was slipping right through his fingers." She wiggled her digits in emphasis. "I tried not to laugh when she ran with open arms to the white light. It was all I could think about when he got drunk off his ass. His mother came over to pick him off the floor and clean up the piss. Never once did he thank her for her tucking him in, for filling his refrigerator, for taking care of his beloved dogs. That was real love smacking him in the face, but he never saw it."

"So, why'd he bother marrying?" I asked, marveling at how weird females were.

"Figures that'd be your question." She huffed. "That's right, you bought the rings but never went down the aisle—couldn't make a fucking commitment."

The accuracy of her guesses baffled me, but I just figured her psychic powers must've been more developed than mine as I prepared to make an exit. "Well, thanks for the uplifting chat."

"Yeah, I'm off to follow him around while he fucks everyone in sight. According to him, they're all crazy. I've yet to understand why I got saddled with a prick just like you. Unbelievable."

"You *wish* you'd been saddled with me." How long had she been undressing me with her eyes in that circle? Pent-up sexual frustration at its finest.

She heaved a sigh. "This is my *second* assignment. *You* were my first, dumbass."

The double entendre of 'being her first' was my initial juvenile focus. Then, I imagined this cute little thing always at my side, with me not being able to enjoy it. Next came the confusion at her hostility. "What?"

"Let that sink into your arrogant skull." Her finger waved in my face. "I can't wait to see which one of us graduates from angel training first. Can't fucking wait." She sniggered. "By the way, you totally deserved to be suffocated in your sleep. I spent many nights wishing I could've done it my-self."

"How angelic of you. You're a model of—"

Then she evaporated with a puff of pink smoke.

Now that was a trick worth learning.

Having been challenged by Miss Pink Know-It-All, I vowed to amass a few brownie points with my spy squad. Game on, bitch.

When a down-to-earth man attended one of Celeste's gallery openings, he seemed like the perfect kind of sensitive-and-doting nerdy type. A certain gleam in his eye indicated a strong admiration, at the very least. I blew tons of metaphorical magic dust around them until she believed in love again, up until they parted ways, leaving her childless and heartbroken. Since I knew absolutely nothing about relationships, I merely watched her splatter her emotions onto fresh canvases. Ugh. Some explosions, some gunfire, some blood and guts—that's what I longed for to pass the time. Instead I got paintings of gothic, tearful angels, of all things.

When Celeste felt ready to resume online dating, I didn't see the harm, until the chat bubble with the familiar asshole's face popped up on her computer screen. She jumped right out of her chair—and not with alarm or wrath. No more torment. Please. Into her ear, I kept whispering wisdom (I know that's ballsy coming from me), reminding her that she'd already given him two chances. "Fool me once, shame on you. Fool me twice, shame on me." But all she heard in her mind was "Three times the charm." Damn clichés.

I nudged her to respond to other prospects. But to her, running into him again was a sign they were getting one final shot. I buried my face in my hands, just like the poster in the meeting room. Art imitating life, or vice versa? Fuck me.

In her car, on the way to his house for a date, I longed to kill the engine. Since I had limited supernatural powers, we went inside. While they caught up, he poured her a couple of shots of Patron, her favorite. That first painting off the easel hung over them on the couch—a blue glow highlighting the masculine face, the shirtless torso licked by red flames. I'd always known she must've seen me at some point. How else could she have gotten my likeness almost exact? The tattooed wings along the arms were the same dimension and placement as mine, reminding me of who I was supposed to be. It weirded me out. I suppose I should be flattered, but I felt unworthy of the tribute. Or was it shame or guilt?

Not sure I've ever wrestled with such emotions. Beats the shit outta me.

When he told her he wanted her to himself, she was so giddy and tipsy she misjudged the width and slope while sitting on the arm of the couch. Falling on her ass, along with all her other clumsy maneuvers, was so endearing. He pulled her up, both of them laughing, and carried her to the bedroom for their 'first time'. I twiddled my thumbs until it was over, since it'd been so long since I'd touched a woman. I immediately switched to revisiting my generous backlog of lovers, refusing to spy on what was going on in the next room. It felt like I'd be violating her privacy or some shit. Or was it something else I was feeling? Nah. Fuck feelings.

Next thing I knew, she moved in with her two cats, which hated his two dogs. It was like supervising a house of bratty orphans who wanted to burn everything to the ground. I saved those cats more than once from being eaten alive. Good grief.

One night, in his idea of opening up, baring his soul while they laid in bed, he told her he liked big tits. What an idiot. Her modest rack was one of the best I'd seen. I know, sue me. Anyway, she was devastated. Her mother had just had a mastectomy. Boobs don't care about you when you're sick, was what she said. And she roared that maybe his dick should've been bigger. She scored a point there. No guy wants to be accused of having a needle dick. He apologized, not wanting to lose 'the only woman he'd ever loved.' I laughed, recalling Little Miss Pink's summary of how he treated women.

Instead of dumping this relationship treasure, Celeste lightened her hair to the shade it had been back in high school and bought stilettos she couldn't even walk in. She modeled lingerie and wore heels to bed, and did all the things he liked in the bedroom, even if she hated them. (For your sake and mine, I'll leave that up to your imagination). But, wait. There's more. She waited for him to come home from work. He rewarded her with a play-by-play of every hot girl who'd thrown herself at him during his shift. On his days off, sometimes he'd go and check on his ex's house when she was out of town. He'd take this ex to and from the airport and carry all her bags. Meanwhile, when Celeste went with him to Paris, she carried her own bags. She had to beg him to be romantic. Insert eye roll here. Or pull out your metaphorical Glock handgun, whichever you prefer.

Post-Paris, he went back to school, which zapped the rest of his time. On his birthday, they took his bike on the twisting neighborhood backroads to the local British pub. She'd savored the thrilling velocity, the night wind making her feel alive. It took me back to when I'd had a motorcycle. I imagined she was grabbing a hold of me, pressing against my back, while I was in control. I recognized then that she turned me on, in a way I'd never experienced before. Once I'd allowed myself to imagine being with her, I got irritated. Angry, even. How can I be objective with these kinds of thoughts? I actually prayed for a lobotomy. Make things a hellova lot easier.

On the way home, an old lady came out of nowhere. Mister Needle Dick slowed down before dropping the bike, preventing a head-on collision. At least he'd done that right. I hovered over the scene, afraid this was it for her. She'd skidded on the asphalt on the skin she'd braved showing that night, thinking 'being sexy' would make him love her. The road rash dripped in blood, her adrenaline making her insist she was okay. When the ambulance came, the guy was attentive, holding her hand. In the emergency room, the nurse cleaned Celeste's wounds, commenting on what a great couple they were. A new look had appeared in his eyes— just for a second. Celeste didn't see it, but the nurse and I did.

He filled her prescription and took her home. For the first

couple of days, he even changed her bandages. But then he left her alone so he could drink with the neighbor. He even made plans to visit his friend upstate. She cried, begging him not to leave. He reluctantly canceled the trip. From then, he planned his exit strategy. She may as well have written him another poem.

After she recovered from the accident, he left her behind to go to Haiti for work. Like some kind of chaperone for his Catholic university's missionary venture. Super librarian helping to save the world. He left Celeste waiting for him at the airport (his cell died and he hadn't memorized her number), while he called his mommy from a pay phone to come pick him up. Real genius, this guy. Then he was off to the mountains on his yearly trip with his father. She was invited, but not bathing for two weeks didn't sound glamorous or romantic to her. I concurred. Not that my vote counts, or anything. But I patted her on the back for knowing they'd need more than a camping adventure to connect. When he left for that trip, he told her to move back to her apartment with her cats. That engagement ring was nowhere on the horizon. She'd said as much. He didn't deny it.

Finally. Three times the charm was coming and going. I couldn't have been more stoked. And then it hit me. I was *him*. Just like him. I finally had something to share when the platinum-haired jackass asked me if I'd any revelations. That is, if I had the balls to open my mouth and humiliate myself in front of the whole damn circle. Would that earn me some extra credit? A relief from my emotions? Something? Anything.

Stunned by everything—him, her, me—I stood by as she packed her things for good. There'd been a missing fleck of paint on that painting of me over the couch. She'd patched the cobalt, her way of leaving things better than she'd found them, which included me. That detail would've been lost on the asshole I used to be. This time I paid attention.

She rounded up her cats with me at her side. He'd almost killed those poor sons of bitches when he poured the Borax on the carpet to get rid of his dog's fleas. He'd thought the trip to the emergency vet was funny. I'd wanted to beat the shit out of him for that. One of many instances I'd had that urge. Supposedly, every motherfucker deserves an angel.

For the first time, I felt truly sorry for Little Miss Pink. My defensive bullshit fell away. I'd never felt so raw or vulnerable. It was like falling through an endless pit. A vacuum sucked at my insides. I feared I would cease to exist any minute now. I begged for mercy to whoever was watching, listening. Make it stop! And, it did. Eventually.

I cringed when the call came. He told her he'd asked her to leave so she wouldn't be responsible for his place while he was gone. There'd been a flood. Fortunately she was spared having to deal with that. It would've been one thing if he'd said that before he left, she'd said. He only wanted her when she wasn't around. Yeah, the fucker. Those were the girls I chased the most, until it was time to throw them back in the discard pile.

I broke another angel rule then, one I managed to catch in my skimming of the manual. That night I left her peacefully sleeping and snooped on him over at his place while he put the wedding photo of him and his dead wife back up. I took a swing at him, fully aware he didn't feel it. But I got it out of my system, not just for me, but for Celeste. Later, that memory of giving him a whack brought me satisfaction. That, and the fact that the picture frame fell, cracking the glass over the image of him and his precious wife-y. My punch must've caused some ripple of energy. That had been enough for me.

Celeste dated, but she never loved again. As she became successful, her artwork graced a few gallery walls and some book covers. Fans emailed her and followed her on social media, and she occasionally got a passing impulse to gloat about it to her old boyfriend. But she never did. In the end, she felt less alone than if she'd married that bastard. Bullet dodged. Or, maybe more like open-gunfire dodged.

However, I'd one hell of a time keeping them apart. You see, he and Celeste had nearly crossed paths many times. In the grocery store, I managed to knock a can of peas onto her foot. At a concert, I splashed her cup of wine onto her dress. At the airport, I pushed a stranger into her path. All with great success. You damn romantics might think they were drawn together repeatedly so they could make it right. Second and third chances? Get that out of your brains. Don't buy into that Hollywood bullshit. Please, save yourselves.

As I laid next to her one night, on the pillow that some worthy chap should've occupied, I felt sorry about preying on starry-eyed romantic girls. Ruining their notions of happily-ever-after. With that thought, I sensed a soreness on my back. I had the crazy suspicion my wings were sprouting. Now you know what a pussy I'd turned into. I might as well have believed in unicorns. Or some other magical shit. I never said I was perfect.

As she applied her eye make-up, emphasizing those gorgeous peepers, which were now framed by crow's feet, I got the vibe this day would be different somehow. She was on her way to meet a dear friend, one who had all the things Celeste had always wanted: a loving husband, grandchildren, a slush fund. But jealousy didn't consume my girl. Would she ever have been creative otherwise?

I sat in the passenger seat. Passing motorists smiled. When she rounded the corner, I spotted him before she did. He scowled, his facial lines scrunching. In that moment, I saw a movie trailer of all my miserably lonely lives—every last person having realized what a selfish shit I was. It took a while. Years, it seemed.

His eyes glazed over as the crosswalk light turned red, but the dogs lurched back.

Her kind, gray eyes sparkled with appreciation for the brilliant blue sky.

I should've done something, but I didn't. He deserved what was coming to him. Say your prayers, motherfucker.

She stepped on the gas, still unaware of anything in her path. I needed this to be over, for her, for me, and for him. Scratch that—not for him. There was the thump of impact and the squish of his guts. Chunks of flesh and blood flooded the air, splashing to the pavement, the car's wheels skidding through a lifetime of regret. As he croaked, he left his body, looking to her, but she couldn't see him. Then, his eyes met mine in confusion. I gazed at him, throwing up my hands and shrugging my shoulders as the tires of Celeste's car screeched to a halt.

She sprung from the vehicle, the eyeliner and mascara streaming down her cheeks as she dialed 911. It wasn't until another motorist moved his face to give him mouth to mouth that she recognized him. Her eyes widened and the phone fell from her hands. Running to him, she wailed. Yeesh, and I'd thought her heart had been broken *before*. She was inconsolable when the medics pronounced him dead at the scene. What was worse was his spry dogs rushed at her like they were hers. As they licked her tears, the faint spark that'd lingered in her eyes disappeared—I feared for good.

Before I had time to process any of it, I was in my chair in the angel-support room. The only other presence was the platinum-haired guy perching on his stool across from me. I took a hateful look at that damned poster.

Something was heavy on my back. Stretching out my arms, I saw the tattoos weren't there, but when I checked behind me, two gray, feathered wings had me flinching in surprise.

"Congratulations, Will. Thought you'd need a few more assignments."

"That's it?" I asked.

"You've exceeded our expectations."

"But I let a guy die right in front of me. What're you talking about?"

"It wasn't your place to interfere. If you'd finished the manual, you'd understand."

"So why reward me?" I said, indicating my new wings, which seemed to have gotten even weightier—a load I'd have to get used to.

"Well, reward is a relative term."

"Okay, so let me go back to finish up with Celeste. She needs me now more than ever."

"That's exactly the sentiment I'm so pleased by." He smiled widely. "But you won't see her again. At least not for a long while."

"What? She's not dead yet—right? I don't understand." I swallowed the lump in my throat.

"You've already been replaced. We do that sometimes."

I couldn't get any more words out.

"It's not for you to concern yourself with."

I'd watched Celeste withstand so much emotional pain, but it wasn't until now that the gloves were off. A gang of grief and emptiness beat me senseless. For once in my whole existence, I missed someone. In my mind's eye, I enveloped Celeste with my new wings. She folded inward, as if cozying into the embrace. The vision was so real, I swiped away a tear. "Now what?" I asked.

"Your prize, my friend, is a new post."

"Another post? I barely know what the hell I'm doing." This oughta be good. Celeste's dead boyfriend in a brand-new life? The soul of a kid I'd never known I had? The jealous bitch who'd suffocated me and put me six feet under?

"Maybe this time you'll read the rules. I suggest you do, since your next assignment will be much more demanding." He pointed under my chair with the expression of a strict teacher commanding the pupil to rise to the occasion.

I didn't have to confirm there was a thick ass edition of the manual waiting for me as my head fell into my hands. More demanding? Sheesh. In what sense?

Although skeptical at first, I've come to believe that someone up there, or up here (I keep forgetting), thinks I've been a quick study. My hunch is that platinum-haired guy put in a few good words on my behalf. A possible reason why I'm in his old 12-step room. After his promotion—well deserved, I must say—he offered it to me.

You got it right. Now I'm the one perched on the stool. I finally studied the damn manual this time. Something tells me I can't half-ass anything anymore.

Celeste apparently had been my perfect catalyst. Maybe overly so. Reading between the lines told me they'd pulled me out for two reasons. One, I was getting too close. Some might accuse me of falling in love, but I wouldn't go that far. Moving on. I think it's more about the second reason. There're an increasing number of misguided souls in need of this angel boot camp. And competent group sponsors are in more demand than ever, prompting my early graduation. Not to pluck my own harp here, but you've gotta admit a good student is a good student. Before you accuse me of getting too cocky, I'm fully aware of what these empty plastic chairs represent. Not to mention, my personal evolution isn't over. That much I'm sure of.

Oh, here we go. The said recruits are entering the room as we speak. Karmically, I deserve an endless cast of characters to be joining my circle. However, I'm looking for one particular familiar face. It doesn't take a rocket scientist, does it?

'Speak of the devil', I want to say to him as he takes his seat. Of course he's no idea who I am. And I'm not sure I'll ever tell Mr. Bad Boy Motorcycle. He can't fathom the ride that's in store for him. Not that watching him squirm will be enjoyable at all. That wouldn't be very angel-like, would it? Oh, let me have a little fun. My worry is he's incapable of self-reflection. Ergot the ultimate challenge. I wish I could say I'll die trying, but that's just silly. Forgive me. Since I'm a competitive beast at heart, we know who's going to win this match. Come on. You know you're rooting for me. Raise that foam finger a little higher in the air, will ya?

All I know is redemption's the one thing we all crave whether we know it or not. I can say that now. If I may throw in a bonus life lesson here—as I glare at that sonovabitch. Whatever you do, 'Don't be a dick'. You can quote me on that. Or, if you prefer the gender-neutral bumper sticker (so I don't come off like some sexist shithead): 'Be nice'. It's really that simple. Especially since you could very well end up in one of those plastic chairs in my 12-step room. I'll reserve you a seat, wink, wink.

GUILTY AS CELL

Andrew kept lifting his cellular from his shorts' pocket.

"I'm gonna drown that thing one of these days," Jorge said, casting a line into the murky lake.

Andrew sneered. After hooking a frozen shrimp and sending it into the water, he belched obnoxiously.

"Dude, you're scaring the fish away."

They laughed.

Jorge burped even louder. "That's what I think of your damn phone."

Andrew glanced down at the screen and jumped, smiling. "I almost missed this," he said, displaying the kissy face emoji. A gust of wind blew his brown hair into his eyes. He shook his head so he could see again.

Puckering up, Jorge played like he was trying to plant one on his friend.

Andrew pushed him away. "Let's go. I'm gonna be late."

They packed up the fishing gear.

Taking off his sunglasses and looking at himself in the rear view mirror, Andrew noticed stark white skin around his eyes. The rest of his face was warm.

"Man, you're gonna get there looking like a freakin' raccoon on your big night," Jorge said.

For a moment, Andrew worried his sunburn might kill the mood. He flipped Jorge off. "It'll be dark, smartass."

The car rumbled off the crab grass and away from the lake.

Andrew's phone chimed with a notification, so he reached for it.

"Come on, man. You're driving," Jorge said.

"I still have to shower." Andrew went to his messages. "Gotta let her know."

Jorge grappled for the device. "Let me do it."

Andrew fumbled to get it back, cringing at the thought of his friend reading through the mushy exchange with Adriana.

The cell went airborne. As Andrew's attention followed the landing phone, he didn't notice the traffic light turning red.

Jorge screamed.

Andrew looked up. Unable to stop, he gunned it through the light. Another car in the intersection rammed into their vehicle, sending them spiraling across the road. The tires squealed. A whir of trees and buildings beyond the car windows passed at lightning speed and slow motion at the same time. Andrew tugged at the steering wheel, vying for control until they smashed into a light pole. The front end crumpled like tissue paper, a stench of motor oil filling the air.

Pieces of the windshield went flying. Andrew's head smacked against the car's interior. Sparkling stars flooded his vision. The side of his skull smarted like it'd been hit with a bat.

Crimson spattered the dashboard. Andrew made himself face the scene beside him. Jorge's head rested against the passenger window, his face sliced up and unrecognizable, a huge glass shard poking out from his bloody cheek.

Andrew fumbled frantically for his cellphone in his pockets, between the seat, on the floorboards, until he found it wedged between his legs.

With shaky fingers, he dialed 911.

"State your emergency."

Before he could get any words out, the phone slipped from his hands and he lost consciousness.

Blips of blood red, flashes of green and silver, and a screeching sound surfaced in Andrew's mind as he woke. His eyes adjusted to the dark room. There were no basketball trophies and his poster of Kobe Bryant wasn't on the wall. Unease shot through him. He tried to turn his head, but the tubes in his nose and the neck brace arrested him. Glancing down, he spotted the IV in his hand. There was a steady beep of his heartbeat on the monitor. It smelled as if someone had spilled a vat of hand sanitizer.

Shit, what happened?

Andrew's clouded mind yielded no memories. His back and head were sore.

The chair by the window was empty.

Where's Mom?

A phone on the side table was just out of reach. Andrew didn't know any numbers from memory anyway. He scanned the room's surfaces as much as he could for his cellphone. Nothing.

There had to be a nurse around—somebody. Maybe in the hall? He tried moving his legs in an effort to get up. It felt like a million needles pricked him. Lifting his arms, they burned with sharp pain.

Sighing, he let his body go limp. The hospital bedding clung to his clammy skin.

The television mounted above the bed flickered on in a flurry of electronic snow. *Shhhhhh...* An image of Jorge and him fishing by the neighborhood lake appeared on the television. They were sipping the Budweisers they'd snuck from Jorge's fridge. Andrew blinked, not sure of what he saw. And then the monitor returned its show of fuzzy nothingness.

I must be on some serious drugs.

He was frustrated that recalling being at the lake didn't explain anything. Jorge had to know what happened—or maybe Adriana. *That's right. We were supposed to go to the movies.* That night he was going to tell her he loved her. *Where is she?*

Andrew felt abandoned. He anxiously wiggled his fingers and toes. Someone in the hospital had to be able to help him understand what he was doing here.

"Hello? Anybody?"

Only stillness.

What time is it?

He yelled again. "Hello?"

A muffled, "Shut up!" came through the wall.

One of the nurses leapt into the room. "It's okay," she whispered. Then she increased the dose of something plugged into his arm.

Everything went black.

A shadow reclined by the window. The chair suddenly turned and slid across the floor. It scooted closer and closer. Andrew's gut tightened. His heart raced a mile a minute. The figure came into view. Whoever it was wore jeans, black Nikes, and a black hoodie shrouding the face.

"Jorge?" Andrew asked.

The person slowly rose up to stand, then pushed back the hood. There was no face, only a slab of flesh. Andrew's stomach lurched into his throat. He swallowed hard, tearing the tubes and the IV from his body, throwing the bedding back as the thing's hand reached for him. Andrew thought he might have a heart attack. He couldn't breathe. The rail on the side of the bed imprisoned him. Just as he got ready to hurdle himself over the metal bars, the mattress violently shook. The entire frame rattled and squeaked as it jumped and crashed against the linoleum.

Andrew opened his eyes, gasping for air. The bed settled to the floor.

"Honey, you alright?" his mother asked, springing up from the chair. Mrs. Walker rushed to her son's side. After she surveyed the tangled mass of dangling tubes, she pressed the button on the wall.

A middle-aged nurse bounded onto the scene, swiftly reattaching Andrew to the medical apparatuses. "We might have to restrain you while you sleep. You can't keep doing this." Her voice was smooth and calm, instead of chiding. With a kind eye, she turned to Mrs. Walker. "The doctor will be in shortly."

His mom smiled. Once the nurse left, Mrs. Walker took her son's hand.

"Mom, what happened? What am I doing here?" he asked.

"There, there. Just rest. We can talk about that later." She pulled an envelope from the pocket of her khaki pants. Her eyes watered. "I've been waiting for you to wake so I could give you this."

The letter had already been open, his mother breaking a minor law to satisfy her undying curiosity. Andrew unfolded the paper. "I got in?" He pinched his arm to make sure he was awake.

"Yes, honey! Your dad would be so proud." She squeezed his hand.

Andrew remembered being ten-years-old, playing basketball in the driveway, dribbling around his dad in circles. "You keep this up, son, and you'll be playing for the Blue Devils in no time!" That had become Andrew's dream—to be a starter for that winning team. Each time he watched a game, it was a tribute to his father and all the basketball they'd cheered on together. Now, he'd have to get in the mindset of going off to North Carolina, leaving his mom behind.

"Where's my phone? I've gotta tell Jorge and Adriana." *Why aren't they here?* He wasn't sure where they'd be attending school next year or if they'd all still keep in touch. Until now, he hadn't thought much about that. Hopefully, it would work itself out.

With a grim expression, his mother gazed at the shiny floor. "You need to rest."

"Mom, what's wrong?"

The nurse entered the room and pushed the mini-table on wheels into place before setting the food tray down. "Enjoy."

Andrew could smell the toast and the rubbery-looking scrambled eggs, even though they were probably already cold. Almost as if she had never been there, the nurse was gone.

"I'm going to get something to eat. You want anything else?" Mrs. Walker asked.

"No, Mom. Just some answers." Andrew removed the foil from the orange juice and drank.

She tried to smile as she walked away, but it was more of a wince.

Adriana greeted Mrs. Walker in the doorway. Standing next to the hospital bed, Adriana's eyes were wide. "Oh, baby." She leaned over and grabbed Andrew's cheeks, kissing him.

The taste of her mouth made him feel so alive. He had a flash of her on the day they went to the beach. After loosening the towel around her, his fingers fumbled to undo her top. Seeing the wounded look in her eyes, he realized he wanted more from her than just getting into her bikini bottoms. His lips had gone to her forehead. He was almost embarrassed that this is where his thoughts went now. It's just that he'd known how he felt about her even then.

His breath hissed through the breathing tubes, so Adriana drew back. "Am I hurting you?"

"No, babes." He wanted to wrap his arms around her, pulling her to him, but he thought of all the medical equipment. "I'm so glad you're here." *Should I say it now?* He decided against it, fearing that an 'I love you' would seem random. Or only a result of his brush with mortality.

"I'm so happy you're okay." She took his hand. "How are you feeling?"

"Been better."

"Me, too." She put her hand on his leg. "I was so worried when you didn't make it to the movie. For a minute, I thought— oh, it doesn't matter."

"That's silly." *I could say it now.* But the words weren't ready to come out. "How's Jorge? That lucky bastard is probably doing better than me."

Tears welled in Adriana's eyes. Her lip quivered. She tightened her hand on Andrew's leg. "Your mom didn't tell you?"

"No…that can't be." Andrew's heart seemed to stop beating. A sudden void consumed him. His throat moistened.

She nodded, covering her mouth.

He wouldn't let himself believe it. Once he got out of this bed, he'd march up to Jorge's front door. His best friend would be there like always. Saturday they'd go fishing. The bait shop would finally have live shrimp. They'd catch a whole school of fish.

The nightmares kept coming. Then there was the real nightmare of the scads of inquiries about what really went down in the car the night of the accident. Everyone wanted to know—Jorge's parents, Andrew's mom, Adriana, the cops. He knew he was the one at the wheel, but there had to be an oncoming car out of nowhere, a stray animal scampering onto the road, a pedestrian he swerved to avoid. It had to be his fault, yet it couldn't be his fault. How could he face the fact that no matter how he looked at it, he killed his closest friend?

He couldn't.

And why was he still alive—how was that fair?

As Andrew washed his face, he wiped his thoughts clean with a towel. After taking a pain killer, he flung the medicine cabinet open, unscrewed a pill bottle, and popped one of his mother's Xanax. Self-medicating seemed to keep the details at bay for most of the day. Since it would be his first Monday back to school, he needed all the help he could get.

He was still sore. The doctor instructed him to wear the neck brace for a few more weeks, but Andrew left it on the bathroom counter.

It was so odd driving a rental to school. The seat didn't feel right, the wheel was at a crazy angle, and there wasn't any window tinting. As he sat there, he couldn't bring himself to turn the key in the ignition. The dizzying spinning, the jarring impact, the blood, the pain. Witnessing Jorge's lifeless body sitting in the passenger seat. He feared that by driving that it would all happen again.

He had to go to school, so he started the engine. At one of the traffic lights, he tried to get his playlist connected to Bluetooth. Nothing but silence. He sighed before checking his phone for messages. The body shop was supposed to let him know the fate of his car. No word yet. No 'good morning' text from Adriana.

Green light. He drummed his fingers on his thigh. Probably everyone knew about the fatal collision by now. Grief counselors would be on campus—maybe even all week.

In his peripheral vision, Andrew spied something. When he turned to the neighboring seat, someone was sitting there.

Holy hell!

He swerved on the asphalt before driving steadily in his lane once again.

Even with his attention back to the road, he sensed the figure still beside him.

I'm losing it.

He tried to focus on getting to school, on ignoring whatever it was in the vehicle with him. His hands shook as he maneuvered the steering wheel. He tapped his foot on the floor mat. He had the urge to turn up the volume of the radio, but that would mean his hand would get closer to his uninvited passenger. What if it grabbed him? What if he crashed again? He wondered if he would he ever be able to forget the accident.

Whoever it was snatched Andrew's cellphone from his leg. His instinct was to fight for it right in the middle of driving, but he had the sense to pull over. That device was his life—all his contacts, private text messages, saved passwords, secret notes to himself, and pics (including a few bathroom mirror shots he hadn't had the nerve to send yet to Adriana).

Whether this apparition was the result of drug side-effects or supernatural shit, he was going to confront whatever it was. Upon examining the figure, Andrew regarded the jeans and black hoodie. The open space around the face was pitch dark.

This person logged into his phone and started touching the screen.

"What the hell are you doing?" Andrew asked. "Jorge?"

The black hood rotated to face Andrew. "We need to talk." The voice was deep and raspy.

Andrew's stomach did flips. "About what?"

"About this." He held the cellular in the air. The phantom faded and the phone plummeted to the passenger seat.

Andrew rubbed his eyes and checked his saved information. No notes, no messages, no contacts, and no photos.

When Andrew entered the hall of the English wing, he ignored the stares and whispers. He had tunnel vision for finding Adriana, hoping she could take his mind off the creepy visits from what he thought had to be Jorge. Yet, he half-expected to see his best buddy in the halls as if nothing had happened.

Adriana leaned against the wall, a light dusting of glitter shimmering her cheeks, making her appear angelic.

"Hey, Baby. How was the family thing?" Andrew's hand clutched the strap of his backpack. The Xanax had kicked in even more. If only he could pretend his life had gone back to normal.

Adriana's braids bounced as her head lolled to the side. She sighed. "I would've rather been with you. So sorry I couldn't."

"It's okay…" He winked half-heartedly, staring at her glossy lips. The taste of her kiss entered his mind. *God, I love her.*

Her cheeks reddened. "Were you able to finish the presentation? It must've been hard to concentrate."

"What presentation?" he asked, trying to keep a straight face.

She bit her lip while pressing her binder to her chest.

"Aw, come on. I said I'd finish it." Andrew picked up one of her braids and played with it. "It helped take my mind off things." He felt strangely like the ghost of himself. His perception of reality was like a dream.

Adriana's eyes beamed with understanding.

The bell rang, sending students scattering in all directions.

She kissed him before running to class. Mid-hall, she looked back. "See you at lunch!"

Andrew strolled into first period. A group of kids clustered in the back of the room while the teacher scrawled the word of the day on the front board.

"Bro, I had no idea you could sing that high," one boy said to Andrew. "And to be in such a great mood today? Shit's messed up."

Several of the students groaned in disapproval. Andrew's stomach felt like someone had kicked it.

"And 'Let It Go'?" another boy said. "You can't just let what you did go—asshole."

One of the girls shook her head. "Who'd you get to film you, anyway? Totally creepy."

Andrew's cheeks heated up. "What're you talking about?" He thought back to before the accident when he'd belted out the Disney song in the shower. He'd downloaded it the morning after his first date with Adriana. It was the happiest time he could remember—before the tragedy hovered over him like an ever-present dark cloud.

"This stuff's going viral as we speak." The student shook his phone in the air and pressed the volume button. The track, Andrew's voice, and the sound of running water blasted from the speaker.

"You're already getting a million scathing comments, you douche."

"Give me that!" Andrew seized the cell and witnessed his blurry form through the shower curtain. Somehow the shaving mirror on the counter was at just the right angle to capture his image in the reflection over the sink. The pitch of his voice sounded embarrassingly high and off key—with moments garbled as he sang with water in his mouth. He scanned the post. Andrew's eyes widened as he noticed it had come from his account this morning. *How the hell?* "That's not me!"

"It's totally you. And that *Finding Nemo* shower curtain— thank God it's covering up your junk."

That *was* a small victory.

"Dude, gimme it!" the kid yelled, clawing to get his phone back.

The final bell for class to start seemed to shake the room. "All right, break it up. Phones away," the teacher said. "It's a hard time for everyone. I need you to settle down."

Andrew sat and slid down in his chair, his undershirt growing damp. If he hadn't felt so vulnerable, he would've removed the hoodie offering him a layer of protection. His heart skipped as he wondered how this could've happened. It's not like he'd pressed record while showering. Where had this file come from? And why had it posted now—and from his own account? But maybe that meant he could take it down!

His mind teemed with worry as to how he might dodge further humiliation. *When I find the son of a...* He clenched his jaw and waited for the end of English class.

I need another Xanax.

The minute the bell sounded, Andrew hurried into the hall where he heard someone chanting, "Let it go, let it go! That perfect girl is gone...Let it go!"

Andrew yanked up his hood and ducked into the restroom. The handicapped stall was free, so he locked himself in and took a few deep breaths. He pulled up the social media site and searched for the delete button.

His phone buzzed and a notification popped up. "Why'd u send a video of us MAKING OUT 2 my mom?" Adriana texted. "& y now? Y???"

What the hell? "I don't even have her #!" he typed.

"I no ur going thru a lot, but jeez!"

"I didn't do it."

Andrew's blood bubbled in his veins. His temples throbbed. *I'm stuck in a damn nightmare.* Two crazy incidents in less than two hours. He massaged his forehead.

"OMG! & I thought u were 1 of the nice guys. I just saw THIS:" Adriana punctuated the message with an unhappy face and attached a screenshot of one of their intimate text conversations. "& THIS is on snapchat right now!" she texted.

"I deleted that from my phone." He knew he had gotten rid of it ages ago so he could pretend it had never happened. And now his phone was empty of data. It didn't make any sense.

"We r over…"

Andrew read the text several times, dumbfounded. What could he say? He slid the cell back into his pocket. 10:30 and he had lost his dignity and his girl. His gut twisted. The agony of missing Jorge intensified. He broke down sobbing, tears streaming his cheeks. Backing himself to the tile wall at the rear of the stall, he slid to the floor.

He wondered if he could get his mom to sign him out early. Surely, she'd understand; but she'd want to talk to him about his feelings. He wasn't sure he was strong enough for that.

Hugging his backpack, Andrew rested his head on it and waited for second period to finish. Getting caught skipping or being suspended from school didn't even cross his mind.

The lunch bell chimed at last. He needed to hunt down Adriana and talk some sense into her. If she saw him face to face, she would know he was telling the truth, no matter how absurd it seemed. He'd never lied to her. Peering into her eyes, she'd have to believe him.

He dashed from the language arts building and under the cover of the breezeway. Dark clouds flooded the sky and the wind picked up. A flicker of light followed the grumbling of thunder. The smell of rain was already thick in the air.

"Andrew Walker to the office. Andrew Walker to the office. Immediately," the principal's voice boomed on the PA.

Aw, come on!

He changed course and headed for his doom. The front office

assistant recognized Andrew and thumbed for him to see Mr. Fuerst, who was buttoning his suit jacket. He motioned for Andrew to shut the door behind him and sit in front of the imposing desk. Andrew's vantage point was much lower to the ground, making him feel smaller than he already did.

"So," the principal said, glaring fiercely. After picking up his cellphone, he pushed it toward the defendant. "Can you explain to me why you sent me such a foul message?"

After Andrew read the screen, Mr. Fuerst snatched the device and stowed it in his jacket pocket. Once seated in his leather swivel chair, he tapped his fingers together. His lips were tight.

"Sir?" Andrew sighed, his face twisting in confusion.

"I won't ask how you got my personal number. I *do* keep wondering what would possess a young man such as yourself to send me something so vile. Maybe you can enlighten me, Mr. Walker."

"What, sir? I didn't send that." Andrew swallowed hard.

"The police traced it to you. So, don't play coy." Mr. Fuerst glowered at him and turned his desk phone around, picking up the receiver. He handed it to Andrew and pointed at the keypad. "Here, call your mother. Tell her why you're here."

Great. That's just what I need right now. "Sir, it wasn't me." Andrew slumped in the chair, crossing his arms.

"You're actually going to deny this? And to act like this after recent events? Unbelievable." The principal slammed the receiver down. "Fine. *I'll* call your mother."

The guilt set in again. Andrew tried to go at least one day without thinking about the accident—the crushed car, the splattering of blood, Jorge's mangled face. "Sir, you've got this all wrong." He willed back tears, yearning to return to the bathroom where he could let it all out.

"No, I believe it's *you* that have it wrong. Get out of my sight.

You're on external suspension until further notice." Mr. Fuerst rose from his chair and pointed to the door. "Say goodbye to your Duke scholarship. They won't touch you after this."

Andrew skulked from the room, actually relieved he could leave campus. His Adidas hit the asphalt so fast, he swore the rubber smoked behind him. He choked back tears, fearing someone might see him. Losing his basketball scholarship was a possibility he couldn't swallow. It was already bad enough that he didn't think he could ever forgive himself for Jorge's death. He just wanted to lock himself in his room, to never come out.

He bolted across the parking lot and got into the rental. The door rattled as he banged it shut. He tossed his phone onto the passenger seat before gripping the steering wheel and bumping his head on it.

"Having a bad day?" Siri's voice chirped through the speakers.

Andrew raised his head. *Is my phone talking to me?* He rubbed his eyes. The keys were on his lap. Realizing that and the fact that the Bluetooth system hadn't worked that morning increased his pulse rate.

"Yeah, I'm talking to *you.*"

After picking up his phone, he looked at the display. Everything seemed normal. He punched in his security code. Then he checked the notifications. *Are there voice commands on this thing?* But he didn't command it to do anything. The stress of the day must have had him hallucinating.

Soon it'll be spouting Latin and levitating.

"I'm not going away, Andrew."

It knows my name? Holy—! He snatched the smart phone from the seat and powered it off.

The phone rang. *Oh, my God! How the—?*

The caller ID read "Mom," so he answered without thinking. *But all my contacts are erased.*

"Andrew?" Her voice sounded tired and hoarse.

"You all right?"

"I'm at Broward General. Please come." She hung up.

Dang! What happened?

He started the car and sped off.

After peeling into the lot and parking, Andrew sprinted to the emergency room desk. He felt jittery, having just been there days before. After hearing the news that he'd lost his best friend, he shuddered to think about how his mother was doing.

His knees wobbled with emotional exhaustion. Panting, he put his hand on the counter to keep from collapsing. "I'm here to see Mrs. Walker."

The nurse scanned the list of patients. "I'm sorry, but she's not here."

"Please look again. Jasmine Walker. She just called me."

"Sorry. There must be some mistake." The nurse got up to retrieve some manila folders.

Andrew paced. Moisture beaded his face. His shirt was soaked at the armpits. He felt his brain go into overdrive. *Where's Mom?*

The reality of standing in this very hospital made him dizzy. His vision hazed. He rubbed his throbbing forehead.

Spotting the restroom, Andrew decided to splash some water on his face. The faucet took a few seconds to run cold. After patting his skin dry, he stood there, gazing at his reflection. The room went dim.

Siri's voice spoke, "You murderer." The words were slow and deliberate.

Taking the phone out of his jean pocket, he saw the screen was black. It was still off. Had it been on when his mom called? He didn't remember.

Where's the sound coming from?

"The world would be better without you in it." The digital voice seemed to be in his head while also bleeding into the room.

In a trance, in some weird meditative state where he was losing control, Andrew tightened his grip on the phone. He smacked it into the mirror, cracking the glass. The shards rained in a clanging symphony onto the tile.

You can't destroy me, Andrew. A loud, maniacal laugh reverberated through the tiny room.

"Sir, you okay in there? Sir?" someone outside the door yelled.

Andrew kneeled on the floor, staring at the glowing broken screen. Fragments of plastic and metal littered the ground. How was it still functioning?

You should off yourself, Andrew.

Without thinking, he took up a piece of mirror. He gazed at his sweaty face and his vacant brown eyes reflecting from his hand. Was there really a reason to live? His dad was dead—and so was Jorge. Everyone at school thought he was a joke. His girlfriend dumped him. The principal hated him. His mom had obviously abandoned him. He wouldn't be going to Duke.

Andrew caught sight of Jorge standing in the corner. Dirt and blood from the collision soiled his shirt. Cuts and abrasions covered his body. Lacerations on his face were so deep that parts of his skull were exposed. His scalp hung in flaps. One of his eyes was just an empty crimson socket. Out of his cheek poked the sliver of windshield.

A crippling grief overwhelmed Andrew as the specter of who he'd killed confronted him. That image, the fact that he was responsible, would never leave him. It would be there at every turn. It would stare back at him from everyone and everything. It would be there in the eyes of his first born, if that was a part of his future—a future that seemed erased. Pointless.

He sliced into his wrist the long way. That was sure to do the trick. Red spurted everywhere. A glistening slick of blood covered the floor. The wall became a Pollock bespattered painting. He felt woozy.

Jorge went to Andrew and helped ease him onto the cold porcelain. He kneeled over him, putting pressure on the gashes.

The door flung open and a stream of light invaded the room. A man with a bandaged head and a nurse in green scrubs hovered over Andrew. The dampness underneath his body chilled him. The smell of iron was thick in the over-air-conditioned air.

"Code blue!" a nurse yelled.

Medical staff loaded Andrew onto a gurney and rolled him down the bright white-walled hallway. The fluorescent lights whirred past overhead.

Jorge's disfigured face hung over Andrew's as Jorge helped wheel him into the emergency room. A bloody finger waved in chastisement before the battered hand pocketed the remains of Andrew's phone.

Regret and anguish overcame Andrew because he knew the doctors would save him.

LOST TIME

I sit in my '57 Chevy in the driveway, not able to feel my feet. The rest of my body is numb, including my mind. All I know is that there's something dreadfully wrong with me. There's nothing I can do about it…

The meeting of the Experimental Aircraft Association ended. Just as I hoped, I gleaned several tips from other pilots also building planes in their garages. Mine is almost fully assembled, but I wanted extra assurance my maiden flight wasn't going to crash and burn. Rachelle secretly hoped I'd never fly it. I saw it in her eyes each time she had brought me just-baked cookies.

In the parking lot of the EAA, I examined my map, looking for a shortcut. Main highways from Mankato to Minnesota Lake were several extra miles. Sure enough, I spotted a direct route on a backroad. Less time. Less traffic. Less speed traps. I'd thrill

Rachelle by arriving home early. One less thing for her to agonize over, especially on a school night when she'd have to teach the next day. And, maybe she'd even be in the mood before lights out.

I drove off the lot, onto the road. As I crossed the train tracks, the car shaking me like a martini, I hadn't seen the massive pothole on the other side. The Chevy plunked and rattled, and I had to hit the gas to get out of the crater. I shot out of the car and stuck my head under it to view the damage. I sighed, noticing the vehicle's one brake line dangled onto the asphalt.

After getting back in the driver's seat, I tapped the steering wheel, convincing myself things weren't really that bad. Having no brakes was all the more reason to take the road less traveled. The plan was to downshift when making any stops, which would be few and far between, at least until I got into my neighborhood.

The twilight pastels of the darkening sky blazed overhead, thick clouds drifting in. Each side of the road dropped off into swamp, and I was glad to be the lone vehicle. I switched on the radio for some company, The Marcel's 'Blue Moon' settling my nerves.

Eventually, I came upon a sign warning 'curve ahead' and fortunately spotted it in time. Had I been going any faster, I'd still be in the swamp. Passing the dangerous turn, I congratulated myself, accelerating on the straightaway. My watch indicated about half past eight. I was making great time.

Having a few close calls that night, I pitied the big black Lincoln tilted off on the embankment ahead. Oddly, it resembled a hearse. By now the night had taken hold and with no streetlights or any sign of the moon. The only light came from my own head-lights and those of the Lincoln. As I rolled closer, two figures surveyed their predicament. My car slowed to a walking pace, and I lowered the window. "Can I help you?" I asked.

A person dressed entirely in black wore an Amish-looking hat, but I couldn't make out any facial features. Somehow his car's brake lights didn't cast a red illumination—there was no effect at all. It was like his skin was immune to even the faint hint of moonlight or twinkling starlight, making me wonder if he had a face at all.

My Adam's apple leapt in my throat. My hands went clammy.

The figure glided toward me, and my brain wasn't processing any of it. I don't think there were any legs under his cloak. He came at me so slowly. The second shadow blocked the Lincoln's brake lights, and the headlights on my vehicle dimmed. A bird squawked, but it was eerily muffled, as was the clock on the dashboard. The radio shorted out. Blood surged loudly in my ears.

"Can I help you?" I asked again. My shirt was drenched with perspiration. I heard Rachelle's voice in my head, reprimanding me for being a hero. *Why did you stop?* And I wondered why myself, my heart beating out of control.

The dark shadow continued to slowly glide at me. I was paralyzed. Even my eyes were transfixed. I thought I'd gone deaf because I heard nothing at all, not even the blood still pounding through my head. Contracting my bladder and bowels, I thought about stepping on the gas and getting the hell out of there. My body wouldn't move. It was the first time in my life I prayed to pass out.

What happened between that moment and the one where my body finally let me gun the gas pedal, I have no flipping clue. All I know is that the night went even darker, even though the moon suddenly came out of hiding. Those dense clouds were gone. My aviator watch, which was supposed to be state-of-the-art reliable, still read half past eight. The clock dial on the dash spun out of control.

As my car sped away, exhaust hazing behind me, I glanced at the rearview mirror. One of the figures floated along, reaching into his cloak for something— a weapon to obliterate me? The gas pedal still pressed down as far as it could go, I finally got out of there. When I checked behind me, there was only midnight black on an open field.

The rest of the drive was so automatic I don't even know how I made it home.

Stepping out onto the driveway, I have the sensation I'm moving on an invisible conveyor belt. And I'm not quite myself anymore. I can't describe it.

The bedroom lamp is still on, but I'm afraid to go inside, afraid of what I might do. I go in anyway. When I see Rachelle in bed, she's reading. She throws the book aside and springs up. Touching my face, her expression contorts, noticeably perplexed. "You look terrible. You eat those pickled pigs' feet again?"

I don't answer, wishing indigestion from my favorite gas station snack was my only problem. My own thoughts fade, and I reach into the inside pocket of my jean jacket. Not thinking of what I'm digging for, I pull out my car keys.

"Wanna go for a drive?" I ask, my awareness slipping away.

HEATHEN

Delvin's mom, close to tears, wildly waved the Satanism pamphlet over her head. As he stood there, she rocked herself on the sofa, lamenting how her bartender's salary wasn't enough for private school tuition.

In the car on the way to the principal's office, Delvin asked if she had even read the leaflet. "It's *Satanism*. What's there to read? I mean, *Jesus*," she said. Those horror movies about delinquent teens and serial killers linked to the occult had done their brainwashing, and so did the priest during Mass every Sunday.

Face to face with the principal, Mrs. Blake, in one of her lowest-cut blouses, defended her son. She went on about Delvin being too smart for his own good. He needed another chance. He'd learned his lesson. Apparently the principal had received too many parent complaints. Showing them the door, he failed to cast one glance at Mrs. Blake's cleavage.

The next day, in her tightest dress, she drove Delvin to the Academy of Holy Angels. This would be his only chance. The head of the school recognized Mrs. Blake upon sight. Behind closed doors, she employed a sultry voice Delvin had never heard before as she referred to 'old time's sake'. Delvin's cheeks heated with embarrassment, but the principal sat on his desk, arms crossed, enjoying the show. She vied for Christian compassion and a scholarship and work-study combination, reminding this man how she counseled bar patrons, just like she had done with him one night. Delvin was another wayward sheep needing to be brought back into the fold. At those words, the principal ushered them to the secretary who immediately registered Delvin.

One month later, Delvin looked at his Marilyn Manson wall calendar while putting on the despised school uniform; khakis and white polo with an embroidered purple cross. He felt much more comfortable in his array of black shirts and jeans that he had worn his whole life in public school. At least his Doc Martins fit the new dress code, so he could keep a sliver of individual expression —that and his silver skull ring and thick silver chain.

Delvin rolled his bike to the elevator. Outside the apartment building, backpack over his shoulder and ear buds in place, he mounted the seat and rode through the spring fog that cast an eerie white on the morning darkness. The glow of headlights and streetlights that were like a sky full of moons stood out among the blur around him. Misty air caressed his face.

Once in the halls of Holy Angels, the smell of urine and bleach reached Delvin's nose while passing one of the bathrooms on his way to first period. He hoped he wouldn't have to scrub toilets the following Saturday. He'd rather pick up trash across campus or scrape gum off desks. He actually didn't mind the work study, since it gave him quiet meditation away from his mother's constant Bible quoting.

A stocky, tall kid wearing a football jersey tapped Delvin as he sauntered by. Delvin wanted to ignore him, but the jock's beefy hand grabbed his arm. "Hey, why don't you *finally* sit with us at lunch? Gotta proposition for yeh."

Delvin arched his brows and shirked free as another student bumped shoulders with the jock.

"Watch where you're going, faggot." The jock brushed his shoulder.

"Leave him alone, asshole." Delvin got into his face and then backed up.

"What, are you butt brothers?"

"Grow up, loser." Delvin snickered.

"Guess I'll have to come to *you* then," the jock yelled, watching Delvin walk away.

Delvin wanted to avoid that scenario by eating lunch in an obscure stairwell for yet another day. This idea of a *proposition* made him cringe. He wasn't sure what high school stereotype he fit, since he was part intellectual, part goth, and part loner—but *zero* part jock. It's not that he didn't participate in physical activities. There was his bike, and the set of weights kept under the bed to pump up his arms so he wouldn't appear so thin and gangly. But team sports were as appealing to Delvin as mainstream organized religion.

After passing through the door to first period, Delvin dropped his bag on the floor and slid into his desk. The pentacle penned on his wrist that morning while waiting for his Eggos to toast seemed to stand out more under the fluorescent lights. He pulled long sleeves down to conceal it.

"Did you hear Principal Jerkins is doing Ms. McDermott?" a kid in a letter jacket asked another with bleached hair. Delvin recalled catching letter jacket boy using his cellphone during the last vocabulary quiz, noting that more private school kids cheated than public school kids. Was it him or did more Christians seem corrupt?

"The *theology* teacher? How'd you know?" the blond boy asked.

"She's always in his office, coming out all—you know." Letter jacket boy lowered his voice. "Plus, them two've been spotted at the Melting Pot, acting like they're on a date or something."

"Now that you mention it, I've seen him in her room after school a lot."

"Yeah, there's something definitely going on."

"Well, she's *hot*, man."

The kid nodded his head. "Can't blame 'em for hitting it. *I'd* do her."

Just before the bell rang, Mr. Hickethier rushed into the room with a Styrofoam cup and an armful of books and papers.

Delvin considered the idea of becoming a teacher himself, since the profession needed more that were free-thinking and inspired. The masses needed to be liberated from their limited beliefs about society and its expectations. It was time to make young people realize they have the power to change the world. Too many sheep roaming around.

The classroom clamor stilled as the senior English literature teacher instructed everyone to turn to the previous day's stopping point in *Macbeth*. "Who can tell me why the witches are significant?" he asked.

Delvin watched as students made themselves smaller or averted their eyes. The fog outside had turned to wisps of white, almost like the school had been lifted into the clouds. Delvin felt like he was amid the three witches on the Shakespearean stage, the fog representing the moral confusion he understood so well.

A girl with fiery red hair was texting under her desk, amusement on her face.

"Cassie? Maybe you can enlighten us?" the teacher barked.

The girl shoved the phone between her legs. "Wha-a-t, Mr. H.?"

Stepping closer to her desk, Mr. Hickethier crossed his arms. He cleared his throat.

Delvin raised his hand. "*I* can tell you."

"Delvin?"

"They're supposed to represent the Devil's temptation because they seem to play on his desire to become king, telling him it's supposedly his fate. But they can be linked to Greek and Norse mythology, too—maybe they're just goddesses of destiny who know what he's going to do anyway. Whether they're really supernatural witches or not, they're a way for Macbeth and the audience to blame everything on the occult. I think Shakespeare was making a commentary on humanity's tendency to shirk personal responsibility." Delvin wanted to add that was exactly what Christians did when they told the story of Lucifer's fall from grace, making him into this evil force wanting to destroy humanity.

Mr. Hickethier's mouth dropped open.

Someone gasped.

"Um, that's an interesting perspective," the teacher said. "But you must know that evil is *real*. It's alive and well all around us. What's more likely is that Shakespeare was saying the struggle between good and evil is as relevant now as it was in the Renaissance."

Was Shakespeare really thinking that far ahead? Delvin shrugged. His teacher probably thought Delvin was acknowledging argumentative defeat, but Delvin knew this man was just like his mother—both were die-hard fans of mass consciousness.

As the class continued reading *Macbeth*, Delvin sketched a pentacle in his notebook. Despite the stigma against Satanists, Delvin didn't feel any shame about wanting everyone to have freedom of thought or wanting everyone to be empowered individuals. He felt sorry for the average person compelled to use 'the Devil made me do it' excuse.

Finally the bell rang.

"Go on," a blonde girl, who was the one Delvin saw making out with some dude the other day, whispered to the red-haired girl.

Delvin noted her long legs as she approached. She rested her hand on his desk. The scent of vanilla and coconut drifted, lifting his spirits like some kind of aromatherapy.

"Thanks so much for the save," she said. "You're always so quiet, I—"

Delvin shoved the books in his bag without looking up, not wanting to encourage some vapid girl's interest in him. "Don't worry about it."

"Yeah, well." She shifted her weight and lifted her hand from the desk. "I like what you said. This place is such a joke. Hypocrisy is everywhere and everyone just accepts it."

Delvin stood and peered into the girl's grey eyes, realizing more stirred there than he had judged. Maybe the school wasn't entirely crammed with Christian drones after all. "Thanks. I'm just glad Mr. H. didn't bite my head off. For a second there, I thought he would."

"No one really ever says anything interesting—especially with senioritis at full-throttle."

"Full-throttle, huh?" Delvin grinned. Not a girly thing to say at all. This red-head was bursting with surprises.

She giggled. "I'm Cassie."

All these weeks in class, he never really paid any attention to names. *Like the Greek prophetess. Nice.* "Delvin."

"I know." She peered at the floor. "So, is it true what they say about your transfer here?"

"I wouldn't believe everything you hear." He shouldered his backpack.

"I *don't* believe everything I hear. That's why I'm asking *you*." Meeting his eyes, her expression was open, hair falling into her eyes.

"Look, I gotta go." Delvin stepped around her, and headed for the door.

The next day Delvin casually walked down the hall to first period when Principal Jerkins stopped him.

Delvin froze.

"How's my little heathen doing?" the principal asked, wearing a suit making him look like a used car salesman.

Heathen, huh? "Great." Delvin was dying to laugh. "Things are great."

"Glad you're adjusting." He patted Delvin on the back. "Don't be late."

"I won't." Delvin strolled away.

In English class, Delvin felt trapped in an eternal cycle of purgatory that would continue for the next few months. *I can't wait to graduate from this hell-hole.* Hell was such an interesting metaphor—one he liked, even if it was merely another Christian invention.

Mr. Hickethier conducted class, but the students fidgeting at their desks and the teacher's voice all faded. Delvin had *The Goetia: The Lesser Key of King Solomon* open on his desk, hidden under his backpack. The book was a grimoire the king used to summon man, beast, demon, and angel. Reportedly, some 72 entities helped Solomon build his temple.

A hand swiped the book from Delvin's desk. "See me after class," the teacher said before continuing his lesson. Delvin prayed the confrontation would be brief, since apparently Mr. H. was fond of hearing himself speak.

After the bell sounded, Cassie approached Delvin's desk. "I'm sorry about yesterday. I didn't mean to be so pushy. *Really*." She swept the hair from her freckled face, her lip gloss shimmering.

"No worries."

Her eyes darted around the room. "So, some of us are going to get together out by the lake this weekend. I thought you might like to come."

"Thanks, but I'm not really into that stuff." Delvin glanced at the clock, wondering how long he could afford to linger before being tardy to next period. He still had to face Mr. H. on the way out. Yet, her sweet smell captivated him.

"I promise you we're not gonna get trashed. We're not like that." Cassie tilted her head, a slight pout on her lips.

"What, are you holding a Bible study or something?" His tone was playfully mocking. He searched his memory, trying to recall who her friends were. Other than the blonde in class, he hadn't noticed her talking to anyone else.

She smirked while crossing her arms. "Hardly. We're interested in something that's right up your alley, if you know what I mean."

Delvin grabbed his chin and cocked his head. He'd been banned from seeing his public school friends, who were the only ones who had really understood him. "Let me think about it," Delvin said, enjoying her flirtation.

Cassie's depth of character, matched with her curvy figure, stimulated his male hormones. He didn't want to admit it, but he was definitely attracted to her.

"And I can always drive you." She slipped him a scrap of notebook paper. "Here's my number." A shy smile lit up her face.

She must've seen him get to school on his bike. "Alright. I'll let you know."

"Delvin?" Mr. Hickethier said from the front of the classroom.

He stepped to the teacher's desk.

"I never want to see you reading something else in class—especially something like this. Do you hear me?"

"Yes, sir."

"Don't mess with this stuff. I'm surprised you haven't learned your lesson by now."

"Sir?"

"Let's just say, you wouldn't want me to tell Jerkins about this, or your mother for that matter." With a scowl, he handed the book to Delvin.

Delvin's mom had just rushed off to her shift at the bar. When he reminded her about going up to the lake for a Bible study retreat with some new friends, Mrs. Blake had been thrilled at the lie and his apparent conversion, kissing his forehead.

Delvin was more curious about whether or not he and Cassie had a connection than feeling guilty about telling his mother a fib.

Delvin paced in front of the window, thinking about how long it had been since he had hung out with anyone. And Cassie seemed to know about his shady past and *still* invited him.

Spotting a light blue Charger in front of the apartment building, he scurried out the door.

"Nice ride," Delvin said as he got into the car, noticing he and Cassie were twinning—both wore black T-shirts and jeans with black boots.

"Thanks. Me and my dad rebuilt it."

Everything that came out of this girl's mouth was a turn-on. "Sweet." Delvin nodded.

"Heard you caused a stir in theology yesterday when you got all pro-choice." She kept her eyes on the winding road flanked now by the beginning of the forest. The canopy of trees enveloped them in shadow.

"Yeah, well, the Catholic church should rethink a few things." Delvin valued human life, but he also understood that some decisions weren't always so simple—rape and incest just to name two. And those things needed more serious attention, in his opinion.

"I take it you're for birth control, too, then?" Her tone of voice was hard to read.

Was she trying to gauge his sexual experience or orientation? "Pretty much."

Cassie glanced at him with confusion—just what he was going for—and then at the penned pentacle on Delvin's forearm. His heart skipped a beat when he saw her checking it out, but she didn't flinch.

"You're gonna like what we have planned tonight," she said, pointing to the marking.

Something in her voice made Delvin uneasy. "We'll see about that." He wondered what he had gotten himself into as he lowered the window and let the country air whip at him.

The cabin smelled musty, and dust danced in the ray of light coming from the ceiling fixture. The interior was a sea of browns —walls, curtains, couch, two recliner chairs, and carpet. The bay window showcased the green lake, which was shaded by a cluster of trees down by the dock.

Even though the décor was stuck in the past, it had a down-to-earth vibe. "Cool place," Delvin said.

Cassie smiled. "Yeah. And, it's so quiet up here."

A car parked outside and the blonde from English class stormed through the front door with the jock who'd harassed him in the hall. The gossipy cheater wore the boy's letter jacket.

Delvin wrestled with his annoyance at himself for allowing his dick to lead him into this trap.

The jock kicked the door closed. "Well, you made it, Del-vin. Welcome."

Delvin noticed how Cassie's seemingly innocent aura became serious and dark as she sat on the couch. The jock mechanically threw his arm around her. If only Delvin had gone to lunch with these fools, he would have known he'd had no chance with Cassie.

"Have a seat, my man," the jock said to Delvin.

With the help of his blonde girlfriend, the letter jacket boy stacked kindling into the fireplace and ignited it.

Delvin took the other side of the couch, clutching his backpack. All eyes were on him. "What's this all about?"

The blonde girl swayed on over and sat on her boyfriend's lap, who was now sprawled on a ratty armchair.

"You don't like to beat around the bush, huh?" The jock stroked his chin.

"No, actually I don't," said Delvin.

The blonde girl got up and touched Delvin's nose with her finger. "Were you expecting some hedonism? Isn't *that* what you're into?" Her voice was high pitched like a three-year-old's.

It took a second for Delvin to register her using such an advanced vocabulary word.

The boy on the chair said, "Apparently, all that bad ass shit isn't just a cover." There was menacing look in his eyes.

Delvin's body became rigid as he considered heading for the door, but they were a few miles from town. His mom's shift wouldn't end until three a.m., and his old public school buddies had been ordered to stay away from him. There wouldn't be anyone to call. And if he'd pussy out, there wouldn't be anyone up here this time of year to hear him yelling for help. Hopefully, Delvin was just blowing this out of proportion.

The blonde got a bottle of Jack Daniels out of the paper bag, took a swig, and passed it to her boyfriend.

Had Delvin misjudged Cassie? "Thought you weren't coming up here to get trashed."

A sinister grin on her face, she said, "Oh, we didn't." She giggled before taking a drink from the bottle, the alcohol sounded melodic as it swilled.

"We came up here to do a kind of exorcism." The jock grabbed the bottle.

Delvin ground his teeth. "Exorcism?"

"Yeah, you know, cleanse you of your *evil* ways." The boy peeled Cassie's hand from his neck, seemingly annoyed she was massaging him.

Delvin gripped his backpack, squeezing the canvas. "If you

knew anything about my beliefs, you'd know all that stuff is bullshit."

"Yeah, right," said the jock.

Delvin rolled his eyes. "You've got this all wrong." He got up, his bag in one hand. "Cassie, take me home."

She shook her head and clucked her tongue. "Sorry, Del. No one's leaving yet."

The jock carelessly pushed Cassie from his lap. He stood at least a head taller than Delvin, and his broad shoulders were much wider. "What's in the bag, son?"

"None of your fucking business."

"This is *my* house, so I say it is." The jock snatched the bag from Delvin and unzipped it. Pulling *The Goetia* out, the boy made a *hmmmm* sound as he read the cover. "That's what I thought."

Just like in the pamphlet incident, Delvin realized there was no use protesting or explaining himself.

"We'll start with getting rid of this," the jock said as he sauntered to the fireplace.

As the book hit the flames, Delvin mourned the book that he'd fortuitously discovered at an obscure second hand store. The paper blazed up like a fireball, and then the ashes disintegrated. Was its destruction as dangerous as burning a Ouija board? Maybe the movies had warped Delvin's mind more than he realized.

"Get back on the couch, son," the jock ordered.

"And if I don't?" Delvin asked, pocketing his effeminate hands.

"Then I kick your ass."

Delvin didn't care what anyone thought, but he wasn't keen on getting his ass kicked. If he just humored them, maybe they'd take him home. No bruises. No broken bones. No cuts. They'd all be graduating soon, and he'd never have to see these dimwits again.

The jock observed the compliance on Delvin's face and signaled to his crew to get the show on the road. Pulling some supplies from the bag, the other teens set the scene. White candles were lit, and the blonde girl pulled out a Bible and a small bottle. Cassie fired up a stick of incense. The boy in the letter jacket turned out the lights.

After the blonde recited the 'Prayer to Archangel Michael', the jock handed Cassie the Bible. She read some of the marked passages that Delvin recognized from either Mass or from films about demonic possession, probably downloaded from the Catholic website.

One of the candles flickered. Delvin hoped that was a sign of a speedy conclusion. As he tapped his foot, he considered sitting in the pew next to his mother at church was much less agonizing.

A drizzle of rain startled Delvin. The jock was squirting the contents of a plastic bottle with a gold cross on it into the air. Delvin wiped the water from his face, spitting some of it from his mouth. The kid in the letter jacket unscrewed a tin. After dipping his fingers in it, he swiped black soot across Delvin's forehead, making a cross, as if it was Ash Wednesday. Not wanting to provoke any of them, Delvin contained his exasperation.

The four teens made a circle around the couch, singing *Amen, Amen, Amen,* for an endless time. When they finally ceased their antics, they all examined Delvin, apparently expecting some physical change. The lone croak of a frog pierced the dead silence outside.

His obnoxious laugh cutting through the stillness, the jock said, "Thou art cleansed."

"I *told* you. I'm not into the occult," Delvin said with vexation.

"Not anymore, you won't be, you pansy," the jock said.

"Pansy?" Where did they get off making up judgements about him? "And so what if I am?"

The boy shoved Cassie aside and leaned into Delvin's personal space. "I knew you were a faggot."

"I think the 'lady doth protest too much.'" Delvin laughed to himself. "Why are you so worried about other dudes? Maybe you should at least *pretend* you're into your girl," he said, shooting a glance at Cassie.

The jock cracked his knuckles. "What're you implying, asshole?"

"Take a few seconds to let your sport's brain get it." Delvin waited for a fist to reel into his face, knowing he should've kept his mouth shut.

A blinding light manifested in the middle of the room, accompanied by a swirling wind extinguishing the candles, as well as the remaining embers in the fireplace. As the illumination dimmed, a male presence of about eight feet tall took form, wearing a short crimson robe. His hulking chest and shoulders wore a sculpted black breastplate, and a red, cape-like cloth whipped in the draft. Gladiator sandals were strapped up to his knees. This being possessed more musculature than was humanly possible, which made Delvin shudder. A thwacking of feathers echoed through the room as two massive, dark iridescent wings unfolded, casting ominous shadows on the walls.

Delvin had never known what it was like for time to stand still until that moment. Anticipation fried his nerves. He couldn't think, breathe, or move.

The androgynous-faced seraph raised his massive sword just like in the famous painting in which he trampled Satan. Delvin had a hard time wrapping his brain around what was happening. He was certain they were about to be sliced and diced.

Instead, the celestial presence shook his head at Delvin's peers whose expressions were that of utter terror. Eyes aglow, the angel focused his power on each one of his victims. One by one, their faces melted like wax, the sagging flesh flopping from the muscle, slumping to the carpet. Their bodies limped forward like junkies after a potent hit, before their blood and entrails heaped into a steaming pool of goop. Each skeleton crumbled like powder and then evaporated. The biological slop on the carpet sizzled, burning and disappearing through the floorboards.

Delvin stretched out his quaking arms to see if he was still alive. A warm sensation in his lap cooled, and he realized he'd pissed himself.

The messenger of light met Delvin's wide-eyed stare and waved the teenager to follow as he headed to the door. All hints of what transpired in the room vanished. The singed couch and the holes in the floor returned to their original state. Gone were the bags and the Jack Daniels bottle. Even the air smelled neutralized, free of any scent.

The night was darker than ever before.

Delvin stood on the porch as the angel opened the passenger door of Cassie's car, motioning for Delvin to enter. Slowly descending the steps, he trembled, fearing what might happen if he didn't comply. After Delvin sat, the being slammed the door and got into the driver's side, starting the engine without a key. Delvin stiffened, staring straight ahead, sensing the powerful vibration filling the car. It calmed his jittery nerves. The vehicle sped along the forest road and into town where they passed through all green lights.

When they neared the Academy of Holy Angels, Delvin realized he was going home. The car rolled into his apartment complex and parked in the loading space. Delvin turned to the seraph, noticing his head grazed the roof of the car, eyes glowing like a golden fire.

He knew he had to ask the question, or forever regret it. "Why didn't you kill me?"

The angel's expression revealed he sensed the curiosity and was impressed with the teen's brazenness. "Well, kid, you must have read about the Pharisees."

The idea of hypocrisy wasn't lost on Delvin, but he was surprised by the nonchalant tone. "Yeah?"

"You understand that one's soul is more important than labels or the letter of the law. Someone upstairs has your back, knowing you'll do great things."

Words escaped Delvin. All of his beliefs and perceptions were shaken. He couldn't be that important. He was just a kid.

"Go on. You'll see me again."

As Delvin got out onto the sidewalk, he wasn't sure how he felt about that. Standing paralyzed, he watched the taillights fade into the night.

STILLBORN

Sylvia's hands shook. Even her eyeballs vibrated.

The rush to save a mother and newborn in the delivery room had fried her nerves—and it was only her second week on the job.

The fact that she worked in the health industry didn't stop her from purchasing a pack of cigarettes in the gift shop. She'd picked up the nasty habit when she'd moonlighted as a P.I.'s lackey, one of the jobs that put her through college.

After tapping the box on her palm on the way past a display of stuffed animals and flowers, Sylvia exited the building. On the sidewalk under the awning, an elderly man in a wheelchair wheezed. A pregnant woman stroking her belly rested on a bench. Her male companion wrapped his arm around her.

The muggy and stagnant air was so unlike the dry, stinging heat in Sedona, where Sylvia had traveled a few weeks ago. That'd been a last hurrah before embarking on her career.

Sylvia fumbled in her purse for a lighter.

The lobby door swung open. A security guard grappled with a

squirming woman whose feet skidded along the sidewalk. A designer handbag dangled from her arm, her brown curls falling into her eyes. "I want to know what happened to my babies!" she screamed.

The guard clutched the patient's upper arms, forcing her to stand in place. "You need to calm down, ma'am."

"I will *not* calm down!" She wriggled free.

"Hey, I don't want to call the police." He widened his stance and put his hands on his hips.

"Fine." The woman backed away, her arms flailing. "I'm getting a fucking lawyer."

He waited for her to turn around and walk away before storming back into the facility.

The patient stomped over to Sylvia. "I remember you."

Her headache throbbing, Sylvia took a drag. "Excuse me?"

"That weird design with the black stone—I remember it."

Sylvia flicked the ash, cursing the scrubs and her striking jewelry that might as well have been a huge bull's-eye. The image surfaced in her memory of a wiry, white-haired woman with brownish teeth who'd convinced her she needed the pendant for protection. She'd claimed the stone came from outer space. No jeweler had been able to identify it, so that may have been true. When Sylvia had handled the piece, a prickle of energy latched onto her, like a stray animal jumping into her arms, begging to go home. *You see?* the woman had said. Well, the charm wasn't keeping the lunatics at bay today.

Sylvia pushed the butt of her cigarette into a nearby ashtray's sand. "I'm sorry. I need to get back to work."

The woman rubbed her nose with the Kleenex. "Which one of you are they firing for throwing away my babies?"

"What?" Sylvia's throat tightened.

"They said one of the nurses would pay."

"Ma'am, I don't know what you're talking about."

"You have to help me."

"I can't do that." Sylvia loosened her ponytail to relieve her headache.

Grabbing Sylvia by the hands, the mother peered into her eyes. "My babies kicked all throughout the last trimester. I *know* they were alive."

"There were complications." The patient had had an epidural; and even without it, feeling everything and remaining lucid during labor was impossible.

Still holding Sylvia's hands, she shook them and sniffled. "A mother *knows*. You have to help me."

Following a gentle squeeze, Sylvia pulled away. "I'm sorry. I can't."

The mother's eyes pleaded, watering. "What if my babies *aren't* dead? What if they're on the black market?"

Sylvia scratched her head, remembering the day she'd found out she was adopted. Getting the records was next to impossible, but she managed. Crooked hospitals existed, selling newborns, telling mothers their children had died in childbirth. Yet, she hadn't noticed anything amiss at this particular facility. "My deepest sympathies, *really*."

"I'll get all of you. You'll pay for what you've done!" the woman yelled.

Sylvia fled inside the building.

Buttoning a cardigan sweater over her scrubs, Sylvia strolled down the hallway to the breakroom. The smell of disinfectant and medicine hung thick in the air, while the fluorescent lights glared above. Dr. Reynolds strutted in her direction, his permanent smirk accented by a strange gleam in his eye. She'd presumed some of his many patient referrals were from women who'd told their friends about the hunky OB-GYN with the chiseled face and cleft chin.

Not wanting to boost his already enormous ego, Sylvia looked away.

"Nurse Falcon."

Glancing up, she stopped in her tracks. "Yes, doctor."

"You shouldn't hide your figure." He grinned, fingering his chin. One of his eyes twitched before coming back into alignment —like someone stressed or who hadn't slept. The movement was something she'd observed on a malfunctioning robot in a science fiction movie.

She swallowed a giggle, thinking this was akin to discovering a male supermodel wore a set of false teeth. "I'm sorry?"

Arching a brow, he eyed her chest.

"It's cold." Sylvia crossed her arms.

"You'll get used to it." He smoothed out the neck of her sweater before swaggering away, his shoes making their distinctive clack along the floor.

Wondering if this was how Dr. Reynolds treated all his female staff, she continued to the break room.

Brian stirred his paper cup of coffee.

"Why aren't you using the mug I got you?" she asked.

"Keep forgetting to wash it. I'll get back to saving the planet tomorrow."

She rolled her eyes, knowing he'd tell her the same thing then. After pouring herself some liquid caffeine, she lightened it with half and half. "Hey, did you see that nutcase who was thrown out?"

"The Yaskov woman? No, but the nurses were yacking about it."

Sylvia nodded. "Well, she begged me to help her. That's the last thing I need to get involved in, being new around here."

"I don't think you have anything to worry about." He squeezed Sylvia's shoulder. His touch reminded her of how touchy-feely he was the other night at the pub.

"What do you mean?"

"No one can keep their mouths shut around here."

"Meaning?"

"Dr. Reynolds picked his new protégés."

"You?" she asked, watching the steam rise from her coffee.

"Yeah, but he's also going with a female for once." He leaned on the counter, elbowing her.

Laughing awkwardly, she bit her lip. "Who's the lucky girl?"

"You're so dense." He put his hands under her jaw in a mock showcase of her face.

Sylvia smiled. "You're joking. After only three weeks?"

"Dead serious."

One of the lights flickered as if in confirmation. It seemed they were the only two people in the entire hospital. The squeaking of gurney wheels, the shouts of 'emergency' in the halls, and the paging of doctors all fell silent.

Without another word, Brian pressed his lips to Sylvia's for the first time. His kiss was soft, oddly familiar, with the promise of intensifying. When a nurse flung the door open, the two quickly separated.

Brian covered a chuckle with his hand. "Enough lazing around. Back to the grind."

"Congrats," she mouthed, trying not to burst into laughter.

He clicked his tongue and gave a thumbs-up on his way out.

The staff's whispering terminated as Sylvia approached. One of the interns averted his eyes.

Dr. Reynolds strolled down the hall with Brian at his side. Brian's head bent toward the doctor, capturing every last inaudible word escaping the man's lips. They grinned, followed by Reynolds socking a fist into Brian's shoulder.

"Right away, doctor," Brian said, spinning on his heel and pointing two index fingers like blazing guns.

Reynolds rested his arms on the counter next to Sylvia, his fingers tented.

Everyone on duty sat up straighter, their bodies angling to Reynolds' gravitational pull. They stared at the doctor without expression.

"Nurse Jenkins, the file?"

A gray-haired woman in scrubs dotted with storks extended her arm, and without looking at the pile of folders, plucked one from the stack. She rolled her chair to Reynolds, handed him the file and resumed her work.

"Nurse Falcon, I need a word," Reynolds said.

Sylvia jumped. "Yes, doctor." After a quick glance at the schedule, she noted it had changed. Her stomach somersaulted with worry of an imminent reprimand.

Dr. Reynolds leered at a nurse's cleavage before turning to his office, waving for Sylvia to follow. Sylvia found it peculiar that the nurse seemed nonplussed. In fact, the perky redhead had squeezed her upper arms into her chest and leaned forward to enhance his view.

"Close the door," he said.

Sylvia did as told and then perched on a chair, embracing her purse like a lap dog.

He stood behind his desk. His light hazel eyes bored into hers. "I'll get right to the point. I can see you're a natural."

The bag squeaked in her grip. Sylvia straightened, wondering if what Brian had predicted could be true. "Doctor?"

"You see, I need someone like you by my side. There've been some accusations, and unfortunately, heads are going to roll. We can't afford a lawsuit." He tapped his chin.

"What's that have to do with me?" All the praise she'd received from the medical staff during her internship flooded Sylvia's mind. Although she'd demonstrated a knack for labor and delivery, she didn't think she'd proven herself yet.

"You're still in the probationary period, and so are two other nurses. That makes this a very dicey time, if you catch my drift."

"Are you trying to intimidate me, doctor?" She shifted in her seat, ready to believe Brian's words had been bullshit.

"Not at all." He grinned. "I'm trusting you. In fact, I've already changed your schedule."

"Oh?" She feigned ignorance, tilting her head.

"From now on, you'll be my primary assistant during all deliveries."

Sylvia thought Brian would have nabbed that honor.

"Thank you, doctor. I appreciate the confidence." Once she swallowed the lump in her throat, she grabbed ahold of her necklace, hankering for its vibration.

"In return, you'll keep what happens in the delivery room between us." His face stiffened.

"Yes, doctor."

Clenching his jaw, he adjusted a frame on the wall containing a photo of himself and the governor. "I realize you're off duty, but I need a favor."

She wiped her brow. "Yes?"

He handed her a key and a Post-It note. "I left a folder in my lab over at NSU. My receptionist already knows you're on the way."

Sylvia, realizing she'd just agreed to be his pawn, glanced at the directions scribbled on the note. Her cat, Isis, would be circling the food bowl by now.

He raised his wrist in an exaggerated manner to examine his Rolex. "It's the only folder on the center lab table. If you leave now, you'll get there before my students log in for their hours. Oh —and remember…"

He placed a finger to his lips.

In Dr. Reynolds' suite, Sylvia contemplated the only door in front of her. Her stomach filled with butterflies for some reason, like this was some covert operation. "It must be in there?"

The receptionist nodded.

Pulling the key from her pocket, Sylvia smiled.

Once inside, she flipped on the light. The room smelled of chemicals, formaldehyde being the most potent. The scent of death hovered in the mix.

It appeared to be a typical laboratory, doubling as a medical classroom. Test tubes filled with different colored liquids lined the center island. A staggered arrangement of beakers, both empty and half-filled, cluttered the counters beneath the cabinets. Several gurneys covered with sheets hugged the walls.

Sylvia had opted for a nursing program that used plastic anatomical dummies instead of cadavers. In fact, had it not been for the required cadaver dissection, she'd have seriously considered becoming a doctor.

On one of the gurneys, a covered mass about the size of a baby bulged. Sylvia slowly approached it before peeling back the sheet.

She flinched, not expecting to see a skinned cat. The head still had its fur, tongue flopping from the mouth. Arms and legs reached as if reveling in a belly rub, but the pickled skin looked like a chicken's at the supermarket. Flaps of the abdomen stretched to each side, revealing pink, gray and brown innards. Upon closer inspection, what at first seemed like organs were curled-up fetuses.

Sylvia threw the sheet back over the corpse. She'd read about how animal farms raised cats, pigs and rats merely to be slaughtered for educational purposes. It pained her to think about innocent life fermented in chemicals, flayed, cut, probed and prodded. She blinked the image of her sweet kitty from her thoughts.

Covering her mouth and choking back bile, she went to the center table, where she spied the file folder. She scooped it up and darted from the room.

In the car, Sylvia thought about how Reynolds had told her to keep what she saw to herself. Although the pregnant cat had disturbed her, animal dissection wasn't out of the ordinary. For most people, it was probably less problematic than seeing a dead person. Brian had told her he used to read all the toe-tags to remind himself the cadavers had donated themselves to medical science.

Her attention turned to the folder on the passenger seat. She picked it up, wondering why the sensitive material hadn't been sealed in an envelope. This had to be some sort of test. As Sylvia flipped through the papers, her body went rigid at the sight of Mrs. Yaskov's medical chart.

Nothing about the paperwork seemed amiss, except for a few corrected items. A whited-out section in one of the boxes had "Stillborn" scrawled over it. Two Polaroids of twin infants stuck to the back of the folder. Their skin had a blueish hue, their lips purple. Umbilical cords hung loosely around their necks, but the visible skin didn't show any evidence of strangulation. The expressions were not of distress, but were eerily tranquil, as if asleep.

When were these photos taken and by whom?

Sylvia shoved everything into the file and turned the key in the ignition.

Dr. Reynolds opened the door as Sylvia lifted her hand to knock. Giving her the once-over, he motioned for her to enter.

She rocked on her heels, finding it odd he hadn't said anything. "Here you go."

He took the paperwork and winced. After dropping the file onto his desk, he sucked his finger.

"You alright?" she asked. It was only a paper cut, but his drama over such a minor injury entertained her.

"It's nothing." He glared at the wound, eyes weirdly rolling like they'd done earlier.

A greenish drop fell from his hand.

Sylvia searched the room for what might've created such an optical illusion. But there was no digital clock, colored lampshade or anything else to create an odd refraction of light.

Reynolds nodded, reaching for a tissue, wiping the surface of his desk clean. With his other hand, he fed the entire folder into the shredder behind him. The machine whirred and crunched before quieting.

"Have a good one, doctor." Sylvia turned to leave. Normally she'd be amazed his abuse of the shredder hadn't destroyed it, but it was only one of many strange occurrences of the day.

"Oh, one more thing. Well, two, actually."

"Yes?" She spun around, hoping she'd managed to tame the growing irritability in her voice.

"One, mark your calendar for happy hour. This Friday."

Her brow furrowed.

He pulled the plastic trash bag from the shredder and tied it. "And two, be a doll and toss this in the dumpster on your way out."

As Sylvia seized the bundle of paper strips, she studied Dr. Reynolds. His pupils enlarged and his expression hardened as he stepped unnaturally close to her. A faint spicy scent reached her nostrils, smelling like Irish Spring soap and a hint of fabric starch.

"Right away," Sylvia said, holding his gaze.

While she retreated, he crossed his arms with the exaggerated flair of a bad actor.

Something in the air made her shudder as she left. She chalked it up to her being punch drunk from the endless day. She possessed zero energy to contemplate the whole happy-hour proposal. That would have to wait.

Downstairs, and out back, Sylvia neared the trash receptacle.

"Disposing of the evidence, huh?" said a familiar voice.

Arm in midair, ready to toss the bag, Sylvia froze. "What?"

"I knew you were in on it. That's why you won't help me." It was Mrs. Yaskov, her eyeliner smeared, her hair mussed.

"Look, I don't know what you want from me." Sylvia hunched her shoulders, wanting to get home to bed.

Regarding the bundle of shreds, Yaskov shook her head,

disgust written on her face. "He's got you doing all of his dirty work. I bet you're even sleeping with the douchebag."

"I don't know where you get off. Here, you figure it out." Sylvia thrust the paper at the woman.

The patient folded her arms around the bag.

"Yeah, you're welcome. Now maybe you can leave me alone." Sylvia threw her hands up and stomped away.

Not able to sleep, Yaskov's desperation haunting her, Sylvia had returned to the parking lot of the hospital as if she'd never left. She sat in her car at the rear of the building, hoping to discern something out of the ordinary. And here she thought her days of investigative spying were over. But instead of earning a crappy hourly wage, this time she was doing it for free.

The clock on the dashboard flashed 3:00 a.m.

Her stomach rumbled, but Sylvia had no interest in food. Poor Isis was probably whining at the window, desperate for human interaction.

Leaning back in the seat, she massaged her temples. The car horns honking in the distance and the whir of the occasional vehicle passing on the nearby road seemed magnified.

Hating herself for it, she lit a cigarette. However, the mere act of puffing and flinging ash out the window kept her from charging into the hospital and interrogating the staff. But then again, who would she ask—and what? If one of the nurses was murdering babies for sport, it's not like the person was likely to confess.

As a nondescript white van pulled up, a shadow wearing scrubs and a black hoodie materialized. The shadow and the driver loaded something into the rear of the vehicle, their movements stiff and mechanical. Sylvia zeroed in on the small bags that could easily have been infant corpses, but she didn't want to get ahead of herself. There was a larger sack, but it was anyone's guess what was in it.

Sylvia's heart pounded as she flicked the cigarette and raised her window.

After the van left, she started her car, keeping the headlights off as she pursued it from a safe distance. Her mother had made fun of her decision to get a black car, considering the South Florida sun, but Sylvia appreciated her current stealth in the early morning darkness.

Only a couple miles from the hospital, the van turned into the university. She tailed it to the back of one of the buildings. The hoodie-clad figure opened the accordion bay door, and the driver helped him lug the bags inside.

Sylvia parked in reverse in a nearby faculty space and tugged the bill of her baseball cap lower.

The two men climbed back into the van. As they drove past, Sylvia ducked out of view. When she heard the vehicle squeal onto the main road, she sat up.

Getting out of her car, she lit another cigarette as she trudged closer to inspect the loading area. There hadn't appeared to be an alarm, since they'd gotten in and out so quickly. She yanked on the handle, hoping by some miracle it opened.

It didn't budge.

After taking the last drag from her cigarette, she ground the butt with her heel.

At the corner Starbucks, Sylvia lounged in one of the faux-leather chairs, the arms cracked and peeling. The air-conditioning blew colder than at the hospital. Florida businesses opted for the *colder the better* motto, which irked Sylvia to no end. Cupping her mug, she watched Brian push through the door, punctual as always.

Under better circumstances, she would've been schoolgirl-crushing over him. He bent over to kiss her and took a seat, dropping his backpack at his feet.

"You look like you haven't slept," he said.

She yawned at the suggestion. "I haven't. I think something fishy's happening at work."

Brian cocked his head before unzipping his knapsack, retrieving a hooded, dark sweatshirt and wriggling into it. "Fishy?"

"Yeah." She imagined how he'd look with the hood on. Trying to recall any other distinguishing features from a couple hours before, she set her coffee on the table and went limp against the chair. She was being silly. Lots of people owned hoodies. Sylvia decided to test his loyalty. Would it be to her or to the hospital? "We have to do something."

"Well, you haven't exactly given me anything to go on." His whine imitated an uncooperative child faced with a list of chores.

Sylvia questioned why a guy who seemed into her wasn't jumping through hoops to be the hero. She always rescued herself, but what was wrong with welcoming a sidekick for a change? Then again, regarding this particular mission, she didn't completely trust him. Too many contracted stakeouts, spying on cheating partners. *Trust no one* was her credo.

His backpack fell over, causing the flap to open wide. A sea of ID bracelets caught the light—or at least that's what Sylvia thought she glimpsed. Normal hospital procedure dictated the parents and infants wore them home, but her facility removed them prior to discharge. The practice hadn't struck her as suspicious until now. But what was the significance of keeping them?

She rubbed her eyes, expecting to see something completely different when she looked again. However, Brian hastily zipped the bag, robbing her of the chance.

What if she grabbed the knapsack and rifled through it? Nah, what then? Accuse him of having some kind of fetish? She didn't have one goddamn idea how any of this made sense. It was better to stay in character in the hopes he might slip up and reveal a valuable clue.

"Look, something's happening to those missing newborns. I don't know what. But I need you to keep an eye out." Without assessing his response, she got up. "In the meantime, I need to get home and crash."

The apartment complex's lot was dark, the trees' black silhouettes creating shadows along the asphalt. Sylvia hung her purse over her shoulder and headed to her building.

A second pair of footsteps crunched through the grass and then onto the pavement. The pace picked up, and Sylvia sensed an urgency in the air. Thinking it was her own jitters, she sped up her stride, focusing on the comfort of her pillow, just minutes out of reach.

The figure behind her sprinted around Sylvia and leapt into her path.

Sylvia halted with a gasp, clapping her hand to her mouth.

A woman in a track suit with reflective stripes stood under the lamplight.

It took Sylvia a few seconds to process the messy bun pulled back the wiry curls. "Yaskov? What the fuck?"

"The answer is in the lab. Get me in there." The patient wrung her hands.

"You've got to stop this." Sylvia wondered where the father of the woman's children was. Apparently absentee sidekicks was an epidemic. Visualizing her coffee cup that read *Cats make more sense than men*, she smiled to herself.

Sylvia tried to pass Yaskov, who gripped her by the shoulders.

"It's not just my babies. Those files … and that was just *one* bag. I know you suspect something." The woman's eyes glistened.

Although Sylvia didn't have any children, she knew the pain of being separated from a birth mother. A nurturing instinct made her wish she could alleviate Yaskov's agony. Goddammit. "Even if I wanted to help you, what can we do about it?"

"Let's not worry about that yet. Just get me into the lab."

"Okay, but that's it. Then you're on your own. You promise?"

Tears streamed down the mother's cheeks. "I promise."

"Dr. Reynolds sent me to pick something up." Sylvia's nails dug into her palms.

The receptionist put down some paperwork and regarded Yaskov.

"We carpool to the hospital together," Sylvia said.

"It's hot as hell out there." Yaskov fanned herself with her hand and grinned.

"He usually calls if someone's coming in. Doesn't he have a lab this morning?"

"He had an emergency delivery." Sylvia quirked an eyebrow

and pointed at the door. "We're late. And I forgot the key. Let's not make the doctor angry, hmm?"

"Alright, alright," she said as the phone rang. "It's unlocked." She picked up the receiver. "Hello?"

Sylvia's heart stopped as she prayed it wasn't Reynolds on the line. Clutching Yaskov's arm, she pulled her into the laboratory.

"What if he's on his way?" Yaskov asked.

"It's now or never."

The mother grabbed a cabinet door and thrust it open.

Sylvia's stomach roiled and her eyes widened.

Shelves and shelves of different sized jars contained various body parts, like artifacts of some twisted museum. She spotted a human foot on the lowest shelf. Pickled hands sat on either side. A uterus and an umbilical cord. An entire container of eyeballs. Testicles. A jaw with all its teeth.

Sylvia slammed the door and opened another, hearing a muffled cry.

When she turned, Yaskov's hand fell away from her mouth before she collapsed. Rushing to her aid, Sylvia felt her partner-in-crime's pulse and verified she still breathed. Were there smelling salts somewhere?

However, when Sylvia stood to view the source of Yaskov's shock, her knees buckled. She had to prop herself against the countertop. Crammed into the cabinet, enormous jars held babies in various stages. Embryos. Premies. Newborns. Stickers with dates stuck to the glass. She stepped closer, studying the faces. One sucked its thumb.

Finally, she noticed two jars side by side. Identical, each one's tiny hand pressed to the glass as if reaching for its other half. One a boy. One a girl. She had to cover a scream as she noticed a "Y" on each of the labels—the date the same as Yaskov's delivery.

The lab's door swung open.

Reynolds hurried into the room, his dress shoes smacking the tile. "What are you doing here?"

He studied the open cabinet and the unconscious body on the floor. As he approached, his face tensed.

Sylvia grasped her supposed lucky necklace. *What a joke*, she thought. On instinct, she snatched a jar of tiny severed feet from the cabinet shelf. Holding it in front of her, she waited to see if Reynolds stopped advancing.

"Put that down, Nurse Falcon. You don't understand." He kept stepping toward her.

"Understand what?" Her sweaty hands started to lose grip on the jar.

"Let's just say human genetics is getting an upgrade. Your illnesses. The untapped power of your minds. All will be improved. Have you been watching the news? You're embarrassing yourselves. Help me help you." He glowered at the charm around her neck.

Sylvia flinched.

"Just think—no more fake social media accounts manipulating you." He waved a hand in the air. "No more tracking of your credit card chips. No more chem trails in the sky. None of that will be necessary anymore."

She half-expected him to confess to being a member of the Illuminati. *What a load of shit.* "What does that have to do with dead babies—*her* dead babies?" Sylvia glanced at the woman puddled at her feet.

"Not everyone passes the selection process. You understand, don't you?" he said.

Her teeth sank into her lip.

"Your mother didn't want you, did she?" Reynolds lunged for her necklace.

Her eyes watering, Sylvia focused her anger at the doctor's

manipulation. She hurled the container, and it shattered against his head. The little feet splashed to the ground. At first, he seemed merely dazed, but the glass had cut into his temples and cheekbones. Emerald-colored liquid oozed from his gashes. After stumbling from side to side, his eyelids fluttered. He tumbled to the floor.

Yaskov stirred, moaning.

Sylvia rushed to her. "We need to get outta here."

"What happened?" She blinked herself into awareness.

"Reynolds … never mind." Sylvia felt as if her sanity waned as she considered what the doctor was. An alien? There was no way she'd ever say that out loud. Life wasn't a science-fiction nightmare. And here she'd thought Yaskov was the crazy one.

Sylvia yanked the woman to her feet, but when they turned, Reynolds had disappeared. In his body's place lay a pool of slimy gunk. It slithered as if alive, the viscosity thickening.

"What the—?" the mother asked.

"Just some chemicals. We don't have time." Sylvia flung Yaskov's arm up and over her shoulders.

When they tottered from the room, the receptionist still sat at the desk. She scratched her head at the sight of the two women. "What's going on?"

Closing the door, Sylvia winced. "We had a bit of an accident. Someone'll need to clean it up."

Yaskov swooned, struggling to stay on her feet.

"Sorry about that," Sylvia said as she hauled her partner away.

"Sweet Jesus. I leave for *one* minute," the receptionist said under her breath.

Sylvia drove Yaskov home, while the poor woman whimpered about what she'd found in the doctor's jars. Sylvia had to pull over. The suggestion that Yaskov take the shredded evidence and her first-hand account to the press finally calmed her down. Surely an investigation would ensue, bringing the guilty and complicit parties to justice. Even if Reynolds had vanished for good, there was no way he'd worked alone. This was the real world. Real life. The scales always balanced—didn't they? After Sylvia tucked Yaskov into bed, she drove to the hospital.

The sterile air of the facility was comforting, the fluorescent lights sobering.

Despite Brian's failure to come to her aid, Sylvia livened at seeing his friendly face.

He massaged his chin before sipping from a mug printed with words *Nurses call the shots*. Today was the day he finally put her gift to use.

"I've decided this planet is worth saving," he said with a smile. "We still on for happy-hour Friday?"

Sylvia pursed her lips. "Did we have plans?"

One of Brian's eyeballs wobbled in its socket, and he knowingly smiled at her pendant. He'd never paid it any attention before. She'd thought it odd he was the only one she knew who hadn't asked her to explain what it was and where she'd gotten it.

In a protective gesture, Sylvia palmed the black stone for a moment. "Sure, we can get a drink."

"Good." His lips met hers, but there was a clumsiness to it, as if they'd never done this before. As that registered, Sylvia felt his teeth piercing the flesh of her mouth, his hand wandering to the back of her neck. She'd bitten her own lip many times before, but this sensation was different. The whole area numbed, like getting an injection of Novocain.

"Ah," she said as she backed away, licking the broken skin.

"Perfect." Detachment had somehow flattened his voice. He passed her a handkerchief.

Sylvia's insides cringed. After forcing a wink, she stepped away into one of the custodial closets. Reaching for the comfort of her necklace, she realized it was gone. Had it fallen off in the corridor? Why hadn't she heard it drop? Could he have snatched it with one hand? Her heart nearly beat through her chest. She fished her phone out of her pocket and dialed her trusty sidekick.

"Wake up," she told Yaskov. "You need to get the ball rolling *now*. Make copies. Send it registered mail." She anxiously tapped her foot, taking the lighter from her pocket and playing with the flint wheel. If only she could have a cigarette without setting off a smoke alarm. Take the edge off. As the thought crossed her mind, her nicotine craving disappeared. Gone, just like that.

Yaskov sounded groggy. "What's going on?"

"You heard me. Get your ass moving. I'm going home sick and catching a plane to Sedona."

"I'm moving my ass, and *you're* going on vacation?"

"It's not a vacation. I'm going to see how we can stop this thing—or *things*. Who knows how many of them there are." Her mind fogged. Details of the past few days slipped away.

"Huh?"

"Yeah, I lied about the green stuff in the lab. It wasn't chemicals." A revulsion at the memory shifted into a curious fascination. That Novocain numbness spread throughout the rest of Sylvia's body.

"You mean—?"

Sylvia pressed the handkerchief to her stinging bottom lip. When she drew it back and inspected it, emerald-colored fluid dotted the cloth. One of her eyes spiraled around on its own, making her dizzy. "I-it's … blo-o-od," she stammered, attempting to steady her wavering voice.

LEGEND TRIPPERS

My reason for still hanging around to tell this story is a selfish one. Technically, I'm done here, but I just can't pull myself away from Jaxon. I've been following him really close, experiencing things through his eyes, which is the best way for me to navigate my purpose. You might call it a mission. But, human nature never ceases to fascinate me, especially when it comes to the supernatural or the unexplainable. People lose their minds. And, they're less likely to notice my presence, even though I, too, fall into that mystical category. More on that later. We don't want to miss anything. Don't worry, I'll do my best to fill you in.

Jaxon knew what the train could do to a living being. A month ago his front end barreled through a flock of sheep, the cowcatcher not doing much good. About twenty animals were cooked meat under the hot traction of the motors, guts and blood on the windshield, bits of wool plastering the glass. The gruesome sight had been enough, the memory of burning flesh stinging his nose. Jaxon thanked his lucky stars the boy on the trestle tonight hadn't suffered the same fate. Damn kid was in some kind of trance, his feet dangling between the ties, oblivious to the locomotive's whistle and various cries for him to get up.

Jaxon had just finished his statement to the police and made sure the kid, apparently named Joey, was safely in the hands of the paramedics now tending to the boy's bloody shins. They had banged against the plow while Jaxon leaned over it to yank him from the tracks just before he'd turned into ground hamburger. But Jaxon couldn't erase the young face from his mind—it had appeared stunned as if coming out of a daydream, every facial muscle had tensed, eyes practically popping out. The boy's life seemed to flash before his eyes as he reached for Jaxon. What the kid said echoed in Jaxon's brain. *The others ran, but my body wouldn't move. I tried to scream, but I couldn't.* The shake in the boy's voice indicated something abnormal happened to him out there. Jaxon was sure of it, too, especially after seeing a shadow with horns and flaming green eyes.

A tall, thin guy in camouflage pants, black T-shirt, and cowboy boots had a video camera propped on his shoulder. He rushed at Jaxon, who was on his way back to the train. "Can you tell me what happened? Is it true you saw the Goatman?" the guy asked.

"Get outta my face, you prick." Jaxon put his hand up over the camera lens and strode away in a huff, impressed that the rescued boy knew Jaxon had seen something, even though he hadn't said one word about it. This goat creature must've been the reason the kids were "legend tripping." Wasn't that what Joey said they were doing?

"Come on, give me something." The guy shimmied to Jaxon, pressing his black-rimmed eyeglasses up to the viewfinder for a second. "Anything."

"No way, asshole." The last thing Jaxon needed was footage of his testimony getting back to his boss, causing public humiliation to the entire rail company.

The cameraman stuffed a business card in Jaxon's shirt pocket. "In case you change your mind. I've been staking out this Louisville Loop for months, hoping to catch a break."

Jaxon pushed past him, tossing the tiny card on the ground, and then lifting himself back inside the cab of the train, where he radioed headquarters.

"You been drinking again?" Frank asked after Jaxon filled him in on the details of the near accident.

Jaxon hadn't touched a drink in two years. Thinking he was safe off the record, he now wished he'd lied about his story. "This wasn't *my* fault."

"Oh, you might as well blame it on Bigfoot." Frank chuckled.

"Come on, man. I know it sounds crazy, but do you think I'd risk mentioning this if it ain't true?"

"I can't write this fucking shit down on the damn report."

"Look, there's a kid missing—and some *thing*'s out there." The brother of the boy Jaxon saved had also brought his girlfriend out to the trestle. She's the one who had vanished.

"I can't believe you're falling for those crack pot stories. Not you."

"I know what I saw. I know what I heard."

"Well, you need to get your head straight. Right now I gotta put you on suspension."

"Fuck, Frank, you firing me?"

"I'll get back to you after the investigation shakes down.

Company'll spring for your motel tonight. Get home tomorrow and shake this off."

"But—" There was a click over the airwaves and static.

Jaxon grabbed his jean jacket and his keys and hopped off the train, skulking past the cameraman who had the lens aimed at the departing ambulance.

Walking down the slope on the side of the tracks leading to the bottom of the trestle, the grass crunched under Jaxon's boots. Shadows of the sparse trees and bushes darkened with the waning light, and the empty lot was eerily devoid of insects or critters. He searched the brush for those green eyes. Had that just been a hallucination brought on by his adrenaline rush? Had he worked too many shifts in a row? Maybe it was just some wild animal.

Whatever it was, he needed to stick around to prove his sanity —to not only himself, but to his boss. And, he couldn't help but think of that poor missing girl. Somehow he felt complicit in her disappearance, although his logical mind told him that was nonsense. However, helping find her might fill the void left by his runaway sister, who narrowly escaped the drunken hand of their father, or his fellow soldiers brutally killed in the Gulf War. All of that had driven Jaxon to the bottle, the alcohol letting him delude himself into believing he wasn't becoming his father.

Following a crossing of the busy highway, he popped into the corner drug store to purchase a disposable camera to capture some much needed evidence.

After checking in and getting his hotel key, Jaxon steered clear of his room. He couldn't afford to stare into the mini-bar. The stuff had already made him hate his father growing up, and himself for drinking away every opportunity and girlfriend he ever had. He'd be damned if he'd lose his engineer job. It was all he had.

Exhaling audibly, he hit the pavement outside the lobby. His adrenaline had tapered off, but the ghost of it ran through his veins. He imagined how some liquor would wash all the nerves away. And how it would make everything worse, too. That was the kicker.

He wandered into the deserted coffee shop on the corner and sat at the counter on one of those old fashioned diner stools with a swiveling cushion. It squeaked with his weight.

For a split second, Jaxon thought he ought to check the closing time on the window. The only sounds were the clanging of pots and pans and the clinking of plates and silverware coming from the kitchen. Stale coffee and sugary dough smells floated to him, accompanied by the faint sound of '80s music.

He had suppressed the reality of what he had experienced for as long as he could. Like a clogged water pipe finally bursting, the images materialized. Jaxon heard an angry snarl as if right next to his ear. The shadow in the darkness at the base of the trestle with horns crouched all over again. Those glowing green eyes locked on Joey once more, the thing's claw pointing up at the boy. Jaxon covered his mouth, to stop himself from crying out *gimmie your hand!* to the kid like he'd done only hours before.

Jaxon jumped in his seat as the front door squealed open and a heavy step stomped the tile.

"Marla?" the man in uniform barked. He faced Jaxon, twisting the end of his white mustache, surrounded by at least a day's worth of stubble.

With a thwack and a slam, a twenty-something Bettie Page-haired woman stepped into view. Her roots were dark blonde, and her arms tattooed with sleeves of roses and pin-up girls. "Hey, Mack," she said, pushing some of her unruly locks behind her ears. After rinsing the brown sludge from the coffee pot, she started a new brew, the strong aroma of coffee beans sputtering from the machine.

Marla looked at Jaxon with bloodshot eyes, a hand on her hip. "What'll you have, darlin'?"

Jaxon examined the bottles of beer in the cooler behind her. "Coffee, and a burger, medium rare."

"Sure thing," she said, going to the kitchen window and patting the counter. "Got that, Al?"

"Coming up," a deep voice said, followed by the sizzle of beef and the gurgling pop of fry oil.

"I see you're stuck with us tonight, huh?" the officer said to Jaxon.

"Yeah." Jaxon rested his elbows on the counter. "Hey, weren't you up there at the scene?"

The cop bobbed his graying head, reaching for the cup Marla had just filled. "Damn kids." Pouring a stream of white sugar from a canister, he clinked his spoon in the cup. "Keeps us busy around here. Damn shame, though."

"Did the girl turn up?" Jaxon asked.

"Nah. Already sniffed 'em dogs all around. Nothing." He pointed his leathery hand to the pastry glass, and Marla plated a chocolate-filled croissant, sliding it along the counter. "None of the tragedies deter them kids—brings even more of 'em out there. I keep saying we need to put up a fence 'er something."

Jaxon shifted in his chair at the cop's cavalier attitude. "They all legend tripping?" He took another gulp of coffee. "Is that what it's called?"

"Beats me. Dumb kid said he took his date up there to scare her, like that's supposed to be some kind of thrill. Said his brother tagged along."

Jaxon tapped his heel on the ledge of the stool, getting ready to ask a question he already knew the answer to. "What're they trying to see?"

"You ain't heard of this place? Pope Lick's supposed to lure victims to their death, straight into an oncoming train." His stout belly rumbled. "Most bastards poke around or get drunk under the trestle without anything happening. The occasional idiot jumps or get shredded on the tracks—it's all the same difference, really."

Jaxon shuddered, remembering the flock of sheep. "What's the story with the—?"

"*Supposedly* a goat man. Some say he's an escaped circus freak. Others that he's some spawn of a devil worshipper, or the devil himself. Who the hell knows."

"You seen him?"

Marla delivered the burger.

The officer munched the last of the croissant. "There ain't no such nonsense."

Something scraped the front window, a sharp screech quickly fading. Jaxon turned but didn't see anything outside, not even a branch. He massaged the gooseflesh along his muscular forearms, wondering why no one else seemed to hear it. "What about the girl? She disappeared after the train had already stopped."

"There might be another reason she's missing," the cop said, rolling his eyes. He stood, his shoes clapping the floor before slapping a twenty on the counter. "Thanks, sweetie."

The waitress picked up the cash and crammed it into her apron before clearing his plate. "Good night, Mack."

"Don't go nosing around out there. That highway traffic'll kill ya when you cross." He patted Jaxon on the back and headed for the door with a hollow-sounding chuckle.

Jaxon chewed a bit of his burger and stuffed the fries into his mouth one by one.

He prayed the goat man was just a prank, someone dressed up

in a costume like his dad did at Halloween, and that the missing girl had somehow made it home safely.

"Do you know those kids that were up there tonight?" he asked Marla.

She wiped the counter with a rag. "Natalie's my cousin."

"Shit, I'm sorry. I didn't know." He pushed his empty plate toward her. "Why didn't you say something when—"

"I'm going to look for her after I close." She dropped his dish in the sink behind the counter with a plunk, his silverware jangling in after it.

"By yourself?" he asked, his leg bouncing so much he forced it down with his palm. "That doesn't sound safe. Don't you—"

"You heard Mack." Her rag swiped in front of him. "There's no such nonsense." She rinsed the rag, her lip quivering, and her hand quaking under the running water.

Jaxon's heart thundered in his chest when he remembered those green eyes, the gnarled claw. He was always glad he never had a wife or a daughter, someone to protect. Wondering what horrors might have befallen his runaway sister was preoccupying enough. Many nights Jaxon woke to the sound of his father calling out in his sleep the details of blood-splatter or chunks of brain-embedded walls from the crime scenes he got paid to clean up. Jaxon couldn't rescue any of those victims either, one of the motivating factors in his enlistment into the army.

Marla must not have anyone stopping her from going out in the dark alone. Or, if she did, she'd managed to lie to them about what she was doing tonight. That urge to save her, to help her find her missing cousin, who was God-knows-where, consumed him. Also, he wanted someone to prove he wasn't crazy. He'd shove it in Frank's face, demanding his job be fully re-instated, his good name cleared.

The front door squeaked on its hinges again.

"Let me go with you," Jaxon said.

"I'm sure you have better things to do." She searched his eyes, appearing to discern his intentions. Blinking, she looked away, perhaps questioning why a stranger might care about her. She adjusted the neckline of her uniform.

"Actually, I don't." He laughed, throwing his hands up. His smiled faded, wondering if he should keep the next remark to himself. "Besides, Mack's wrong."

Her face paled. "What do you mean? Have you seen something?"

A camera clunked down on the counter. Jaxon noticed the camouflage pants on the chair next to him. "Yeah, you see something?" he asked, tilting his head.

Jaxon clenched his jaw and glanced at Marla.

"Hey, I'm not the enemy here," the cameraman said, pointing to the pot of coffee.

Marla set a mug in front of him and poured a cup.

"No? You don't care about that girl out there—or who you make look like a fool with that." Jaxon waved at the camera. "You're just after the story at our expense."

"Oh, and you're not thinking about using her to get your job back?" The cameraman smirked.

Jaxon squinted, searching his memory for how this guy could possibly know that.

He pushed the bridge of his glasses with his middle finger. "I heard you tell your boss what you saw. Let me help."

"Fuck you." Pulling out his wallet, Jaxon laid a few bills on the counter.

As Jaxon got up, the cameraman grabbed him by the arm. "Seriously, you don't know what you're dealing with. I've been tracking this thing for years."

"Get off me." Jaxon glowered.

The man peeled his hand from Jaxon's arm.

"What *are* we dealing with?" Marla asked.

"Shapeshifting. Mind control, to name a couple," the camera guy said, taking a toothpick from the dispenser and poking it between his teeth. He patted the camera. "From what survivors have told me, you gotta look away. And the more of us at the trestle, the better. It can't get all of us at once."

Jaxon got to his feet and leaned toward the guy. "Who's gonna be the bait, then, huh?"

"Can we all play nice?" she asked in the tone of an elementary school teacher.

The two men, now both standing, glared at Marla.

"Let's close down the joint, Al." She turned off the coffee pot and didn't wait for his answer.

Marla untied her apron and retrieved her purse, slinging it over her shoulder. "Hey, how 'bout you brief us on the way?" she asked the cameraman. Then she met Jaxon's eyes. "We've all got something to gain here."

The cameraman exited first through the diner's door. Marla sidled up to Jaxon whispering in his ear, "And we can use him as the bait."

They'd dodged the traffic just fine, despite Mack's lame warning. Jaxon wished he'd had his handgun that was in the glovebox of his truck as he led the way over the open field. By the light of the yellowish moon, his gait was hesitant, his hands in the back pockets of his jeans.

Jaxon heard the flick of Marla's lighter.

She puffed the cigarette to life, the embers firing up.

The cameraman paused to check his equipment.

"Can I have one?" Jaxon asked.

She slipped a stick from the pack and lit it.

"And, you better blur out my fucking face on that feed," Jaxon said to the camera guy.

"You got it, chum." He wiped the lens with his sleeve.

"What're you filming for, anyway?" Jaxon asked.

"Trying to pilot a new show called 'Legend Trippers'."

Jaxon chuckled. "Perfect." He flinched at a crunching sound in the shrubs. "Did you hear that?"

Her hand unsteady as she inhaled smoke, Marla shook her head.

The cameraman began recording.

Jaxon surveyed the open space and the rusted iron base of the trestle. Graffiti decorated the beams and empty beer bottles hid in the dirt, gum and candy wrappers littering the ground. He tossed his smoke and extinguished it with his heel.

"You okay?" he asked Marla.

She nodded, drawing in the last drag before tossing the butt to the trestle base.

Extending his hand, Jaxon waited for her take it. Then he plodded into the woods, Marla staggering along behind him.

Crickets chirruped. Leaves swished in the breeze.

At the sound of a sudden rustling, they paused, scanning the area.

Marla grimaced and grabbed ahold of Jaxon's upper arm, squeezing it. Her breath tickled his neck, and the hairs rose along his body. He wasn't sure if it was because she was close, or because he was afraid.

The outline of a girl wearing a dress appeared between the trees, her arms limp at her sides. As she waddled closer, her dark hair shone in the moonlight and her eyes twinkled with a neon green.

"Natalie?" Marla asked, letting go of Jaxon and taking a couple of steps forward.

Sections of her dress were tattered and flecked with dirt. "I'm alright. I'm going home."

Marla dashed to the girl, throwing her arms around her. "Oh, thank God."

The girl didn't react.

"Come on, let's go." Marla let go of her cousin and watched the darkness as if expecting to see something. All was oddly silent and still.

"I want to walk. It's so beautiful tonight." The girl swayed on her feet.

"I don't think that's a good idea." Marla tilted her head and wrinkled her nose.

"No, really." Her shoulders drooped. "I'm fine."

Slowly turning away, Natalie's steps were so light she left no imprints in the grass. Her skirt swooshed in the returning wind.

Marla bit her lip as she looked at Jaxon. She tried to speak, but nothing came out.

The girl disappeared into a thicket.

Jaxon knew he had to do something and lunged forward.

The cameraman whispered, "No! What are you doing?"

But Jaxon went anyway. When he scurried into the shadows to scoop her up, she wasn't there. The moon broke through the cover of branches, speckling the vacant space with a dim leopard spotted illumination.

Marla gripped Jaxon's shoulder upon his return, pressing up against his back. Her head bobbed and weaved like a confused animal. "Where'd she go?"

He put his hand on hers. "I don't know."

They stepped cautiously in unison. A stillness invaded the night once more. Out of the corner of his vision, Jaxon saw a tiny glint like two eyes. Hoping to spy an owl or even a bat, by the time he turned, whatever it was had vanished.

Jaxon looked to Marla, her face wide with terror.

Putting his hand to his jaw, he glanced in the direction of the eyes. A fleeting shadow of something wielding an axe passed through the trees. For a brief second he could've sworn it shifted into the outline of his father, a stern, vacant stare searching for him in the darkness.

Jaxon stiffened. "Now what?" he whispered.

Her unsteady finger pointed in the direction where Natalie had wandered off, and she shook her head. "Let's go back." She tugged on his T-shirt.

"Shit, I think I got something!" the cameraman hissed.

Neither Marla nor Jaxon acknowledged the remark.

The thought of going back, of being the ultimate coward, wasn't an option for Jaxon.

Marla hesitated, as if confronting her fears. Just as Jaxon was shrouded in the shadow of canopied branches, she caught up to him.

As they marched on, Jaxon served as Marla's shield. A dense structure stood amid the brush. It was a thatched bunch of sticks and branches woven thickly together. Through the bushes, someone or something breathed heavily through blocked nasal passages, creating a viscous sucking sound accompanied by an intermittent snarl.

Marla plastered herself against Jaxon. Her shivering vibration making him jumpy, yet he continued to push them forward. He didn't know if she still shook, or if it was him. He bit his tongue.

The ground seemed to have a stronger gravitational pull, making Jaxon strain to lift each leaden step. His whole body was like a pile of stones he had to drag along with Marla, who still hung onto him. When they closed in on what appeared to be a lair, they heard a soft moan from within. Twigs snapped inside.

"Natalie?" Marla muttered.

"Marla? Stay away!" the girl replied in a jittery voice.

Jaxon whirled around and clutched Marla's shoulders, glowering at her. "Don't move."

"What are you doing?" she asked.

"Just don't move," Jaxon said with his hand outstretched to her, before drawing toward the enclosure, holding his breath. His heart pounded with each step until he planted his feet in a wide stance. There was no time to wonder what the monster wanted with Natalie, what it'd already done to her.

A heavy thud made the ground tremble. Hot breath heated the crown of Jaxon's head. Marla screamed so loud it echoed.

"Natalie?" he yelped.

"Huh?" She gasped.

"Natalie, I need you to run. Do you hear me?" He heard himself sound like his father when he had managed to contain his rage.

Unwavering, Jaxon was a wall between her and the thing at his back.

The girl escaped from the woven mass of twigs, some of them cracking as they scraped her arms and legs, ripping the sides of her dress. She scuttled like a crab under Jaxon, scrambling to her feet, sobbing uncontrollably.

"Run!" he yelled.

"But—" Marla said.

"Just run!" Jaxon repeated.

"Holy shit!" the camera guy exclaimed, peeking out from behind the lens.

At the sound of their immediate departure, Jaxon gulped and

faced the creature. Its knobby horns reached for the moon, its snout angled downward as if sniffing the terror oozing from Jaxon's every pore. Matted and greasy fur covered its humanoid upper form, hulking shoulders and defined arms. Its lower body was a pair of massive goat-like legs ending in cleft hooves. Slatted green lava-eyes glowed supernaturally in the night, steeped in anger and flashing hypnotically like a neon sign shorting out.

Jaxon was struck dumb, his thoughts and instincts ebbing from his mind. They were replaced by an overwhelming rage, laced with jealousy and a stinging sorrow. These weren't his feelings. "What do you want?" he asked in a daze, not really sure he verbalized anything at all.

The answer was a crooked claw extending toward his face.

Jaxon closed his eyes, as if avoiding Medusa's gaze, the scent much like a wet dog offending his nose. He gradually backed away, one foot after the other, eyelids clenched tight, as he pretended this thing was only his father in a Halloween costume. Stumbling over the rocky ground behind him, Jaxon opened his eyes. It was then he glimpsed the rusty axe hanging at the beast's side.

The creature's ability to invade his mind erased the urge to spin around and run. Jaxon slowly forgot who he was, why he was here, even what was happening. His futile strain to hold onto his thoughts was like sand slipping through his fingers. Even the awareness of his body and his vision were disappearing. He dreaded that he might die tonight, but not like this. He stood there, a hollowed shell of a man, staring blindly at nothing at all.

"Holy shit! Holy shit!" the cameraman murmured in the darkness.

A booming snarl filled the air as if the only sound to ever have existed. The human-like lips on the oily-haired face upturned into a demented grin. Sharp fangs glistened in the moonlight. For a moment, Jaxon wondered if this was the actual devil as its eyes brightly flamed before turning away.

Jaxon charged the colossal abomination.

The axe whooshed through the air at Jaxon.

But, its focus turned to the bold cameraman who had closed in on the scene to get a better shot. Their eyes met in confrontation, the Goatman wearing a demonic smile. Frozen by the realization that this was the end, the camera slipped off his shoulder. The monster's dull blade sliced into his victim's neck, skidding through his tissue and bone as the camera clattered to the ground. A pitiful shriek died, as his head hurtled and then rolled until it bumped into a tree trunk, blood pooling where it landed. Blood spurted and rained from his body that stood on its own before crumbling to the earth.

Adrenaline making Jaxon sick, the gore of the decapitated journalist compounding it, he dove for the camera. He'd be damned if the cameraman died in vain, the evidence of this urban legend going to waste.

"Jaxon! No!" Marla screamed from the trees.

A rippling hairy arm snatched Jaxon's jacket as he sailed through the air. The Goatman pulled Jaxon up so they were eye to eye, Jaxon's legs kicking for solid ground. One of its hoofs stomped the camera over and over, shattering it to bits.

Okay, so, I'd joke that I'm here to get my wings, but it's no time to poke fun. Plus, that's not how it works anyway. But I might as well tell you why the hell I'm here, or why I have been sent here in the first place.

I've been sent to save Joey. It's not for me to question why. Here's the thing. You see, this Jaxon seems to be worth saving, too. Even though I know this won't end well for him, I can't leave. Nor can I interfere with the chain of events, or interrupt the laws of karma. Although, I sometimes think karma is more than a bitch—she's not even real.

But there's no time to get into any of that, since the creature's ear perks in the direction of the train whistle in the distance. Look at those flashing yellowed fangs, and how the creature sets Jaxon on his feet. Before the guy can run, the monster's blazing eyes bore into Jaxon's. As if an unseen hand on his head spins him around, Jaxon turns and wanders to the slope leading to the trestle top. I can hear his spliced bits of memory: his father slurring that Jaxon was a worthless piece of shit, that he should have been the gunshot victim at the crime scene that night—he wished he was wiping down his own son's biological waste. Jaxon's sister screams she hates him for not protecting her, her last words to him. His best army buddy, his face burned beyond recognition, his ear dangling from his head, only gurgling as blood filled his mouth. Jaxon, after a twelve pack, stopping his balled fist from swinging at his fiancé, her wide eyes of incredulity and horror, wailing about how she couldn't do this anymore. All of it replays in his mind, creating a loathing of himself and his life—yet it's tainted with a curious jealousy for having lived a life at all.

I cringe. If only I could disconnect the creature's hold on him while its twisted claw is outstretched, targeted on Jaxon's back.

A female scream erupts from somewhere in the night.

Stepping onto the tracks, Jaxon isn't the least bit phased by the rumbling locomotive shaking the trestle. The whistle howls frantically, joined by the screeching grinding of the brakes. "Get outta the way, man!" someone shouts from the train.

Rubber squeals on pavement and flashing red and blue lights

flare. A man in uniform speeds up the slope, stumbling over himself.

There's another shriek as the front of the train rams into Jaxon's body. He looks like a lifeless dummy falling upon impact, but he then gets sucked under the wheels. Blood sprays into the night, meaty chunks and scraps of clothing flying. His greatest fear was to witness someone mangled by his train while he was on duty, but he could never imagine this. I can tell you that no one ever gets it completely right. Even those who have that final intuition about how they're going to go. It's never what they think it is when they get to the other side. That's where all the answers are.

Now that you know there's something to see, I warn you against dragging your friends to the trestle. There are more ways to feel alive than putting yourself in harm's way. Because you won't ever get any proof. You see, when the waitress takes the cop to the Goatman's lair and then looks for the tape, none of it will be there. No one will ever understand what happens at the Louisville Loop—that is, except you and me. And maybe the victims yet to meet their demise.

DYING FOR AN INVITATION

Mama discovered a six-year-old Dacie twirling and dancing in her bedroom. Her arms were outstretched, her tiny hands clasped by unseen larger ones that pulled her around in circles. Noticing her mother in the doorway, Dacie rapidly drew her hands back and sprung on her heels. That following Sunday she was baptized yet again and a newly blessed cross placed on her little neck.

Another time her mother stumbled upon her playing with a doll that was posing on its own midair.

"Dacie?" her mother called, concern in her voice.

The doll quickly dropped to the floor.

"Yes, Mama?"

"Who's there with you?"

"No one, Mama." Dacie picked up the doll and hugged it to her chest.

Her mother entered the room and bent down, taking her daughter by the arms. "You can tell me. Who plays with you?"

Dacie's gaze lowered to the area rug. "I don't know."

She lifted her daughter's chin. "What do you mean you don't know?" Her eyes darted about the room. Squinting, she said, "Listen to me. You need to stop this. Command whatever it is to leave you alone. Do you understand me?" She shook her daughter's shoulders while glaring at her.

Dacie slowly nodded, her eyes wide with fear.

"Come, you're sleeping with me tonight." She yanked her daughter's hand. Dacie trailed along, her doll dangling behind.

She knew her mother suspected the paranormal activity continued, but Dacie vowed to be more careful to keep her secret.

"You need to go away when Mama comes," she'd told him the next night, as she stood underneath the giant wooden rosary newly nailed to the wall.

Not quite twenty years later, sitting in the back of the cab, Dacie wondered if her unnamed playmate still lurked in the corners of the family mansion. The memories of him seemed like a dream, although napping now in the car on the four-hour ride to Bran village appeared to be as useless as stealing any sleep on the plane from New York to Bucharest. Normally the passing fields of corn and long grasses dotted with white and yellow flowers proved a visual lullaby. She'd watch the occasional farmer, dressed in cioareci pants tucked into boots, a linen shirt, and straw hat, feeling like she'd somehow traveled back in time when things were simpler. There was something comforting about a place where time stood still, while simultaneously feeling eerily unnatural. Now, in winter, the landscape was a blinding white. Everything was silent, cold, frozen.

None of her friends believed that Transylvania was an actual place, much less that Dacie grew up in one of its villages. Even the origin of her unabridged name, Daciana, was a history lesson. So she told people it meant "wolf." Technically, that was only one of the etymologies.

The truth was she was named after her grandmother, who'd disappeared at the age of twenty-three. Speculation regarding her fate had circulated in the family for years, but Dacie refused to believe anything dreadful had happened. She always imagined her grandmother had escaped from her ordinary life and was doing something extraordinary somewhere. That was the spirit that had prompted Dacie to step on a plane headed for the United States when she turned eighteen. She wanted to leave behind her childish fantasies and meet a real man and have a normal relationship. And, as fate would have it, it was on that very flight where she sat next to Zane.

As the cab twisted along the driveway, past the dry fountain coated in ice, she coaxed the sketch pad from her bag to compare her memory with the real life mystique of the manor. Despite her preference for drawing human subjects, she'd captured the spired turrets, all the straight edges, as well as the correct number of windows. She grinned in satisfaction until a drawing of Zane slid from the pad's pages when the car hit a bump. Trying not to look at it, recalling sitting with him at a Parisian café near the Eiffel Tower where she'd put pencil to paper on the very trip he proposed to her, she stuffed the image back in the book.

Once the driver had helped unload her suitcase, she paid him. He scanned the façade of the house before appearing to shiver, his breath like smoke in the air. Hastily tipping his fedora, he scrambled back into his vehicle. The car jerked into reverse and drove away.

Dacie stomped the snow from her boots onto the mat.

Opening the front door, she smelled the odor of old wood and dusty curtains. Her mother could never keep up maintaining such a large place. Dacie suddenly sympathized, thinking about how she'd trouble keeping her studio apartment clean. Although, now it was easier to tidy up since Zane had taken all of his stuff.

The latticed rectangular skylights sent rays in ribbons. If only she could feel more of that light in her life. She dropped her luggage on the polished floor in the entryway. Even if the rest of the house was not in tip-top shape, the entrance needed to give an immaculate impression—especially since superstition spoke of a correlation between it and the type of visitors one attracted.

Practically toppling down the steps and throwing her arms about her daughter, her mother cried, "Dacie, my baby!" She was still her petite, solidly built self, her long gray hair framing her animated face.

Dacie leaned forward for her cheeks to be kissed.

The jet lag had her feeling cranky. A year had passed since she'd been home, and her mother'd be rabid with inquiries. Sprinkled into the conversation would most likely be the typically ominous remarks about the local legends she grew up hearing. *I hope she spares me the dark tales tonight.*

"It's been too long. Come," Mama said.

Dacie groggily shadowed her mother into the sitting room where she took out the decanter of palinka from the antique cabinet and poured two drinks. Her hands wavered with age as the plum brandy filled the glasses.

Dacie recalled a time when her mother's hands had been steady. The years had passed so rapidly that Dacie had a hard time believing she was out of the nest and on her own.

They clinked a toast.

"To you finally being home," her mother said with a smile.

They swigged the alcohol in unison. Dacie had forgotten how strong it was and covered her mouth, repressing a cough. Her throat burned. While she studied at the Academy of Art, she'd indulged in the occasional wine, but there was no palinka to be had—and even if she'd found a bottle, it would never have been homemade moonshine.

Her mother tugged at the drawstrings of her dress, making sure they were perfectly symmetrical, as she lounged in one of the leather chairs. "My, you're rather dark." Her eyes darted about the space around her daughter as if scanning for something in her aura.

Dacie's brow crinkled. "I wear a lot of black, Mama. You should know that by now." She sipped.

"That's not what I mean." Mama lifted her hair from her neck and moved it to one side. Patting her chest, she said, "Something troubles you here."

Dacie yawned. Her eyelids were heavy.

"No answer and now you're yawning in my face?" Mama crossed her arms.

"I'm just tired." She flopped onto the loveseat and stared out the window overlooking the hillside. The last time she'd sat here, her fiancé had his arm around her as she rested her head on his shoulder. They had swapped stories with Dacie's mother late into the night.

"What's Zane up to?" her mother asked. "I thought you'd be bringing him with you—and we were going to plan the wedding."

Dacie's eyes watered and her heart ached. "We broke up." Saying it flat out made her face the finality of it. She hated endings, especially this one, an ending that wasn't supposed to be an ending.

Her mother's eyes widened as she got up to pour herself more liquor. "How can this be?"

Dacie twisted the butterfly ring on her finger.

"What happened? You looked happier than I've ever seen you." The tone of her voice was flat as if she was saying one thing, but thinking of something else. Her eyes narrowed while she straightened one of the picture frames on the coffee table. It was a selfie of Dacie and Zane in front of Bran Castle.

Glancing at the romantic picture flooded Dacie with regret, a longing for the return of the blissful times with Zane. "Lots of things happened, I guess," she finally said. Spending long hours apart hadn't helped. Her studio hours, his researching for his next big court case. They were supposed to go back to Paris for the honeymoon. Dacie had even called the travel agent.

"You two should work things out—you have to work things out." Her mother put her glass down as if it'd suddenly become too heavy.

"It's not that simple." Dacie noted the lack of inquiry about the details of the split. Startled by the touch of a hand on her shoulder, she turned her head. There was an imprint of fingers on her T-shirt. She pressed her shoulder to her cheek in acknowledgement as her emotional anguish dulled. Maybe part of her heart had always been here with him. As his presence retreated, she recalled the first time she'd sensed his comforting hand. Standing in the living room the night of her father's funeral, tears streaming her chubby cheeks, she felt that same touch on her shoulder. Instead of being afraid, she wondered for a moment if it was her father's spirit. But her six-year-old intuition told her this was not his stern, mature energy. It was a younger man.

"You're more vulnerable now than ever. And, you're the exact age my mother was when she vanished. This is unbelievable." Mama squeezed her age-spotted hands together.

"I'm not going to disappear. You need to relax about that stupid nonsense." Anger flared inside Dacie as she resented that her mother cared more about vampire lore than the fact that her daughter was suffering a heartbreak. She stared at the framed black and white prints of the nearby forest on the wall, noting their precise alignment. Mama had nagged her father to get the measurements just right until he did.

Mama's face tensed as she frowned. Her expression faded while she surveyed the room and rubbed her arms. "Do you feel that?"

"What? How much palinka've you had tonight?" Dacie smiled, deflecting attention away from her. It was one tactic she used to cover for her supernatural friend, just like when she was little.

Her mother scowled while nervously looking around. "I thought that with Zane you'd finally be safe—you would've had a husband to protect you."

That's just what I need—to feel even worse because I might become a vampire. Dacie clenched her teeth, reminding herself that her mother wasn't employing old world sexism dictating that a woman needed a man to take care of her. The risk of turning into a strigoi was equal opportunity for both genders. Anyone who died unmarried could become one of the undead. "I'm doing my best not to die," Dacie uttered in a huff.

"You never know when your time will come. Look at what happened to your grandmother. Tomorrow we'll visit Father Dimitri for a blessing."

Dacie sipped her drink and bit the inside of her cheek. "We don't know anything about what happened. You act like she's out roaming with Vlad Tepes somewhere, sucking blood."

Her mother shook her head. "That man saved us from the Turks—but also turned some of our ancestors. Don't take this so lightly. We're going to church first thing."

She thought Mama probably feared her daughter wasn't only

in danger of becoming a strigoi, but that she was also being visited by one. Dacie didn't think her unseen companion was one of the undead. He'd played with her and wiped her tears. Those were not the actions of a predator. "Fine, if that helps you sleep at night. But I can't live in fear. I won't ever be—" She was going to say "like you," but she stopped herself. The light prismed like diamonds in her empty glass. "I'm going to bed."

Her mother's gaze clung to Dacie's with intensity. "I pray you'll take this seriously." She got up and pulled a vial from the side table drawer. After pouring out the last drops onto her hand, she flicked her fingers at her daughter, creating a tiny rain shower.

Dacie blinked, amused. *Good old holy water.*

"Good night," Mama said. "Oh, and put this under your pillow." She opened a drawer and pulled out a long knife. Its shiny silver glinted in the light.

Dacie stifled a reaction and took the blade, wondering if there were already strings of garlic waiting for her in her room. At least the invasion of lore and its suffocation dulled the emotional agony afflicting her soul.

After kissing her mother's cheek, Dacie entered the foyer leading to the staircase. She forged her way up the steps and down the hall. Pausing before one of her paintings, she recalled how her art professor had hated it. "Create something new. That's so Hellenistic." He'd pushed his nose in the air.

But the piece mesmerized her as if she hadn't been its creator. One summer she'd hauled all her paints home, just in case creativity struck. And sure enough, a compelling force held her captive at the canvas, the brush seeming to glide without effort. Once her mother saw the finished product, she claimed it and made space on the wall. An undressed Psyche clutched at her beloved Cupid while he sprang from their bed. The oil from the lamp in her hand had scorched his shoulder, his hand soothing the wound stinging from her betrayal. Psyche's unwillingness to believe he was the perfect man, her god, was her deepest regret. None of Dacie's other works had captured emotion in such fine and masterful brush strokes. Had a muse held her hand?

She longed for that feeling again as she entered her moonlit room and plunked the luggage on the floor. Artistic inspiration had always filled her with life and energy. Now she was tired all the time from her grief.

She combed her fingers through her long, dark hair and fell fully dressed onto the bed, hoping to sense her supernatural friend. There was nothing but stillness as she slid the knife under the mattress. The last thing she needed was to slice up her face while she slept.

"Where are you?" she whispered, in case her mother was eavesdropping.

Silence.

Disappointment filled her. It bled into her drowsiness. She looked to the rocking chair in the corner. Sometimes it creaked against the floorboards ever so slowly. But not this time. *I guess it's just me and my luggage tonight.* The emptiness in her heart deepened.

After removing the sunglasses from her head, she went to set them on the nightstand. In her sleepy clumsiness, her placement missed, and they toppled to the floor. Afraid she might step on them in the morning, she fumbled for them. When she didn't feel anything, she leaned her head over the side of the bed. She managed to grab the glasses while spotting something white lying on the floor.

It was an old black and white photo, with a border around it like early prints had. She studied the portrait of a young woman in a high-necked dress. Her hair was piled in waves. Her hands rested in her lap. Although she maintained a seriousness, there was a brightness in her laughing eyes. They were the same eyes Dacie and her mother had. She wondered if there was a photographer leaning to the viewfinder at the top of a tripod, a cloth draped over his head while he snapped the frame.

Dacie brought the image with her into bed. Examining the photograph more closely, she noticed an indentation in the shape of a hand on the woman's shoulder. *Could it be him?* Dacie felt jealous, wondering whether her invisible man was hers alone, or if he manifested to all the women of the house. For the first time she thought about how he never seemed to age on those rare occasions when he materialized. His hands were always the same size, and his presence was somehow consistent. She noted a watermark on the edge of the picture and rolled onto her back.

Before she knew it, she'd drifted to sleep. The snapshot slipped from her hand and disappeared under the bed.

Just as the dawn crept into her bedroom, Dacie's mother knocked.

She could feel Mama's tense energy through the door and heard the tapping of her feet on the floorboards. Dacie rolled over, putting her pillow over her head, the scent of detergent filling her nose.

More knocking. The door creaked open, letting in the smell of coffee brewing downstairs. "Dacie? We must leave soon."

"Okay, okay," Dacie said through the pillow. So much for sleeping off her jet lag.

After showering and getting dressed, she gulped the cup of coffee and munched on the pastry her mother had left her on the kitchen table, knowing Mama would act like they were thirty minutes late any minute now.

Her mother entered the room, clearly having come from where she kept the potted roses during the winter. Dirt dusted her blouse. Her grimy hands were full of thorned stems that she unloaded onto the table before taking some and laying them across the threshold, one of the many ways to ward off vampires.

Mama washed her hands without acknowledging her daughter. After grabbing the keys off the hook, she jangled them. "Ready?"

Dacie finished the pastry while noting the fresh tar cross scrawled above the door. No doubt all of the manor's other entry points had been marked for protection. "Do we really have to do this?"

Mama propped a knuckle on her hip and cocked her head.

Dacie sighed, got up, and took the keys.

The daylight was making the snow bright and highlighted the dormant rose bushes outside that looked like skeletons topped with powder. It was quite a long walk to the Queen Mary Chapel, but a short drive. Dacie felt grateful for the ride, at least, and was looking forward to getting the whole ritual over with.

"I so wish you understood that the *Nesuferitu* must be feared." Her mother crossed herself as if merely saying the word might summon one from the darkness.

Dacie kept her eyes on the winding road covered in ice, thinking about how medical conditions like porphyria, the abnormal sensitivity to light, fed those myths. She envisioned someone afflicted with the disorder. He cowered from the sunlight as blisters formed on his skin, his mouth dropping open in pain, revealing what looked like blood-stained teeth. Then she imagined this poor soul slipping into a coma, being thought dead and then buried—fingernails eventually clawing the inside of a coffin. This was probably how her mother thought her unseen playmate looked. "Yes, Mama."

"You remember Petre Toma, don't you? That wasn't even that long ago."

"Yeah, and the family served time—because the court thought they were out of their minds." *I sure hope things don't get that bad around here.*

"And what if they hadn't burned his body? He might still be among us." She folded her hands and squeezed them tight.

"Come on, they didn't just burn his body. They cut his heart out, burned him, *and* drank his ashes. Custom or no custom, that's just crazy." She thanked God that this blessing she was about to receive from Father Dimitri would probably hold her mother off for the rest of her visit.

"They did what they had to. It has never come to that, but if your father had come back—"

"But he didn't, praise the Lord."

"Probably because of all those millet seeds and garlic I placed in his coffin."

The domes of the gray stoned chapel came into view amid the evergreens. Only a couple more minutes until they rolled onto the gravel driveway. Bales of hay smothered in white were like corpulent snow men, left abandoned in the fields.

"I'm so glad you staved off Papa's coming back." Dacie immediately regretted the remark. She glanced at Mama whose brow had scrunched in frustration. They were now on the chapel's grounds, and Dacie parked the car near the entrance.

Her mother pursed her lips before getting out of the vehicle.

Dacie followed as Father Dimitri came out to greet them, her feet crunching snow. He wore his usual priest vestments which she had always thought looked like a long black dress with a white collar. His stringy silver hair fell to his shoulders, the creases on his face were even more pronounced than Dacie remembered. He touched Mama's shoulder and waved them inside.

Incense had already filled the air, and a warm candle glow illuminated the religious paintings and gilded accents surrounding the pews. They stepped to the altar where Father had lined up his arsenal.

Dacie's mother sat in the front pew, her rosary in hand. Dacie knew to follow the priest and stand there while he performed the blessing.

Father Dimitri chanted several Romanian prayers, the leather-bound volume seeming light in his hand. With his other, he swung the censor around Dacie, allowing the frankincense to waft over her. She closed her eyes to avoid them stinging. Then, she felt the sprinkling of holy water, knowing the rite was almost complete. A series of Amens signaled the conclusion, and she opened her eyes.

The priest stood before her, crossing her with his hand. Then he looped a rosary over her head and nodded.

Mama rose from her place and rubbed Dacie's back. "Thank you so much, Father. I'm so glad you met us so early."

"It was of importance. I understand." He handed Mama a small bottle of water. "For you."

Dacie's mother pressed the holy water to her chest. "Thank you."

"You must still be vigilant," Father Dimitri said to Dacie. "They glamour you—and the seduction is hard to resist. When you are at your weakest, he will beg to be invited in."

"Thank you, Father," Dacie said, wondering if the priest even knew about her breakup with Zane. Although she was acutely aware of her vulnerability, no one had been asking to be invited in. She turned, but then stopped to face the altar again. "Father, did my grandmother have a weak moment before she vanished?"

There was the hope she'd get an objective account of what might've happened.

His eyes met Mama's. He folded his hands before looking back at Dacie. "That is something to ask your mother."

Of course it is.

Once back in the car, Dacie asked, "Why haven't you told me?"

Her mother crossed her arms. "Because I only have suspicions."

"What are they?"

"She went missing. That's the important part of the story. And she never came back." Mama's eyes watered and her lip quivered. She wiped her tears on the sleeve of her dress.

Maybe Father Dimitri would tell her more in private. Why hadn't her mother fallen victim to the strigoi? Surely she suffered vulnerable moments in her life.

Back at the house, Dacie excused herself and went up to her room. Lying on the bed, she thought about how her sudden curiosity about the family history was a distraction from the pain of losing her fiancé. Even though she'd never met her grandmother, she felt somehow they were kindred spirits. This very room had been one of her favorites, her place of solitude where she reportedly wrote poetry while gazing out at the rose garden.

A thick layer of clouds masked the sunlight, making the room darker. Shadows of branches looked like scolding fingers on the wall.

Dacie remembered the photo she'd found the night before. She searched the nightstand and the floor. On her hands and knees, she explored under the bed. Her hand finally touched a paper square that she dragged into the light. Once she sat on the hard wood, leaning against the mattress, she read the words. "My true love, in my heart, I know you are my real destiny."

Before falling asleep the previous night, she hadn't thought to turn the picture over. Now that she had, what did it mean? *...my real destiny.* Dacie wondered if it was meant to be found by someone in this house. The thought intrigued her.

Staring off in contemplation, her gaze fell to the base of the nightstand. There was a rectangle cut into its base she hadn't noticed until now. She got the knife from under the mattress, the one her mother gave her to ward off evil. After digging the silver tip into each side of the rectangle, it popped onto the floor. A hidden bundle of papers tied with red ribbon sat in the open space.

Dacie's heart beat faster as she grabbed the stack and unfastened the letters. A faint smell of perfume escaped after she opened one of the envelopes delivered to Igor, her grandfather. She fanned out the pile, revealing each one had his name penned in neat and feminine cursive. Some of the ink had been smeared with drops of what must've been tears.

The dates of correspondence were from the late 1930s and early 1940s, which were the years he'd been off fighting in the war. As Dacie read through them, feeling like she was invading a private conversation, she couldn't stop. The messages began in an almost platonic manner, like they could've been written by a friend or sister, but then signed "forever yours, R—." About halfway through the batch, the tone shifted to desperation. "Your sweet words are with me always. I can't wait to feel your touch again, like your promise. Come back to me soon, my darling. I ache to see you and share the most wonderful news that will bind us together always." Dacie could only guess he was conflicted, since the last few letters were even more direct. "Little Igor and me have found an apartment in Bran. We count the moments as each is closer to your return, when we can be reunited at last."

Dacie imagined she was her grandmother, reading through each and every word, her heart splitting in two with jealousy and betrayal. She recalled the romantic story of how her grandparents had met. They'd been traditional dance partners at a church festival one season, years before the war. Both had described the electricity they felt when they touched and when they looked at each other. Somewhere along the line, that magical bond must've been severed.

Was this gran's moment of weakness?

Then it all clicked for Dacie. The woman she'd always remembered being around her grandfather in his old age…what was her name? Ruby! And Mama's brother was named Igor, which had never been a second thought until now, since sons often bore their father's name. But now it made so much more sense that Dacie's mother always joked her brother didn't look anything like her, so it was no wonder they didn't get along. Whereas she'd embraced village life, he'd always had an aversion to Bran, and was now reportedly off somewhere in Europe. No one knew exactly where. "My Crazy Brother Igor," Mama would call him when recounting childhood stories.

Does she know the truth?

Dacie assembled the letters, winding the ribbon around them, before folding them to her chest. Letting the revelations from the past sink in, she hadn't heard her mother's footfall on the stairs, nor the steps to the door.

Mama knocked, making Dacie jump. She was in the process of shoving the letters under the bed when her mother flung the door open. "What're you doing on the floor?"

"Thinking."

Mama examined the room, the creases on her face accentuating as she squinted. "And what's under the bed?"

Dacie looked away. "Nothing." The photo lay right next to her thigh, so she discreetly pushed it with her thumb out of sight.

"I saw something. What're you hiding?"

Knowing she was caught, Dacie pulled the stack out.

Mama's hand went to her heart and gasped. "I've combed through everything in this house."

"So, you've read them?"

"No, I saw her crying over them when I was a child. I always knew they'd have answers, but when I didn't find them, I thought they'd been destroyed."

"There are some answers." Dacie needed to dig more into what was behind the photo. Did her grandmother take the portrait herself? Had anyone else seen it? How much did Father Dimitri know about any of this? Her intuition told her that there had to be a connection between the entity standing beside her grandmother in the picture and her own invisible playmate.

"Give them to me," her mother said.

Dacie furrowed her brow, wishing she could disobey the orders. But she scooped up the bundle and handed them off.

"And whatever is under your leg, too."

Not the picture. She knew it'd only worsen her mother's fear of the strigoi.

Mama stashed it beneath the letters, as if saving it for a grand finale. "Well, I came to tell you lunch is ready."

"Thanks. I'm going out for a while to clear my head. I'll eat when I come back."

Food was the last thing on Dacie's mind, and she suspected the same was true of her mother. The ghosts of the past had been stirred up, hanging thicker in the air than ever.

Dacie hoped Father Dimitri was still at the chapel as she drove past Bran Castle that looked like a gothic winter wonderland. The dark walls and towers contrasted with the sparkling snow. She recalled more innocent times when she worked summers there, steeped in the fictional world of Bram Stoker, watching all the tourists gawking and taking photos. She'd catch the occasional crow flying overhead while walking the tour along the grounds. And the stray black dog she often petted in the yard at the manor seemed to follow her to the castle to catch her spiel to the visitors. She'd never felt threatened by anything, especially with her unseen guardian protecting her at home, and her overprotective mother on constant vigil.

As she parked in the gravel lot at the Queen Mary Chapel for the second time that day, a vague and constant terror took hold of Dacie. She didn't know exactly what she was afraid of, yet the vague dread simmered in her blood.

Jittery, she dropped the keys after she got out of the car. After picking them up and taking a deep breath, she went for the door, clutching her coat closer.

The smell of incense calmed her nerves once she stepped through the threshold.

Father Dimitri tended to the candle stand where parishioners lit votives for their intentions. Flickering flames brightened his face. "Dacie, is everything alright?" he asked without looking up.

"Do you have a minute, Father?"

He extinguished another low burning taper before sitting next to Dacie on the pew. She gazed at the Madonna and child hanging above them, the paint faded to dark hues, making the joyous image seem grave. It fit the black cloud following her as of late.

"What troubles you?" he asked.

She didn't like the feeling that she might be succumbing to her mother's superstitions. And Dacie was certain Mama would find a way to strengthen her convictions even more after reading through the letters and seeing the photo of her lost mother. "I'm worried about Mama."

"She worries for you, my child."

"But, I've never been afraid."

"She's gone through much to watch over you."

"Yes, I know. I think she's always felt that whatever happened to Grandma would happen to me."

"The fear is a real one." He clasped the wooden cross dangling from his neck.

Dacie bit her lip. "I know you know something, Father. Please."

"Has she told you about your connection to Vlad Tepes?"

"What?" Dacie had to close her mouth.

"It goes back to when he was imprisoned in the castle for two months by the Hungarian king."

She leaned forward, loosening her scarf.

"Before he was captured—while he was going back and forth to Brasov—he fell in love with a young peasant girl. She was pushing a wagon of wares and was so beautiful that he offered to help her, and did so almost daily. Knowing who he was and the extent of his power, she was eventually seduced by his charms. In fact, she told him she was pregnant with his child before he was locked up here in Bran. To gain leverage with Vlad, the king discovered this girl. He tied her up and put her on display outside of Vlad's prison and cut off all her hair. She was almost killed, but Tepes agreed to the king's demands to save his love."

"There's nothing scary about that, Father. I don't understand."

"Well, this girl was of your blood." He squeezed his cross. "There's more."

Dacie's head pounded. "Oh?"

"You see, Vlad had never felt this way about any other. He planned a life with her, only to discover she and the child were dead. His heart was broken beyond repair."

Dacie shifted her eyes. "What happened?"

"She'd been told he was executed. Devastated and without hope of her and the baby being able to survive—she was without a husband or means to support her newborn, or so she thought—she attempted to kill her child and managed to kill herself."

"That's awful." Dacie tugged at her scarf. "The child lived?"

"Indeed. Found by a gypsy, and eventually found by Tepes. According to legend, once he became immortal, he sought out other women in his soulmates' family line in the hopes of having another chance at love. Her soul was gone forever, but her blood still ran through her descendants' veins. He's been obsessed with acquiring everlasting love, even though it's been perpetually eluding him."

"How do you know it's been eluding him?"

"Because I know." The milky film in Father Dimitri's eyes seemed to clear for a moment.

"Please, tell me." Dacie's heart thudded.

"Your grandmother came to me before she disappeared. Just a week before, she'd come to church forlorn and deep in prayer. Suddenly, she was giddy—like I'd never seen her, even before her wedding."

He'd known her family for so long. She'd never considered his age before and guessed he must've been eighty. "Happiness isn't a sign of doom, Father."

"It is when it's unnaturally so. When I asked her the cause of her bliss, she merely said her prayers had been answered. I pressed her further, only for her to say no more."

"You don't think?"

"I do. And now that your mother is convinced there's been a presence lurking around you for some years now, I can only surmise that love has eluded him once more. He's back to try again."

The candle flames leapt up as if in confirmation.

"But this all sounds so ludicrous. And why not Mama?"

"Oh, don't assume. You must not remember, but the two of you stayed in a room at the monastery for several months after your father died."

Dacie searched her memory and nodded, vague remnants of sleeping in a sparse room, her mother tucking her in, telling her it was only temporary. Mama had wanted to let the image of her husband's lifeless body to fade before going back to the manor. Or, at least that's what she'd said.

"Once she told me about the wolf-dog that started showing up at your manor and the apparition that looked like your father. She said she knew it wasn't him—those hadn't been his eyes or his mannerisms. I knew then she was in danger." The priest rose and pulled out a small plastic bottle from his vestments. "This is no joke. Take heed, but do spend some joyful time with your mother. She needs it."

"Thank you, Father." Dacie glanced at the gold cross on the bottle, mulling over whether or not shapeshifting was possible. Maybe it was just a dog—the same friendly one she'd also seen as a young woman. And, why wouldn't Papa be visiting his wife from beyond the grave? Maybe Mama was just paranoid she'd seen something evil.

Dacie entered through the back door and set her purse down and draped her coat over one of the kitchen chairs. The cold polenta with cheese and cabbage rolls with sour cream were still on the table. After finishing her portion, she went in search of her mother.

Mama hadn't been tending her potted roses when Dacie came in. She wasn't in the sitting room either. In fact, her mother wasn't anywhere to be found in the downstairs. It struck Dacie that the house was unusually quiet, which filled her with unease. Mama would normally have detected her daughter had come in and would've joined her in the kitchen. Even if she wasn't hungry, she would've poured herself some of the coffee that Dacie noticed was still on the burner.

Once she ascended the stairs, taking the railing to steady herself, Dacie knocked on her mother's bedroom door. No answer. She rapped again. Nothing.

Dacie's heart seemed to stop. Taking a deep breath, she turned the knob. What she saw made her knees buckle. Her mother lay motionless on the bed, her eyes staring into space, her mouth agape. The letters were scattered all over the bedspread, some of them on her stomach, and one still in her hand. Between the fingers of her other hand was the photo. Dacie knew its shades of gray from fixating on it for so long.

Running to her mother, she screamed, "Mama!"

Dacie swept her arm over the bed, angrily sending the papers flying as she knelt down and grasped her mother's hands.

"I know what happened to her," Mama said in a raspy voice.

"What?" Tears welled.

"Dust," she wheezed, "dust." Her voice trailed off.

What's she talking about?

"Mama?" Leaning over her chest, Dacie listened for a heartbeat. Then she put her ear to her mother's face, hoping to hear breath. Nothing. She took her pulse, even though she knew there'd be none.

Collapsing onto the body, Dacie sobbed uncontrollably. She cried until she didn't have any more tears. Finally, she gathered the letters and envelopes, the ribbon, and the picture and took them back to her room. A fresh string of garlic had been lined across the headboard. Dacie picked it up and sniffed it like a bouquet. *Oh, Mama.* Anger fired within her, and she'd a vision of watching the letters burn in the fireplace, flames consuming the parchment until there was nothing left but ashes. That would have to wait. She needed to call Father Dimitri.

The priest came right away and called for the doctor. It was determined that Mama had suffered a stroke. When asked what might have caused it, Dacie said she didn't know. All of this strigoi drama had caused nothing but stress and suffering. To think Mama was so embroiled in it that she died at its hands was beyond Dacie's comprehension. She couldn't let that be known because it would only perpetuate the fear. It was time to let it go. Dacie wanted to be rid of the irrational beliefs once and for all.

She made arrangements to extend her stay, as there wasn't anything pressing to get back to in New York. Besides, the ground needed to thaw enough for the burial, and that'd take weeks.

Father Dimitri had begun asking what Dacie wanted to do with the body. Did she want to impale her mother with iron or wood? In the heart or the navel? Would she prefer the corpse to be buried face down and in reverse? Dacie told him she didn't want to do any of it. Then he urged for her to consider burning Mama to ash, mixing the remains in holy water, so Dacie could drink it. That might be the only way to save her from an attack of the strigoi. Apparently, doing this would not only prevent Mama from becoming one, but her ashes would be a kind of antidote against other vampires. He whispered a reminder about her family legend.

All Dacie had to do was make it through the funeral alive, and she could go back to the United States where none of this lore mattered.

That night Dacie sensed she wasn't alone. Embers in the bedroom fireplace radiated a comforting heat. The flames had just finished curling the bundle of letters into black remains, and the photo suffered its final distortion before melting into oblivion.

"It's me," he said softly.

A tingle running up her spine, Dacie glanced about the room, but saw no one. Her hand went to her chest, feeling her heart pumping. *Is it really him?* She'd never heard his voice and wanted to hear it once more. "You're back. I thought I'd never see—rather, never feel you there again."

The covers drew back suddenly. Dacie climbed onto the left side of the bed. She listened for his breathing, but there was only silence in the darkness. Though the bed was empty, the edge of the mattress held the impression of an invisible form. In the past, he'd never touched the bedding or sat so close to her. She felt their connection was different, frighteningly intense, even though underneath it all he was as familiar as one of her child-hood toys.

Dacie's felt at ease, even though her heart raced. "What do you want?" she asked, pulling the covers to her chin. She bit her lip as her whole body tensed.

"I've been waiting for you."

She sat up, inching her back toward the wall, not knowing if she should feel flattered or disturbed.

"You've never been afraid of me before."

Dacie's eyes teared.

Even though her invisible companion had always been here, part of her always wished they'd talked. Their unspoken closeness had never deepened with verbal communication. And she didn't know if she was ready to know more. It was easier to leave things as they were, at least for now. She was just relieved he was back. That was enough.

"I've never left you."

Dacie's sorrow faded as she considered his silent loyalty. "Don't leave me tonight." She reached for him in the moonlit darkness. He took her hands. His were cool to the touch as if he'd just come in from the storm outside. After pulling him to her, she wrapped her arms around his unseen form. She shivered at the contact with his body and questioned whether this was her mind's illusion to distract her from her anguish.

She gently pushed him to the mattress and snuggled into his chest. A primal protectiveness consumed her. He kissed the base of her shoulder. His arms around her soothed her emptiness, and she fell into a deep sleep.

Eventually, dawn intruded into the room as if the brocade curtains had been ripped from the windows. The spirit had vanished.

Dacie ventured downstairs the next morning.

Wind groaned against the windows. Snow flurries gathered on the ground.

While sitting in the breakfast nook, she waited for the teapot to whistle.

Dacie's thoughts turned to her father. Before he died, he emphasized how they'd meet again. "The soul never perishes, only the borrowed bag of flesh," he'd said. She wondered if he'd found Mama already, and if they both would find her when her time came. Until then, she was grateful not to be completely alone.

The kettle whined. She snatched it from the stove. Following a generous pour of water, she steeped the tea bag. A peppermint-and-clove scent floated down the hall as she took the mug to the sitting room. The grandfather clock chimed eerily as if trying to speak to her. Etched feathers carved near the top reminded her of the accent on one of her father's old-fashioned hats. She missed discussing his insights on life as he chewed on his cigar. Too bad the clock didn't have any answers for her.

There was a crumpling sound of the leather chair in the corner. Her hands cradled the cup. Steam coiled into the air.

"Why can't I ever see you?" she asked.

The lack of a response made her uneasy. Her heart galloped.

"You haven't asked," he said. "Don't you believe in the adage 'ask and you shall receive'?"

She drank her tea. "Actually, I don't."

"That's a shame. You've never invited me into your life, even after all this time."

That word invitation was like a trigger, making her swallow hard. All those warnings to be vigilant replayed in her mind. Yet, there was a yearning to connect with someone who knew her, who had always been by her side, especially now that her mother was gone. "Who are you? How do I know you aren't a vampire?"

"You know the truth. Don't let anyone else's fear of the unknown keep us apart."

"But I don't know the truth—I haven't even seen you. I don't even know your name." Mama's and Father Dimitri's admonitions were like devils on her shoulder. However, here in this room was an angel who understood her like no other.

"I've been in your heart, in your dreams. You remember those, don't you?"

She did. They strolled along the misty hillside. When she looked down, he was at the end of her hand, holding it. His form was always blurry, but she knew it was him. "When can I really see you? I have to know you are real."

"I've waited so long for you to ask, to be ready. I can wait awhile longer, for you to be sure."

Mama's scowling face surfaced in her mind. "I'm ready," Dacie said, a hint of hesitation in her voice. The ending of her relationship with Zane meant heartbreak was always imminent. At the same time, this otherworldly connection promised to transcend all of that.

"You sure?"

"Yes, I'm sure." She was bravely accepting his invitation, after remaining passive for all these years. This could be a transformative intimacy that could sustain her no matter what else she'd have to face.

Why can't I see him yet? Maybe he has something to hide. Maybe he is the one who isn't ready.

A squeaking of the leather chair told her he'd stood up. Just the faintest hint of the sun peeped on the horizon.

"Where're you going?" she asked.

"I'll return when you're completely sure." His steps headed for the door.

Dacie plunked down on the loveseat, her tea splashing up on her nightshirt. Thankfully it had cooled enough that it didn't burn.

That night, the restless wind pushed at the window panes. Yet inside, the house was silent and at rest. She moved the family photo albums to the nightstand. Spending the day with the memory of her parents had been bittersweet. She wondered if she'd find Uncle Igor to tell him of his sister's passing. He was all the family she'd left.

Dacie dressed in a black negligee she'd found in her mother's closet. The lace detail plunged toward her naval, accenting her generous cleavage. Dark satin hugged her curves in all the right places. She sat at the vanity, admiring her reflection in the mirror. Romantic love seemed so much more fragile than familial love. *What if I've driven him away?* It would be cruel to have felt whole and wonderful only for it to be taken from her. She poured herself some wine from the bottle on the dresser. Swirling the liquid, she watched the moonlight play with the garnet color.

As she examined the horizon, she glimpsed a harvest moon rising. The glowing orb crept up, birthing itself into the sky. "The bigger the moon, the bigger the wish," her mother had always said. And tonight Dacie wished more than ever that her mystery man would manifest in the flesh.

The idea struck her to treat this night like St. Agnes Eve. Her

Scottish grandmother on Papa's side had told her to slip her hands under the pillow while looking up into the heavens. "Agnes sweet and Agnes fair, hither, hither, now repair," Dacie said as if it was an incantation. *I'm inviting you into my life for good.* Climbing onto her mattress, she lowered herself down onto her stomach, repeating the words under her breath. Her hands disappeared beneath the pillow. She propped her head up to watch the moon rise.

Dacie'd already gone through the motions of St. Agnes Eve at six-years-old. Soon after that special night, a shadowy figure had appeared in her dreams for the first time. And her unseen play-mate had held her hands the next day, making his first physical contact.

She imagined what he'd look like. He'd be dark haired with eyes able to pierce the midnight, and strong arms that could hold the world. The superstition advised not casting a glance behind, so she had to repress the urge when she felt a presence. The vanity mirror held nothing out of the ordinary. Then it dawned on her that he might not have made himself visible yet.

She shut her eyes in a moment of preparation before saying, "I know you're there."

Branches no longer rustled outside or tapped on the window pane. The wind no longer stirred. In fact, Dacie had trouble breathing. It was as if there was less oxygen in the room.

A tall, dark form of a man materialized.

She hid her head in the pillow while waiting for her heartbeat to slow. Once she looked at him again, she felt a current of excite-ment. His dark hair complemented the symmetry of his pale face. Obsidian eyes welcomed her home. A peacefulness emanated. She half-expected him to resemble the portraits of Vlad Tepes she'd seen so many times, but his nose wasn't as sharp and he didn't have that striking mustache. It couldn't be Vlad himself.

Dacie sat up and stroked his cheek with the back of her hand, unable to take her eyes off him. *He's real. And so beautiful.*

The mattress dipped as he entered the bed. He put his fingers to her mouth. Her whole body tingled as if he were magic.

He lay back, drawing her to him. "It's you who's beautiful."

She was startled that he seemed to know her thoughts. It unnerved her, but also made her feel more one with him. This had to be a love to transcend the depth of mortal-to-mortal connection. What had she done to deserve such bliss?

Her lips met his.

She basked in his salty taste, not caring about anything but the moment. Tonight she honored herself and the here and now. None of her ancestors mattered. This profound bond existed just for the two of them. No one else.

"Is this what you really want?" His fingers traced the side of her face. "There are consequences."

"Consequences?" Her chest tightened, not knowing if she could take the risk. *Nothing ventured, nothing gained. It's better to have loved and lost than to have never loved at all.* Father Dimitri's words interrupted her thoughts: *They will glamour you.*

He pulled away and sat up. "I understand."

It was as if her heart forgot to pump. Her stomach contracted. The feeling of abandonment, her real fear, set in. Her eyes watered.

His gaze locked with hers, his eyes flashing with desire, a desire so captivating she had trouble thinking of anything else.

This being—whatever he was—had always been near. There was no glamouring. Even now, he seemed like just a man, a man who loved her. "Don't go," she managed to say.

He kissed her deeply, holding her tighter. Lost in his embrace, her hands roamed over a body she could finally see. And what a specimen he was. His smooth, muscular physique called for her to explore every inch. The electric chemistry was nothing like she'd ever felt before. She wanted desperately to be skin to skin, surrendering all her human inhibitions. With that thought she undid the buttons of his shirt, one by one, each seeming like an eternity.

His lips traveled over her cheek and down her neck where he lightly nibbled. Covered in goose bumps, she writhed in pleasure. The satin of the nightgown began to feel like an imprisonment. Then he bit into her skin, a sharp prick and a trickle of blood dropped onto the sheets.

This must be the consequence.

Her lover pulled back and licked the blood from his lips with his eyes closed, savoring her taste. The black of his eyes had lightened when he opened them.

She knew he must've felt an uncontrollable passion for her to linger in the periphery of her life for so long. For a moment, she felt light-headed, her vision losing focus. The swooning sensation trumped any pleasure she'd experienced prior.

"I've always loved you, even when you went off with *him*."

Had she unwittingly forsaken him? Was he riddled with jealousy? Dacie hoped he would forgive her for loving Zane, especially since her memory of him faded with each passing day. Zane's devotion paled in comparison to the palpable emotion filling the room. And if this entity had loved her ancestors, wouldn't he need forgiveness, too? They both had a past.

Soon, her questions didn't need to be answered. His powerful hands swept gently over her breasts, past the curve of her hips, and down her firm thighs. "Our love is timeless," he said, seeming to know she loved him equally in return. Next, he began inching the satin up, slowly revealing her bare skin.

Dacie kissed him eagerly, removing his already unfastened shirt, thinking of their unspoken vow. Her invitation solidified this union, which she asked her brain to record in consummate detail.

Time ticked slowly and swiftly all at once. As he inched the nightgown up and away from her body, she thought she might black out from such anticipation. His breath brushed her neck, igniting an army of goosebumps, and a wetness between her legs.

When her hands ventured to his loins, she discovered he was rock hard. Such immediacy had never struck her like this as she undid his pants, peeling the fabric from his gloriously smooth flesh.

His fingers explored her swelling need for him, knowing the exact pressure and rhythm to coax her excitement to its limits.

"I want you," she whispered.

"Now, that's an invitation I can't refuse." His voice bellowed in her ear as he gently pushed her to the mattress and went to straddle her. The inches separating his manhood and her throbbing desire seemed endless. She rose to pull him to her faster. She needed him so badly she feared she might die before he entered her.

"Please, take me now," she pleaded.

And with that, he closed the space separating them, thrusting himself inside of her. The fit could not have been more perfect, her gorging womanhood swallowing all of him. As she let go, she'd never felt so open, so uninhibited. They'd truly become one. Any separation had been lost to the surrender of her mind, body, and soul. Her broken heart suddenly restored itself in this promise of eternal love.

She woke with a surge of energy. From the moment she opened her eyes, her body was high on adrenaline. Her veins pulsed. Her heart pumped vigorously. She'd never felt so present, so willing to meet the new day. Everything in her line of sight was crisp and vibrant as if she'd a new set of eyes. The outline of the wine bottle they'd emptied the night before was strikingly bold. The glasses sparkled. Tiny orbs of light speckled the room.

He'd somehow erased all of her heartache and loss. Was it because his devotion could breach the past, present, and eternity?

She brought her hand to her mouth and grinned as she remembered their passionate love making. Even her lips were sore. Her entire being hummed with the need to be caressed and fondled again. *I can't wait to spend our lives together.*

When she rolled over, Dacie was startled by the empty bed. She noticed something on the pillow. After picking it up, she turned it over, realizing it was the photo of her and Zane in front of Bran Castle. Before, looking at the picture would've roused a sadness of love lost, of what could have been, what wasn't meant to be. Now, she knew she'd completely let go. With that thought, she set the snapshot on the nightstand, unable to shake the unease of finding it here and now.

She rose, pulling the sheet to wrap around her nude body, wondering why the photo had been left for her. As she slinked past the vanity mirror, she didn't stop to see her reflection. Despite her confusion, the sensation of being so alive fueled her impulse to rip back the thick velvet curtains and feel the sunlight on her face. She'd never felt so good, so happy.

Through the distortion of the leaded glass, she scanned the snow-covered lawn, deeply shaded by towering trees. A figure sprinted, entirely shrouded by a black hooded cloak.

That had to be him. Ah, him. She touched her chest, where her heart beat wildly.

Where's he going?

Before she could think through anything, radiant beams of the morning sun reflected through the glass and struck her like a million blazing pinpricks. Unbearable pain paralyzed her. Her skin sizzled and smoked. Dacie dropped the sheet and shrieked. Her cry could have woken the entire world, but she was alone.

Betrayal stung her. *They'll glamour you.*

There wasn't time to reflect on whether or not they shared true love, or why he'd done this to her. A tear rolled down her cheek as she felt herself disintegrate. The tear dissipated in a tiny wisp of steam as her body turned to dust.

HOMECOMING

I never thought I'd have to bring Melanie back in a box.

It's not a pine box. That much is a relief. I just couldn't leave what was supposed to be our dream vacation without her. Hence the reason I went through the trouble of packing her up in that tank. It sounds cruel, but it's not like I could've boarded her on a passenger plane in her state. I worried sick about how she was holding up on that other aircraft. Not for nothing, but she wasn't coming with me willingly. I tried that route, believe me.

On the return flight, I researched Scottish legends, wondering if there was any truth to them. The innkeeper had tried to warn me about the creature he claimed was coming for him. Maybe I'm better off not knowing his truth. Schrodinger's cat and all that. Melanie's eyes betrayed that she wanted me. And bad. I saw it there myself. I know it's still her. Most importantly, now we can be together. Sure, things will never be the same—but they never are, are they?

Now, my feet dangle off the dock. The moonlight pings off the lustrous surface of Lake Superior. She's swimming around out there somewhere. She only emerges well after sunset—the reason I am here in the wee hours. Solo. Just me.

While Melanie and I sat somewhere over the Mid-Atlantic, I knew what a lucky bastard I was that she agreed to travel with me across the pond. Only a few nights prior, I'd snuck in late to her performance as Christine in *The Phantom of the Opera* on closing night, her biggest role to date. When I got to her dressing room, her pretty boy co-star's face soured before he hauled ass in a huff. Melanie shoved my gas station roses into an empty vase—right next to another dozen. That's when I whipped out two plane tickets, urging her to book the castle of her choice. It was proof I'd been paying attention to something she'd mentioned in passing. However, if you'd ask when that was, I couldn't tell you.

"I still can't believe we're here." Melanie reached for the seat pocket in front of her.

Grabbing her hand, I said, "Now that I got the grant, things will be better. I promise."

Her glassy eyes met mine. "I'm happy your work's paid off. But *I* need you."

"I know." I needed her, too, but the words backed up in my throat. As usual.

Touching the pocket with the ring box, I fought the impulse to propose to her right then and there. You see, I envisioned something epic, something she'd never forget. Having the flight attendant make an announcement over the speaker system wasn't my jam. It had to be when we were at the castle. I'd plot a romantic surprise after a good night's sleep. Plus, I did my best work under pressure. Procrastination, the ultimate champion.

I kissed her forehead as she nestled onto my shoulder. Shit, how could I forget how good that felt?

She lifted her head to kiss me. Her lipstick tasted sweet, but the tenderness got my juices flowing—definitely not the obligatory peck of the last few months. My hands fingered her hair, our breaths getting shorter. She pulled back, remembering we were in public view. We knowingly smiled at each other, having the decency to wait until we got to our hotel room. Still too many hours away.

I'd soaked up those few moments. That returned spark reminded me of the day we'd met at the coffee shop five years ago. Noticing the research lab logo on my shirt, she'd asked about my job. Wouldn't you know, we both are passionate about animals. She'd protested dolphin captivity when she'd read they were committing suicide. I'd bragged how my study aimed to help free the creatures from their pain, while also better understanding how humans developed and dealt with depression—and losing the will to live.

Melanie's voice broke me from my thoughts and the hypnotic drone of the aircraft's engine. "Isn't that Mrs. Halverson?" she said, pointing to a photo of an elderly woman in the in-flight magazine. It was the spitting image of our neighbor—minus the threadbare housedress—gesturing to the eye-popping Scottish scenery, a plate of local food in her other hand.

"Yep, looks just like the charming lass," I said, trying to forget how the neighbor had recently stopped watering her plants to blab about another dude leaving our house right before I'd gotten home. Should I have assumed the worst? Should I have confronted Melanie about it? Decisions. Decisions.

"Well, her name *is* of Viking origin," she said without looking at me.

"Are you a Viking, too?" I wondered if I'd missed that detail about her.

"May-be," she said playfully.

It'd been a million years since I'd heard that in her voice.

"Some role-playing in our future, then?" Chuckling, I visualized some of her best skimpy bedroom costumes. And a few of our sexual positions.

"No so fast, mister." Her hand brushed past my pocket while grabbing for an eye mask sitting between us. She patted my chest. "What's that?"

"Nothing." I handed her the mask. "Rest up. You're gonna to need it."

This vacation was going to be unforgettable. I could feel it.

Had Melanie pieced together the imminent proposal? That's what bounced around in my mind as the driver finally rolled into the gravel lot outside Mingary Castle. The name reminded me of the villain from *Flash Gordon*, but I knew she'd picked it for some other reason. Maybe she'd found out some ancestor of hers had lived here. I looked forward to finding out. My attention was all hers. Finally.

The expanse of grass and trees defined the essence of green. The crisp air carried the scent of clover. A faint rumble of waves murmured in the distance. My watch indicated almost ten in the evening, yet it was barely dusk. This was a fucking fairytale.

When my feet hit the ground outside the cab, unease struck me. The surrounding wilderness opened its arms wide, but not the fortress' property. No sir-ree. Once we stepped closer, I shuddered at the chill from the stone walls.

The iron hinges of the door screamed open, and a short innkeeper waved us inside. His sudden coughing distracted me from his stringy hair and crooked posture. The luggage wheels wobbled on the cobblestone, creating a rickety clack reminiscent of an '80s song's backbeat. I repressed the urge to hum along. I had my masculinity to preserve, if I was going to pull off this knight in shining armor business.

Sconces barely lit the dining hall we passed through. Various swords and axes clung to the walls, along with portraits of smug nobility and tapestries of battle scenes. A painting of a mermaid—with a desperate come-hither look—caught my eye. Her hand clutched the sailor's shirt. His expression of lust and apprehension. I snapped out of a kind of trance, fearing I'd fall behind. Man, that innkeeper was just zipping along.

Our host failed to lift a finger when it came to our bags as we climbed a steep, claustrophobic stairway. When Melanie and I panted in front of our room, he handed me the key, which iced my palm. He invited us to breakfast in the morning, and then he practically evaporated into the shadows like a leprechaun. If not for my utter fatigue, I'd swear I saw a green puff of smoke in his wake.

After unloading our luggage, Melanie took off for the staircase, continuing up to the turret. I followed.

Trying to catch our breath, we gaped like idiots at the sea and mountain panorama. Standing next to her and seeing the beauty of the landscape, we could've been in a movie with a CGI backdrop. It put those photos in the in-flight magazine to shame. I refused to peer over the wall, afraid I'd get vertigo or start imagining toppling to my death, like a sissy.

"Happy anniversary." I kissed her eyelid.

"Happy anniversary." Her hand clasped mine, her long red hair taking flight in the breeze.

Despite the ring in my pocket, I hesitated. I wanted to wow the shit out of her—candles, champagne, the works.

Clouds blanketed the setting sun. The dimness unnerved me, or maybe it was the moan of the wind against the fortress. Back home I had nerves of steel. Not here.

I scooped her up just as she pointed to the stairs leading to the shore.

"But—My Lo—" she said.

She'd almost uttered it—her pet phrase for me: *My Love*. For once, I missed her treating me like a goddamn little boy. Was there a way to play this on a loop? Forever.

I lowered her to her feet. She'd seemed to have ditched the idea of exploring the water's edge. Her face turned serious. "There's something I have to tell you."

"The jetlag is strong with this one. Can it wait 'til tomorrow?" I didn't want anything to muck up the way things were going. I sucked up every drop of hope, savoring it, postponing reality setting in.

The crease in her brow relaxed. She nodded.

That night I carried her to that four-poster bed. I had the whole trip to tell her about the future I'd planned for us. Completely winning her back would take more than a castle or a ring, but it was a place to start.

When I woke, it took several seconds for my vision to adjust to the darkness, and to the stone masonry walling me in. There was no sign of movement in the room. Stark shadows mimicked monster claws and deformed profiles. My hand searched the crisp sheets, feeling around the empty mattress and finding the imprint of her body still there. The bedding was peeled back. Melanie was gone.

My heart jumped in triple time, knowing her history of sleepwalking. I sprung up, stuffing my feet into shoes and grabbing my jacket. If anything should have happened to her…

Tripping down the steps leading to the jagged shoreline, I wondered how she could've ghosted me like this. At home, a cat yawn could jolt my ass up.

My gut tightened. Squinting into the night, I prayed I'd see her somewhere.

After shining a cellphone flashlight over slippery patches of moss, for a goddamn eternity, I took a rest at the water's edge. The rock I rested on was cool and wet. Leaning my arms on my knees, I sensed someone watching me. I spun around but saw no one. I glanced up at one of the fortress windows to see a hunched silhouette. I wasn't sure if the innkeeper's stalking me was a comfort. At least I wasn't alone. Also, he'd be able to lead me through every nook and cranny inside the fortress. Since he was awake, that would be handy.

Gazing up at the velvet sky and brilliant stars, I berated myself for being so stupid. All those theater performances I'd missed. All the romantic dinners when my mind was somewhere else. Forgotten dates and times. The whole nine yards.

Was she hurt? Her neck broken on one of these blasted rocks? It'd all be *fine*, she'd said when she chose this castle. Besides, not once had she sleepwalked off the dock at Lake Superior or gone overboard when we anchored the boat for the night. Let go of some of your *control issues,* she'd said. She'd convinced me the worst of her nocturnal episodes resulted in having a midnight snack or sitting on the couch with one of our cats in her lap. I could always steer her back to bed. All the more reason to turn the inside of that fortress upside down.

I folded my arms across my chest and felt the bulge in my jacket pocket. Pulling out the box and flipping open the lid, I studied the glittering carat inside. Would I ever get the chance to pop the question? I held onto that box, stashing the hope back into my pocket.

Then, while I blankly regarded the sea, the glassy water stirred as if a tiny earthquake trembled. A few drops levitated in the air, and I rubbed my eyes. When I opened them, more droplets had gathered, hovering and swirling in a liquid mass. I was a damn statue. The glimmering blob stretched upward and assimilated into a human-like form. A familiar hourglass figure materialized. A heart-shaped face framed by spiral tendrils regarded mine, and I recognized her at once. Was it really Melanie? Did this mean she was dead? Was any of this real?

Come be with me, now and forever, My Love, I heard a voice say inside my head.

I closed my eyes, considering whether I was still back in the room having some crazy dream. A faint wind brushed my face, and nothing mattered but the immediacy of Melanie. Here and now.

A touch chilled my cheek. Devoid of lifelike color, the watery Melanie was as tangible as the one made of flesh and bone. Even the scar on her lower lip was a strikingly accurate watermark. Her kind eyes evoked an uncontrollable desire, one that only reared its head during our most passionate moments. Transparent locks of hair twisted like tiny snakes, the ends tickling my neck under my chin, leaving a faint wetness.

I longed for her to say more, to embrace me with liquescent arms, or drown me with her mouth. Instead, she moved backward, leaving footprints on the stones. Strangely, she stepped back without glancing behind, her every footfall landing firmly on the next rock, avoiding the mossy areas or puddles. Her gaze never left mine. A fluid arm raised and then the other, both summoning me. One foot met the surface of the sea, followed by the second, her hands still signaling.

I stood, thankful she'd forgiven me for my shitload of sins. Just as I got my footing and lunged forward, a hand gripped my shoulder. Practically flying backwards, I watched Melanie's doppelganger dematerialize, flowing into the sea that lapped softly until the surface calmed.

Her vanishing left me dumbfounded.

I turned to find the innkeeper standing behind me.

"If you're out here too long, the land starts tricking you," he said. His bulbous nose shone in the moonlight. His reddish hair, beard, and even his distinctive eyebrows swayed with the breeze.

"Have you seen my girlfriend?" I hoped he'd fess up to spotting either the human or the aquatic version of her. I didn't care which.

His unsteady hand twirled the end of his wiry beard. He scanned the span of the sea. "She's probably taken a stroll to clear her head." He yanked a handkerchief from his trousers pocket and almost coughed up a lung into it.

"I doubt that." I transferred my weight from one foot to the other. Beads of sweat dripped along my brow.

"You haven't learned that women often don't make sense?" He met my gaze.

Although he did have several years of life experience on me, he hadn't spent five of them with Melanie. "What doesn't make sense is how I didn't hear her leaving the room."

"Well, there's that secret passage," he said, jingling the change in his pocket.

I snorted. "What?"

"It's one of the reasons she reserved that particular room."

His hand clapped me on the back a couple of times. Suddenly we were best pals.

As I shirked away from him, I wondered if Melanie had really swallowed that sleeping pill. Had that been another of her dramatic performances? What reason would she have to slip out in the middle of the night? And what about that version of Melanie coming out of the sea?

Thoroughly flabbergasted, I asked, "Where does the damn thing lead?"

"Around there." He pointed to the right side of the fortress' foundation. "Let's have a looksee to settle your mind."

We headed back to the castle and up to the room. After he opened the lock with a key around his neck, he quickly stepped to the bathroom and tugged on what appeared to be a built-in case of shelves. It squeaked as the bottom grazed the tile, and it thumped when hitting the opposite wall. While he unlatched a hidden panel within the opening, I doubted if Melanie had had the time to investigate any of this.

As I ducked into the passage after the innkeeper, it struck me he might've been distracting me from the real truth. We were in the land of fairies and the Loch Ness monster... Had something supernatural happened to Melanie? Or did the innkeeper have a hand in this?

The narrow and winding staircase smelled musty, the stone wall skimming my shoulder. If it wasn't for the sliver of illumination eking in from the slats in the masonry, I could have fallen to my demise on the uneven steps along the descent. Maybe that was the freaking point. If I died, this guy's problems—suddenly solved. There'd be no one to report Melanie's disappearance. Crouching through a dwarfish door and into a bath of moonlight, we both halted at the foot of the castle.

"You see, the coast is clear." The innkeeper threw up a jittery hand, waving it from where we'd just exited and across the entire shoreline. He avoided my eyes, coughing into his handkerchief.

Glowering, I got in his face. "Where is she? What about the rest of the castle? Take me through it. Now."

"Every door is locked. And, I would've heard her in the halls." His expression appeared sincere, but I was still skeptical. "Look, get some shut-eye. If she doesn't turn up when you wake, we'll call the authorities."

I had no intention of going to sleep. I'd contact the police myself and ask them to investigate this shady sonofabitch. I nodded in feigned agreement, passing him without a word, and headed back to my room.

When I went to use my cell, and then my laptop, both were dead, even though they'd been charging while I was out. The electrical outlets were fine, yet I was powerless in many ways. This irony did not escape me. There wasn't really anywhere I could walk to. Not to mention I'd become a slave to Google Maps. The paper map on the bureau was utterly useless.

I peered out the window, cursing my isolation, thinking I might as well have been stuck at Alcatraz. Along the surface of the water something was tracing letters that spelled out "I love you." However, there was no visible source—no bird, insect or fluttering leaf. I wanted it to be Melanie somehow sending me smoke signals, but reasoned the mirage had to be a sign I needed to lie down.

When I passed her suitcase, I noticed a lace negligee on top of her clothes, which wasn't there earlier. The proof that she hadn't given up on us made my knees buckle. I picked it up and pressed it to my chest as I eased onto the mattress.

I was out for so long that the sun was high in the cloudy sky. Standing at the window, nothing but Melanie's absence seemed out of the ordinary. Recharged, I decided to confront the innkeeper.

I found him in the common area downstairs, sprawled on one of the couches, his feet propped up on the ottoman, a beer bottle dangling precariously in his thick fingers.

"I should've told her we were booked," he said without glancing up.

"Why would you do that?" I sat on the opposite couch.

"One of the last things Beverly said to me was she never wanted to leave this place." He sniffed. "And she hasn't."

Beverly? There wasn't a sweater or purse, or any other sign of the female persuasion. For some reason my body tensed.

"Did you know your girlfriend inquired about buying this place?" He drained some of his beer. "All I need is her signature."

Why hadn't the asshole mentioned this before? "You're shitting me." Then, I recalled Melanie had wanted to tell me something. And, she was so giddy on the turret. Damn her.

He rubbed his forehead. "Melanie mentioned you two needed a fresh start… something else Beverly had said, word for word."

I squeezed my hands together. "I'm not following you."

"On our first night here, Beverly dropped two bombshells on me—one, that she'd put a down payment on this very castle, and two, that she was expecting our first child." The corners of his mouth drooped. "I told her we should sleep on it."

My eyes widened. Now I wondered if Melanie's news might have included being pregnant. Holy shit. "What else did Melanie say?"

He coughed up blood into that blasted handkerchief. "Look, I don't have much time. That thing out there wants me, once and for all." His head lolled, and his eyelids appeared heavy.

"What are you talking about?" I ground my teeth.

"You think it's her—" He seemed to be choking, gasping for air. "You can't refuse, you know." His eyes rolled back so just the whites were visible. He fell limply against the couch.

My heart thudded, and I leapt to my feet, frantically examining every inch of the room. "Where's your phone?"

He moaned, a finger pointing to an open door in the corner. "I-it's to-o-o la-a-a-te…" The innkeeper convulsed, blood and fluid oozing from his mouth.

I sprinted into an office crammed with bookshelves and an immense claw-footed desk. Picking up the receiver to the old rotary phone, I dialed the operator. "Hello?" There was a lot of static on the line. I pressed on the receiver again, hoping to get a better connection. After hearing a woman's voice, I spoke as loudly as I could. "Yes, at Mingary Castle—it's a medical emergency. Please hur—!"

The line went dead.

By the time I returned to where I'd left the innkeeper, he was MIA. Spotting his crimson-soaked handkerchief on the carpet leading to the hall, I ran after him. How he'd managed to escape seemed impossible. Freaking ancient piece-of-shit phone.

When I shoved open the castle door leading outside, there was no one there. I hopped along the rocks like a goddamn bullfrog to the shore. At the water's edge, I glanced down at the skeleton key at the end of a dull, coiled silver chain.

With communications still down, I hitchhiked into town and reported the innkeeper's disappearance.

Then I began plotting my departure from Scotland. Being a marine biologist has its advantages. First, I arranged for urgent delivery of the specimen tank under the pretense of conducting an important experiment. When the seamen arrived the next morning at the castle's pier, I tipped them extra to help me buoy the tank against the pilings. And a bit more to keep their traps shut.

After they'd gone, I waited inside it, up to my neck in water. The tips of my fingers had shriveled by the time Melanie appeared. She craned her head over the rim, inspecting the interior and my demeanor. There was something animal-like in her movements, like a skittish kitten sniffing an empty box.

My arms outstretched, I blurted, "Baby, I've never loved anyone else—and I know I never will. Please, let me make it right. Just trust me this last time."

I didn't give a shit that she was different now. We'd figure all that out.

Her head tilted, her expression unchanged.

I lowered my arms, a rush of defeat overwhelming me. Why couldn't I get anything right?

She slithered inside and moved toward me.

I gasped and almost freaking collapsed with relief.

We were mouth to mouth, body to body. She was cold and wet and so smooth. Exploring each other excited me like never before.

My feet lost touch with the floor, and I floated into her arms. It was as if she fed off my warmth as she wriggled against me. Her groans were soft, and when I locked eyes with her watery ones, it was like an endless hall of mirrors reflecting countless hues of blue. Her innocence, her ability to embody each of the characters she played on stage, merged into my consciousness. She'd portrayed their beautiful and relatable imperfections with unparalleled empathy. All of it made sense in that very moment, and I was ashamed I'd never noticed it. What a loser I'd been.

Her lips tasted and smelled like rain. I immersed myself in her dazzling depths just as her translucent locks of hair rose up and coiled, as if ready to wrap around me. Her form became even more slippery.

On instinct, I splashed my way backwards and up through the hatch, slamming the tank closed. The desire to re-experience that feeling of unconditional acceptance kept needling me. But I needed to catch my breath, to be myself for a while. It was too goddamn much.

The walls thumped as she pounded from within.

Don't take me from here. It's the only place we can be happy. Come back inside so I can explain... My Love, listen. Please, or you'll be sorry...

Her pet name for me was hypnotic—*My Love*—proof it was really her. But I needed the comfort of home—my things, my family, my friends, my routine. And even my work. Was that why she went behind my back to buy the castle—to have me all to herself? Or, would she have stayed here anyway, had I refused? I pondered those questions as I fell asleep in the castle, where I dreamed about making love to Melanie as a water sprite. The ultimate role play.

It wasn't until the flight home that I had reliable Wi-Fi. In my Google search of Scottish legends, I came across a description of an *ashray*, which absorbs its victims and is able to take on that human's physical form at will…That completely amused me. Kind of like my own superhero. Or super-villain. Either way, we're crazy about each other. This whole fucking thing was crazy. I had no choice but to go with it.

Whatever I've brought here with me, I have the home advantage. My turf, my rules.

To my left, the lake's coastline bears the twinkling lights of the year-round residents. The illumination from the summer-houses is still a ways off. Something's not right, though. I have yet to hear Mrs. Halverson squawking for her mutt. Come to think of it, her place is quiet and dark. No sightings of her in that dreaded house dress. That much makes me glad. Maybe she's finally on a holiday.

While I zone out at the sparkling surface, something snags my attention in the distance. Movement creates a rippling trail, like a giant fish swimming for the dock. My heartbeat quickens as I swing my feet in circles, stirring up two small whirlpools.

I pray it's Melanie. I already feel her pressing against me. The memory of her kiss tasting and smelling like rain floods into my mind. That sensation of becoming one with her is all that matters. *Be with me forever*, she said. I think forever isn't long enough.

The water gathers, like a sculptor's creation. The lake in front of me animates, a crystal glob of liquid rising into the air and becoming the womanly configuration of my Melanie. A primal yearning swims in her eyes, her shapely breasts and hips begging for me to caress them. Her lips part, yet she doesn't speak. They pucker slightly.

I lean forward, ready to rush up and unleash my need for her.

But as she moves closer, Melanie transforms into a murky version of herself. The back hunches, the arms and hands growing crooked and misshapen. The breasts shrivel and elongate into hanging bags. The hips slant, legs the texture of ancient tree trunks disappearing into the lake below. As the facial features sharpen, the eyes deaden. Wrinkles spread like roads on a map, the cheeks sinking in and hollowing. Her prominent nose and chin are now too close together, the mouth withdrawing into a toothless abyss. Stray hairs branch up like jellyfish tentacles.

My heart drops. I should run, but my feet are two hunks of heavy iron submerged to the ankles.

The eyes flash bright green.

I pull my legs up and scoot the fuck back. The thing keeps advancing, devoid of any expression. At that moment I realize it's my neighbor, the details of her mustache and assorted moles right in my goddamn face. My eyes close as she presses into me. I lower myself backward while smelling putrid garbage. Bile rises in my throat.

Where's Melanie?

I cringe as its hands travel along my body. It climbs on top of me, legs flopping at my sides. The slick of pruned skin brushes mine. Instead of facing the sight of it, I swallow and keep still, holding my breath. A hand unzips my fly. My pants slide down my thighs. The dank evening air meets my nakedness. Goosebumps prickle my legs.

Paralyzed, I wince as a hand grips and manipulates my dick. I strain to block the sensation, but to no avail. The memory of Melanie and her every effort to please me—her lips gently brushing my face, neck, and chest—disappears like an elusive dream. Reality is a crone on top of me, pinning me to the dock. I lay motionless while the nightmare plays out. Her ancient genitals swallowing mine is more than I can bear. She wriggles and bobs unceasingly, trying to force an erection.

Suddenly, the she-fiend is still.

When I finally take a look, the creature's green eyes go dim, but the glow of the sun peeps along the horizon. An unnatural orange halo surrounds the swamp-like form, highlighting bits of algae swimming within her.

Her distorted legs restrain me with superhuman strength, while I try to conjure a desperate notion to roll away or break free. But that time never comes.

She gurgles, and foam escapes her mouth. *You didn't listen to me. I didn't want to leave.*

As the rays of dawn creep across the lake, the liquid monster disintegrates. All of the water cascades over me. My body feels less solid, like Jell-O—and getting thinner in consistency. Everything in my mind fades, my love for Melanie some distant thought bubble from a time before we met. Even before we existed.

The remaining rain of that thing blends with what's become of me. Together, it all splashes up from the dock's planks and then runs off through the slats and off the sides. Every one of our molecules is dripping, vanishing, leaving only a shallow puddle that will soon be dried up forever by the unforgiving sun.

STAY TUNED

By the time you hear me out, you'll be thinking it'll only be a matter of time before we're caught. My prep school buddies and me discussed that when making our business plan. We agreed it's worth the throng of subscribers on the DarkNet who appreciate our efforts, some even posting specific requests or giving us leads for upcoming episodes. We've become anonymously famous. It's glorious.

Our teachers, and later, professors, accused us of lacking focus. Follow through. Ambition. You name it. We were too busy skipping class to drag race or walk the perilous ledge of the clock tower—anything to feel more alive.

In the end it was clear the establishment's cards were stacked against me when I got kicked out. Apparently rescuing the headmaster's daughter from gang rape is a sure way to get blamed for it. Well, it's not like any of us need Shakespeare. Or stiff, meaningless corporate jobs. Fuck them. I literally roll around naked on a stash of Benjamins. Whenever.

I'm the brains of this operation. My instincts for the right

targets has served us well so far. The ideal age range is somewhere between five and eleven, although seven and eight have
proven to make the best videos. I know you're thinking I'm some
pedophiliac sicko, but that is just as revolting to me as it is you.
So cool your jets.

Before I tell you about the type of footage going on here, let
me cue you into the process. You see, camping outside suburban
gas stations, scoping out expensive cars and logging the ones with
child passengers is boring. But somebody's gotta do it.

I study the family dynamics, noticing who's at the wheel and
body language and all that crap. Believe it or not, the degree of
forcefulness when handling the pump and the cap on the gas tank
reveals quite a bit. That, and where those eyes roam while filling
up. What's carried out of the convenience store is noteworthy—
cigarettes or beer for himself, or candy and sodas for them? After
collecting data, I can tell how photogenic and interactive the
family is. Most importantly: how suggestible and easy to over-
power, if it comes to that.

Next step: log license plate and tail the vehicle home.
Surveillance goes on for as long as it takes.

Helpful hint: don't be sloppy. Just imagine there's a 'Smile,
You're on Camera' sign on the bars of the security gate. And there
usually is. At this stage of the game, I'm looking for something to
think about when I go through with it. I mean, I'm not a complete
asshole. So when I think about a father slapping his daughter on
the ride up the driveway, or sniffing his side piece's panties before
stuffing them back in his pocket—or throwing a rolled up rug into
the trunk, I feel way less guilty.

There's no actor, I don't care how Oscar-worthy, who can
perform as well as real people. That's why viewers pay us the big
bucks. The cherry on top? These reality stars pay *us* for it.

The kid on deck for this week's film always watches his dad's every move, his brain calculating how to respond accordingly so he won't get beat. I've seen his little bruised arm hanging out the passenger window. Far. too. Many. Times.

Anyway, before I punch a hole in the panel of my car door, let's continue. Once I've committed to the target, one of us raids the garbage for carelessly tossed information. Any gaps are just a few clicks away in any public computer. As luck has it, little Timothy's birthday is on this page of the calendar. At times, we're not so lucky.

Word to the wise: don't try to do it all alone.

When all the groundwork is laid, it's time to gear up for the money shot. A month before the event, the campaign launches. A flyer under the windshield. Wait a day or two. Flyer in the crack of the window. Promotional emails. Everyone loves a freaking discount. This 'unique' and 'custom made' party favor is guaranteed to be an experience "remembered for a lifetime."

That's an epic understatement.

Fast forward to my chat with the little whipper snapper when I catch him alone. What kind of unique whiz-bang would snaz up his party? A piñata, he says—in the shape of a rocket. Filled with an ocean of Jolly Ranchers. Then my mind films the scene. I can't keep from shaking. They won't know until the day of the party how much behind-the-scenes labor is behind the cinematic effect. Speaking of which, the set-up of the venue determines logistics. It's best to get up close and personal. We see if the parents want a face painter or magician for an additional 'promotional rate.'

We all take turns in the coveted spot, the live moment that makes it all worthwhile. Today I'm the clown and balloon-maker extraordinaire. It's the typical getup—the boiling hot red wig and thick makeup. Red nose and a beanie with one of those spinning things at the top. Polka dot suit that's as big as a tent. With the goofy glasses with the crazy swirls in the middle, I safely hide behind a high-pitched phony voice.

The kids gather around the piñata now dangling from a back-yard oak.

"It's so big!" one partygoer marvels.

That it is. It has to be for everything to go off without a hitch. For a second, I worry about my craftsmanship. The piñata only needs to hold up for a few more minutes anyway. But the anticipation is nearly killing me. Pun intended.

The birthday boy holds the stick while his mother ties the blindfold over his eyes. His hair fans out around the bandana circling his head. He stumbles along the grass, tottering closer to the rocket with rainbow-colored streamers all over it, while brandishing his weapon. Something in him is driving that thing through the air with violent force. All his pent-up anger and hatred flies. You see, his father's a no show. This little boy's been staring at the sliding glass door, preparing to cower. But it's been over an hour since everyone has arrived. His sister has been gabbing with her friends and taking her balloon unicorn for several flights.

This is the moment we've been waiting for. I could almost pee my damn polka dot suit with excitement, the hidden camera in my glasses recording each magnificent moment.

The kid finally takes the winning whack to the piñata. Out comes a shower of red dripping onto the birthday boy and several bystanders. Some wipe the spray from their eyes.

There are a few nervous and confused screams.

That stick is still a-whacking. A new wound in its side rips wide, chunks and bits spraying out. Partygoers lunge forward, picking up what they think is candy. A girl in pig-tails yanks her hand away, yelping as she runs into her mother's arms. A boy with thick glasses slips in the grass, the liquid splashing all over his face and covering his lenses with what looks like watery tomato sauce.

The birthday boy slides the blindfold from his eyes, glancing up at his handiwork as a severed hand falls from the piñata. He jerks aside just in time, not noticing the familiar watch on the wrist or the distinctively roped silver wedding band landing at his feet.

By now, it's pandemonium, but the screeches and commotion of the guests fleeing is all muffled background noise. My mind plays a soundtrack of Drowning Pool's "Let the Bodies Hit the Floor" and my veins pulse and throb.

I've side-stepped to the door like a country western clown, pausing as the notes in my brain build to a piercing climax. Nothing is so satisfying as witnessing brother, sister, and mother in a huddled mass, a decapitated head plummeting to the ground with a squish. She covers her children's eyes with her hands, bawling as she must've recognized the bloody face and sopping hair of her husband—the whites of his lifeless eyes crimson, his mouth agape.

Well, that's not how it went down. That was how it played out in my head.

The reality was more like this.

The little fucker had no aim whatsoever. Even though I rooted for him to save the day. Be a hero. Be the child superstar he was destined to be. As his weapon sailed aimlessly through the air, a crimson drop splatted onto mom's cheek. She wiped it and put her fingers to her nose. It seemed she considered tasting it just to be certain.

If only the piñata's innards had fallen then.

Instead, maternal instinct urged her to scoop up her son and yank her daughter by the arm. The mythical balloon creature popped, pieces of white and blue latex wilting on their way to the soon-to-be trampled earth.

"Everyone inside!" mom yelled with a craze-filled immediacy.

The blood saturated papier-mâché finally weakened, the piñata contents fighting for freedom. A red seam on the belly of the rocket spread wide as one of the other mothers corralled children with cake and frosting covered faces to the sliding door. Some fingers dangled lifelessly, blood trickling, then streaming.

"Come on, kiddies!" I called, my body in slow-motion, feigning helpfulness, still hoping for a last minute shot.

Trent had already cut the wire-fence, motioning to me to make a run for the idling getaway van as sirens wailed in the distance.

For a number of reasons, it was time to switch gears. Time to take a break from punishing terrible parental units. And, we set up a brand new base of operation, which is always smart. Keep the trail cold, just in case. There are enough empty warehouses all over the country to stay off the grid. A generator is really all you need.

It wasn't long before we got a lead from a fan. Her girlfriend was hot to do something special for her husband for their anniversary. What a cluster fuck, right? Not to mention I know what it's like to be slighted. Back at that party when I'd pulled a bunch of drunk dudes off that headmaster's daughter, even my own girl-friend didn't believe my side of the story. Like there's no such thing as a good guy. Ahem… whatever people want their realities to be.

Back to our regularly scheduled programming.

Our van was packed with the party supplies and audio-video equipment. Trent and I were already in our monkey suits with the ear pieces. He had on a realistic-looking blond wig and some blue contacts. I'd gotten a buzz cut and was wearing a pair of Clark Kent glasses with the camera. Oh, and the gloves. This was an occasion for gloves. Be sure to overthink all the ways one can get caught—hint, hint.

Right on schedule we pulled up to the rear of the mansion.

Trent and I got to work lugging out the enormous cake. The trick was to make it look as real as possible, even though no one was really going to eat it. I crossed myself in the hopes this contraption was up to snuff.

"How do I look?" the hostess asked.

Obliging her with a once over, I took in what must've taken a few hours. The faultless hair swept up and makeup, both clearly done at a salon, and her black satin dress clinging to all those exquisite nips and tucks. Her shiny new stilettos. "Smashing."

I gave her the okay sign and turned to Trent with raised eyebrows.

"Absolutely." He grinned, a twinkle in his eye, probably thinking about his mother decked out like that in her heyday when she was a groupie for '80s and '90s bands. For all Trent knew, his dad was Mick Jagger. If I even breathed a word about Reznor, he threw a hissy.

We rolled the sugary-looking monstrosity to the kitchen.

"Okay, so how do I get in?" she asked.

"Let me show you." Trent opened the trap door.

"Oh, pretty," she said, rubbing her hands over the sea of velvety red fabric.

Typical. I grabbed her wrist, fearful she'd trigger something prematurely.

We unfolded the step stool and helped her inside, reminding her one of us would tap on the side to give her the signal. The timing was bound to sort itself out much better this time around, especially if Trent and I could help it.

No one had to wait long.

The stiff-walking man of the hour clanked through the marble foyer and into the dark living room. Huffing to himself, he must've wondered why all the drapes were drawn for once. "Goddammit, Marla! What the fuck?" he said as he tripped over a lamp cord.

In the dim light, I caught a glimpse of Trent's smile.

Someone cued the lights. Another party-goer blasted some big band music from a record player in the corner.

Loosening his tie, Marla's husband craned his neck at the room-full of guests. The liver spots on his face stretched as he opened his mouth and ran a hand atop his comb-over.

Trent pushed the cake from the kitchen and into place, right front and center on the Parisian rug. I patted the side.

Almost forgetting to take a few steps back, I recalled the importance of angles and jumped to an appropriate spot. Her heels thumped into position as Marla got ready. A series of clicks and cranks sounded as the hinges creaked.

The loving wife popped upwards, reaching her arms above her head and striking a pose, which was a poor parody of one Marilyn Monroe would've executed flawlessly. Her red lips spread into a beauty pageant smile. "Surprise!" she exclaimed.

Curiously, the champagne glasses didn't shatter all around me.

The cake's timer ticked and then sputtered as all the appropriate mechanisms released.

A clean shriek of steel on steel. A series of blades raked Marla from head to knee, slicing through her cocktail dress and scraping her fishnets. She managed to moan. Blood ebbed from the gashes and the rivulets made her look like a human Twizzler. Another artillery of knives shot up at various angles. When the blades pulled away, hunks of Marla plummeted. Blood sprayed the onlookers, some frozen. Others howled or screamed as they scampered away.

A couple of crimson-covered bystanders looked our way, but Trent and I weren't too worried. The champagne had been laced with drugs, so there'd be quite a bit of doubt regarding their testimony. Plus, an explosion of confetti and smoke detonated from the lower tier of the cake. People coughed and hacked, rubbing their eyes. Tiny strips of multi-colored paper fell like snow.

I'd already given my buddy the nod for us to make a run for it. We'd stashed a change of clothes under the kitchen sink. It'd then just be a matter of hopping into the van.

Back at the lair we'd edit the footage and anticipate the thank you message from the jilted lover who sent us there in the first place. Cheers, little lady. Here's to a future girlfriend—who won't be some fake piece of shit.

What might be our next production? Our next lesson of vigilante justice? The possibilities are endless.

Stay tuned.

WHILE MY GUITAR GENTLY WEEPS

I chucked my work phone into the gutter, watching it shatter into a small shit storm of fractured plastic and metal. A feeling of satisfaction pumped through my veins. *Ha! They'll probably take that out of my paycheck—bastards!*

When I looked up to find out where the hell I was, a sign reading 'The Rising Sun' hung overhead. It was just the sign I needed. *Time to get shitfaced 'til dawn.* I could almost feel a buzz coming on. I realized I'd walked past this pub a few times while heading to my hotel, so I could stumble back there without much effort.

I passed the textured glass lit up from within the pub. The words above the corner door said 'Public Bar,' making me wonder if some bars weren't public, and how I might get an invite to one of those places.

Inside, chandeliers cast ominous shadows on the wood paneling. The joint was too classy for any neon signs—not the kind of hole-in-the-wall I was hoping for. My dress shoes clacked on the floorboards as I approached the bar, the glasses stocked on its overhead canopy leered at me.

A couple sucked each other's faces at a corner table, the woman's bare leg thrust up in her boyfriend's lap, her hiked-up jean skirt giving me a view of her black panties. One of the man's eyes opened and met mine in a warning to look away or there'd be trouble. I had no interest in ogling anymore of that side show. I could fire up the internet later if I wanted to see something worth getting hard over.

I parked my ass on a stool at the bar, trying not to spin on the seat as it rumbled and wavered. I felt like a kid on some kind of ride. Someone must've really loosened the thing. Maybe one of the regulars was Thor or some shit. Not too many regulars out after midnight, apparently. All the other stools were empty.

In a heavy British accent, the bartender spouted, "What ya hav'n, chap?"

"Whisky on the rocks." I crossed my arms and planted them on the bar.

He didn't ask what kind, but grabbed a bottle and glugged some of the amber-colored liquid over cubes of ice in a short glass. Loneliness hovered around me like buzzards waiting for the rest of my life to collapse. They wouldn't be waiting long. My personal phone was still playing dead in my pocket. No one would be messaging me. My instinct was to dial up Jamie. Old habit, but I had to break it. She was probably deleting every trace of me from her digital and actual life. Hopefully, she wouldn't smash all my old vinyl records while she was at it, but I knew I had to be prepared to kiss them all goodbye.

I needed to get my head together, figure out my next move. Getting the band back together crossed my mind. And not to play covers, but to create our own material. That had always been a kind of musical masturbation, but not just us jerking ourselves off.

Someone else would hear that shit and say, "That turns me on, too." That's music. That's what I missed. The days of playing with the band were long over. My life was spent.

Out of the corner of my eye I watched someone sit down next to me. *Of all the goddam places to sit, you couldn't give me some space?* Turning would be an invite for conversation, so I stared into the mirror lined with shelves of liquor. Next to the back of the bartender's bald head, I caught a glimpse of the stranger. His pretentious haircut fell over his weathered face. His red collared button down must've just come right out of the damn package. There was something about this dude that was oddly familiar, like maybe I'd seen him in a billboard somewhere.

"How's it going, mate?" The man made eye contact with the bartender and pointed to the vacant space in front of him where there should've been a drink.

Is that a pick up line? Maybe I do know him. Regardless, I didn't go in there to be bothered, but didn't want to be an asshole. "Do I know you?" I didn't turn my head. *Yeah, I'm being an asshole.*

"We're all connected somehow or another." Even his deep voice sounded familiar.

"I suppose." *This guy is so gay. Either that, or he's about to appear on Oprah's "Super Soul Sunday." One good thing about the divorce—I wouldn't have to hear any of that garbage on TV anymore.* My gaze was still fixed on the reflection ahead of me.

I'd be damned if I was going to get sucked into a philosophical conversation tonight. I couldn't recall anyone I ever knew who actually gave two shits about any of that crap. Well, maybe Jamie. With her, in the beginning, it was fun—to see her face light up, probably thinking about how we were deeply connecting. I pushed her out of my mind again.

A few minutes of silence allowed me to watch the water from

the ice mix with my drink. The glass felt cool to my lips, and I slugged most of it back. The stranger studied me in the mirror's reflection. Maybe he'd pay up his tab soon and get going. He didn't.

The couple at the corner table had come up for air, both of the woman's legs now draped over her date's lap. Couldn't they just go somewhere and screw already? Now that I could see her face as she rested her head on his shoulder, I thought I'd need to be paid to even consider tapping that. But, hey, there's someone for everyone. Right?

As I looked down, the dings and gauges in the wood of the bar made me wonder if Shakespeare had once set a pint of ale down on it. I picked up my second glass and rattled the ice, then sucked a cube into my mouth and crunched it. When I set the glass back on the bar, it slid along by itself for a few inches and stopped. The trail of sweat from the glass shined before starting to evaporate.

"The place's supposed to be haunted," the stranger said.

Did he see it too? I don't believe in that bullshit. But then again, my glass had just acted like it was slowly sliding into home base. "Yeah?" I didn't want to hear about it, but thought it might take my mind off things while I waited for the bartender to return. They always seemed to disappear when you wanted your check.

"Yep. Used to be an inn. The family that ran it killed some of the visitors and sold the bodies to medical science—a real bloody body snatcher scenario."

"No shit."

He traced the rim of his glass with his finger. "Kooky occurrences are always happening in here, especially after closing. Can't keep the bartenders too long. They eventually get spooked and literally throw in their towel."

"I see. You the manager?" *Where's that damn bartender? Or maybe I should just throw down some cash and be done with it.* I fumbled through my pocket for my wallet and slapped it on the counter.

"I'm the owner. Family business. Grew up with all the specters. They're family, too, I guess you could say." His finger still circled the rim because I could hear the slight hum.

I drummed my fingers on the bar. "I'm sure you have some good stories." *None of which I want to hear. Guy's friends are ghosts? I somehow attract all the crazies.*

"I don't mean to put you on edge, mate. But I have to say that you came in here with a pack of demons on your heels. Life's been beating you down?"

I threw back the rest of my booze. "You don't even want to know," I muttered. *Here we go. This is how he's gonna suck me into yapping with him.*

"Try me."

The whisky burned in my throat and also burned away most of my giving a rat's ass about what I might say and not say to this weirdo. It's not like I'd ever see him again. "Last business trip of my life."

"Congratulations?" He smirked, his cheek dimpled.

I laughed, swirling my drink that I thought I'd finished. Maybe I hadn't. "Yeah. Congrats, alright. You've no idea how much corruption I've seen over my lifetime."

"You'd be surprised." He sneered, slurping the rest of his liquor and wiping his mouth.

"You don't want to hear my problems."

"That's what I do—almost became a psychotherapist." He motioned for another round to the bartender whose bald head gleamed.

"Therapist, huh? Okay, let's see what you've got. Well, I should've never listened to my parents and walked away from that music scholarship." I wondered if the dude behind the bar would do another sleight of hand and feed me more whisky.

He had this blank look like he'd heard all this before, but being in the pub business probably lent itself to hearing a whole bunch of shit. "Good old folks probably just didn't want you to starve." He chuckled. "What'd you end up studying?"

I wasn't so sure what he was laughing at. "Business law." Just saying the words made my veins twitch and my stomach crawl.

"What happened after graduation?" His green eyes bored into mine as if this question held the meaning of life.

I looked away and back to my glass. The bartender poured more whisky over the ice. I lifted my chin in thanks. "Married the love of my life."

"Brilliant. Then what?"

"After years of my having to answer the phone on Thanksgiving, Christmas, and during sex, she left me." I paused, swallowing some of my refill. "I suppose I drove her to it. I mean, I wasn't even around to give her any kids."

He grunted and I could see him nod out of the corner of my eye. "So, after all that sacrifice, I bet your company sold you down the river."

"Yeah. Never got any thanks for it. Plus, I got so tired of covering up their cheating and skimming money. I finally snapped."

"So, what'd you do, have to put up your own 'employee of the month' picture up?" he asked.

How could he know I did exactly that a few weeks ago? "Yeah, in the hallway outside my office. You've obviously read my book on midlife crisis survival." I played it off with a jest.

"I'm somewhat of an expert in that department myself. Did you destroy your business phone yet? Your arch nemesis?"

This is getting creepy. Is he psychic? "Just smashed it on the sidewalk tonight."

"I figured." He beamed, swishing the whisky.

The oaky scent made me think of my basement where we had our jam sessions. My mom would always turn the lights on and off to signal that we were playing too loud. Lost in the past, strumming my guitar, the bar's wall fixtures flickered. I noted how the timing of that was pretty cool. *Somebody upstairs is having some fun, or maybe someone from the other side. That's a hoot!*

"So, what're going to do now you've quit your job?" he asked.

"My impossible dream would be to get the band back together." *I've got no wife to object. Might as well be out all hours and sleep all day.*

"Where're the other guys now?"

"Not doing much. Mick's living in Key West, drinking himself to death. I'd have to convince him to give up playing his guitar every night at Mallory Square. James's a retired paramedic the last I heard, but who knows if he also retired his drum sticks. Billy's probably still writing greeting cards, but he'd have to get used to writing lyrics again. We couldn't have that simple, sappy crap seeping into our songs. And poor Paul. We'd have to fill his spot somehow."

"Died, huh?"

"Yeah, hit by a car six years ago. He was the only noble one—used his lead singer charisma to become a priest." I took a closer look at the stranger and thought there was something about the shape of his eyes and the fired up enthusiasm that reminded me of a teenage Paul.

"I know."

He knows? He knows what? I felt my whole face tense in confusion.

"It's hard to lose a friend." He averted his eyes.

"Yeah." *This guy's a whacko.*

"Well, I seem to be your missing puzzle piece."

My eyes met his. "Excuse me?" *No, dude, you don't 'complete me'—or us, for that matter.*

"I'm proof there're no coincidences in life. I'm your singer."

"You sing?" I sputtered, slamming my glass on the bar.

"Pretty damn good, too." He started to sing "While My Guitar Gently Weeps." The tonality and range of his voice was so magnificent that it made me question what music really was. I lost myself in the words, to the point I no longer heard them or registered their meaning. For a moment I lost awareness of time and space, a chill running through my bones. The experience affected me so deeply I realized I never wrote a note of music in my life.

I took a look around the bar. Everyone had stopped to stare. The bartender held a glass and tilted bottle in midair. The couple that should have gotten a room had broken away from each other's lips to follow the source of the song. I felt my mouth had dropped open, so I snapped it closed. My eyebrows raised. "Damn."

His smile revealed crooked, but white teeth. "In the end, it's just a couple of notes."

"That's what you call it?"

He laughed. "Bring the guys here, where a lot of bands've found success."

"To London?" How the hell was I going to convince them? I'd have to ask for a recording of his voice. That would seal the deal for sure.

"Yep. We can practice here. And, I'll call in my industry contacts. Gotta chap over at the 100 Club who'd give us go."

Dang! That's where the Sex Pistols, the Clash, the Stones all played. I tried to silence the teen boy inside of me bouncing off the walls. "That's sounding pretty good." Minutes ago he had been bugging the shit out of me, talking of spirits disturbing the peace and getting up all in my business. One listen to his voice and it was all erased from my memory. "You've a band name in mind?"

"Soul Retrieval?" He smirked. "That'll come when everyone's together. Here." He pulled his wallet from his jeans and then handed me a business card embossed with a sun.

I took it without reading it and slid it into my shirt pocket. Something else had landed on the bar that I picked up. It was a concert ticket stamped "May 3, 1980, International Amphitheatre, The Who." Suddenly I was seventeen years old, listening with Paul to Roger Daltrey sing numbers from the *Who Are You* album. He and I stood out in the rain at the crack of dawn on a Saturday morning to score those tickets. *How the hell did this bastard have one? And what the hell had he been doing in Chicago?* I flipped the stub over and noticed it was signed, just like Paul's was. We had run into the lead singer on his way to the band's tour bus. It was one of our big moments as music fans.

"You were there?" I asked in disbelief.

"Sure was." He grimaced. "Kept thinking of how much I missed Keith Moon on drums."

"Yeah, he was awesome." I really didn't know what else to say.

"You see, our paths seemed to have crossed more than once, mate." After lifting the stub from my fingers, he tucked it back in his wallet.

"I don't believe it. And you got it signed?" I really wanted to press him for all the details, but I didn't. Maybe I was afraid they'd be exactly like what happened with Paul and me. Maybe a part of me didn't want to know. *Is that ticket even real?* Why someone would have a fake stub in their wallet suddenly seemed the stupidest thought I'd ever had.

"Yep, was a pretty wicked moment, I must say. Seems like you know exactly what I'm talking about."

"I certainly do." Funny thing was, I was getting more confused by the minute. The opening rifts of "Won't Get Fooled Again" played in the soundtrack of my mind. I remember thinking how weird that was—but then again, this whole night had been weird.

"And here we are—two musicians about to live a dream." He patted me on the shoulder. "You see, everything happens for a reason." The ice cubes jingled in the glass as he shook the last drops into his mouth.

Ignoring the Oprah crap spewing from his mouth, I was still drinking in the excitement of the band reuniting.

In those few seconds when I regarded him in the mirror, he suddenly looked distorted. His facial features seemed to drip like a waxy mess, and his sharp red shirt blurred and wilted. After rubbing my eyes, the reflection resumed its normal appearance. *For shit's sake, I haven't had that much to drink.* The stress of the day must have screwed me up more than I had realized—or, I was really losing my mind. Maybe that suggestive talk about this place being haunted was doing a number on me.

"Oh, there's only one thing. We'll have to give up our souls in return." He chortled loudly, throwing his head back.

"Oh, yeah. No problem." I laughed along. *This guy's got personality. Playing with him should be fucking fantastic.*

HEIRLOOM

Rachel tilted back in her office chair, trying to shake last night's nightmare. The shock of her stomach being a round mountain of nine months had her patting her flat tummy when she woke. This was a common dream for women, merely symbolic of birthing anything new. The only thing new today was a patient, hardly warranting this kind of anxiety. And, she had been testing her motherly inclinations by volunteering to hold abandoned and premature newborns at the local hospital. Although it seemed she was making a difference, by lending her human touch, the experience confirmed she didn't possess a maternal instinct. The nightmare didn't make sense.

Rachel turned her attention to the mirror on the opposite wall, bequeathed by her mother who seemed to float in the reflection with an air of poise, pressing her opera glasses to the living room window like always, scouting for exotic birds with her bright green eyes as sharp as an eagle's. But the image evaporated like a hot shower's steam once Rachel touched the glass.

After the antique was delivered to her office the previous day,

Rachel had to tip the maintenance man to secure the huge piece to the wall. The wood frame of the family heirloom was complexly hand-carved, the gold paint still bright in spots, but tarnished in others, dark grime deposited in the grooves. Edges of the glass near the frame were speckled with age. Its old character contrasted with the clean walls and Ikea furniture. But this was where Rachel spent most of her day, and it was where she wanted the reminder of her mother, the person who had encouraged her to study psychology.

Rachel's phone vibrated with a message from John. His full name popped up: *John Johnson*. His parents' lack of creativity still made her smile. He was free tonight, most likely eager to ask if she'd considered his marriage proposal. She sighed. He was too accommodating, too attentive, too understanding, and too open. It was smothering. When she had told him she couldn't have kids, he had graciously said that they'd adopt. Then, he had nervously twisted his mouth into the cutest contortion. She didn't have any interest in having children, no matter how adorable his lips were.

Hearing the outer door open, Rachel went to the waiting room, her heels clicking on the tile. This first appointment of the day was pro bono. The client had lost her job and insurance, but something about her story resonated with Rachel, who'd insisted that she keep coming for sessions.

"Good morning, Ashley. Come in."

Only in her twenties, Ashley dragged herself into the room in a wide-stepped waddle, reminiscent of a giant spouting *fee, fie, fo, fum*. Some days this amused Rachel. Today her thoughts cast a cloud of seriousness, something she shared with Ashley, who wore the expression of a pouting toddler.

"Bottle of water?" Rachel imagined Ashley as a kid, her now short choppy hair once long, bouncing with a child-like enthusiasm, and her khaki pants and striped T-shirt once a frilly dress.

Ashley clasped her hands in her lap after collapsing into the client chair. "I did it again." The red and black checkered rug stole her attention. "I'm pregnant."

Rachel gnawed the top of her pen. "I thought we talked about this." It was Ashley's third pregnancy since she'd been in therapy. Disappointed in her client's state, Rachel put her hand on her own stomach, details of the nightmare suddenly assaulting her thoughts. She had woken on a mattress in a primitive cave, the odor of earth and blood in the air. Rachel rubbed her forehead.

Ashley's gaze didn't leave the carpet. "I know."

"What happened?" Rachel refrained from inserting expletives, her disappointment in Ashley turning to anger, followed by a wave of empathy for the difficult decisions ahead. Rachel's dream fetus squirming and crushing her bladder was an uncomfortable blurring of the line between her and Ashley.

"The guy bought me a few drinks and the next thing I knew we were in the back of his van."

Exactly how many was a few drinks? They'd talked about waiting six dates before sex, the barest minimum being three dates. She watched Ashley spiral out, giving a play by play of the details. Peppered in between was commentary on what she should have done instead and how she was ashamed of herself.

Meanwhile, Rachel's mind kept running her nightmare's script. An old crone with striking emerald eyes had said this was Rachel's third baby—didn't she remember? *This one's destiny will be great.* A shaky hand had poured a half-shell of murky liquid into Rachel's mouth. An overwhelming fear for the unborn consumed her—a strong cord connecting her subconscious and conscious mind. It was all so vivid—she even smelled the herbs and something putrid in the concoction.

"Have you decided what you're going to do?" Rachel asked during a pause, unable to will away her queasiness. Was this what morning sickness was like? It was possible Ashley was going through it already. But Rachel didn't know why she was so sick.

"I have to have it." Ashley balled her fist and put it to her mouth.

Why this one and why now were questions for another session. "Okay. So, it'll be more important than ever that we continue your inner work." Rachel pressed her lips together. "We don't have time for a regression today, but it will be a priority next time." Her forehead heated.

Ashley uncrossed her legs and doubled over, moping.

"So what's your plan for the next couple of days?" Swallowing a lump in her throat, Rachel eyed the garbage in case the contents of her stomach came up.

"Keep looking for a job." Ashley's hand cupped her stomach. "And stay out of bars."

"Good."

Ashley nodded and got up to leave.

As Ashley closed the door, Rachel thought about her own patterns. The passionate romantic love of equals was always out of reach. John's helping her up and down the stairs of her condo, and washing and folding her laundry while she recovered from her hysterectomy was sweet. But it made her weak, needy, and even worse, his kindness made him too feminine. So far no man had possessed the right dynamic, the right fit.

Rachel sipped the cold coffee on her desk to combat the emotional exhaustion. She had ten minutes until her next client, who according to his file had only been giving one-word answers during sessions. Fortunately, her petite frame and youthfulness, which made her look like a teenager from afar, had something to do with her ability to break tough cases. That was the reason for the picture of the cat admiring a reflection of a lioness sitting on her desk, a gift from John, who also happened to be a therapist.

Rachel tapped into that energy, walking taller, as she went to the door.

The patient's arms and chest filled out his button down, and his jeans were on the tighter side. Intense dark eyes were framed by neatly styled brown hair—a very deliberate flair at the hairline, probably done with styling gel. Black rimmed glasses, magnifying his eyes, were perched on his face.

"Mr. Wilcox?" She extended her dainty hand and his swallowed it. "I'm Dr. Conrad." Something about him made her insides jumpy. Scads of clients had a criminal past, so it wasn't that. He triggered an incredibly disconcerting uneasiness impossible to explain.

Stepping further into her personal space, he smelled of cigarettes and maybe scotch.

She endured the uncomfortable closeness while he gave her the once over. He smirked. An apathetic recklessness lurked in his glare.

She kept a professional expression, which was rather like resting bitch face, and fiddled with her earring. "Would you like a water?" After motioning for him to help himself at the mini-fridge near her desk, she grabbed the manila folder and legal pad from the side table.

He took the water to the window, setting it on the sill. After pulling out an airplane-sized bottle of alcohol from his pocket, he proceeded to mix himself a cocktail.

Almost laughing out loud, Rachel confiscated his drink. "You're not doing this here." It was an effort to sustain her expression as she dropped the bottle into the trash can. "Have a seat."

He shrugged. Once he ran his hand through the side of his hair, he sat. He leaned back in the chair, his legs spread eagle.

Rachel took her seat. While she glimpsed the antique mirror, she thought the glass trembled. It wasn't the first time her mind had played tricks on her under duress, so she dismissed it.

She tapped the pencil on her lips. "By now, you know how this works." Earlier in her career, she would have started with something simple like whether or not he easily found her office, or maybe how long he had lived in Ft. Lauderdale. That only wasted the appointment. The goal was to expedite wellness. "What brings you in?"

He crossed his arms. "Got to be here, else I won't see my kids."

Rachel sat stiffly upright, hands folded. "Okay, so tell me more about that. Why is it mandated?"

His face relaxed, and his eyes softened. Her directness disarmed him. "Maybe I have *mommy* issues."

Rachel's eyes widened. "It appears more serious from the documents I have here." She tapped the pad and folder in her lap.

"It's complicated." He twisted the old-looking silver ring on his pinky, his eyes narrowing.

The fact that he possessed the air of a mafia boss planning his next hit amused her. The way he kept playing with the ring made her think he either had a form of OCD or it was an extension of his manliness.

The mirror jangled on the office wall, putting it off kilter.

"Did you see that?" She leapt up to prevent her family heirloom from crashing to the floor.

Her client might have continued speaking, but Rachel didn't hear it. The room was like a wind tunnel. She slowly put one foot in front of the other until she faced the mirror. Her reflection stood in a charcoal gray pantsuit, her straight chestnut-colored bob curled up at her sharp jaw. An unseen hand pulled her through the mirror. Her vision blurred—everything was funhouse trickery, colors and shapes morphing, until the world crisped and focused once again.

She stumbled onto the dirt, now in sandals kicking up some grit between her toes, and looked down to see her usually pale skin was bronze. Thick, wavy brown hair cascaded over her shoulders.

She blinked. Her bosom was more ample, and her hands lacked the pink polish she always stared at while on the phone back in her office. Supple suede covered her body. Silver armbands coiled around each bicep.

Sweat pearled all over her.

The day was sunny. A market bustled at her right, and an open plain lay silent to her left. Thatched roof buildings dotted the horizon. A wicker basket dangled on her arm. A horse-drawn wagon heaped with fruits and vegetables hurtled past her, the gravel stirred by the hooves and wheels disappearing in the distance.

Only a few steps away, a burly man emerged through a dust cloud. He wore a dark and tattered robe. His skin was tan, or grimy, and so were the rest of his features, his eyes shadowed by his protruding brow.

Weathered hands with dirt-encrusted nails swiftly gripped her by the arms, and forced her over a firm shoulder. She dropped the basket and screamed. He scurried to the covered wagon rolling closer, and threw her inside. Her legs brushed something hard suspended at his waist.

Then everything was like scraps of memory from a drunken night out. A dry rag was stuffed in Rachel's mouth. Rope bound her wrists and ankles. As the binding tightened, scraping her, she moaned. There was more than one man in the wagon, but she didn't know how many. Their faces floated around her like levitating severed heads. One of them had a maniacal, toothless grin.

Closing her eyes, she thought of her office—wishing to be

back there. But instead of the scent of the vanilla plug-in, a rank stench of body odor and booze hit her nose.

"I hope we got the right girl," one of the captors said in a husky, faraway voice.

His hands outlined the generous curves of a woman before lifting Rachel's chin. He nodded. "Blue eyes. It's the right one."

She shook her chin free, wondering if this was a psychotic slip. The wagon bumbled along as the wheels struggled over the crude road. She longed to see the landscape in order to memorize any landmarks in the slim chance it might be useful.

Someone pulled her off the wagon onto solid ground. One of the men untied her ankles and another pulled her by the rope at her wrists.

Rachel struggled for air, noticing the altitude change. A blanket of clouds swelled in the sky, and a wall of black rock disappeared up into the thick, puffy haze. The base of the mountain housed a row of rounded openings.

One of the assailants yanked her leash, forcing her into a cave, her sandaled feet leaving grooves in the dirt. The damp atmosphere hung thick. Goosebumps ran up and down Rachel's arms before she warmed from the torches mounted overhead. A rusty odor of earth and blood pervaded the pitch darkness. She flinched and her eyelid twitched when she realized it was the same smell from her nightmare.

At the back of the cave was a sheen of an iron linked chain coming from the wall, appearing serpentine along the floor.

The hairs raised along Rachel's arms and neck. Her heart pumped wildly as she recalled something at her captor's waist.

Disappearing into the rolls of his flesh was a scabbard. She knew what she had to do. These circumstances seemed vaguely familiar like a scene from a movie.

The jailer loosened the ropes at her wrists. As if she'd done this before, everything unfolding in this very sequence, she jerked free and slid the ropes off. Grappling with the folds of the man's belly, she ripped the dagger from its sheath. It was oddly comfortable in her hand. Gripping it tight, she swiftly plunged the steel into his heart, leaning on the blade, driving it deep.

He fell in anguish. His eyes bulged in surprise as he groaned. The chain clinked to the ground, and his knees buckled. Rachel pushed him onto his back, pinning him with her legs. She drew the dagger from his chest and stabbed him again and again. Blood sprayed her face and neck, dripping along her skin.

His hands fell limp at his sides, and his eyes lost their life.

Coming out of a trance, not fully realizing what she'd done, she let the weapon thump to the ground. At the sound of a commotion at the cave's entrance, she picked up the dagger and slithered into the shadows.

"Find her!" one of the men cried.

She had a sense she had lost time. Someone clutched her wrist, squeezing it until the knife thudded in the dirt.

She tried to wriggle free, but hands were all over her. Fingernails gouged her skin as the men yanked her arms and legs into the air, carrying her. At the wall, the chains clinked as they secured her wrists and ankles. She slid in resignation to the floor, hanging her head.

"She's *not* like all the others," the captor said.

"Apparently it's not just them blue eyes." The other one snorted and wiped his nose with his filthy hand as he ogled Rachel. "She's a fighter. Wonder if she has any *other* talents." His laugh betrayed impure thoughts.

Rachel curled into the fetal position. The sound of the chain echoed and faded into the recesses of her mind. Everything got smaller and smaller until she closed her eyes.

When Rachel came back to awareness, she lay on a coarse and lumpy mattress.

Mottled in her head were bits of a dream. She was blonde, long flowing hair spilling from under a silver headband encrusted with red stones. A silver belt cinched a leather bodice and short skirt hanging in strips. She swung a leg over a man sitting in a crude throne-like chair, her thigh high boot brushing his hilted sword. Pulling the blade from its sheath, she set it down on the banquet table. He smiled in anticipation, eyes turning black as if possessed by a demon. She held onto his face, putting her lips to his, his excitement evident beneath her.

Why her subconscious chose some Xena Warrior Princess fantasy, Rachel had no idea. Her mind was like the endless reflection of two mirrors facing each other. She was in a dream, having another dream. It was extremely disorienting, especially since she had no way to tell how much time had elapsed. For a moment, she identified with someone with multiple personality disorder.

Where she lay now, the walls were animal skin instead of stone. Cast iron caldrons of light stood at the four corners of the tent's dim interior. The flames rhythmically blazed up and dipped.

The tent flap peeled open and a man in a black robe strode through it. Whether he came from outside or from some other dimension, Rachel wasn't sure. He poured himself ruby-colored wine into a cup from a dulled iron pitcher. A prominent silver ring on his pinky finger shimmered in the firelight as he cast his head back to drain the liquid. He wiped his lips with an "Ah-h-h" and fingered the ring.

Rachel's heartbeat sped and her body trembled. She clutched the woolen blanket covering her. Her naked body was sore, especially down below. Her abdomen seemed tired and loose, her breasts swollen and full. She guessed this was the sensation of a new mother. Could she really have been in this place for over nine months?

After running his hand through his dark hair, his eyes narrowed. A twinge of unnerving memory struck Rachel. She knew she had seen that gesture before, and those deep-set eyes hiding malice and mayhem. Here, his penetrating glare burned with ownership.

As this familiar man stepped with determination to Rachel, her every muscle tensed. He squatted beside her. Fighting the urge to look away, she surmised she didn't get this tent upgrade by being meek and malleable. Boldly, eye to eye, she gulped deep breaths.

He stroked her like a cat while she gently took his hand and studied the ring. A blood-colored stone sparkled. Filigrees and scrolls decorated the silver setting. What could have been ancient symbols were marked on either side, continuing to the underside. She rubbed it with her thumb, recalling Wilcox fiddling with his ring. This man exhibited the same obsessive connection with his object of power.

"I am very pleased," he said as he freed his hand. "You have delivered your promise."

"My promise?" Rachel asked.

"Yes, this time a son, a protégé." The corners of his mouth turned up slightly, like a gladiator who had just slaughtered his foe in the middle of an arena.

How could she have made such a promise? Then she remembered her pregnancy nightmare. *This one's destiny will be great.* Is that what the ancient woman had meant?

"In fact, I'm *more* than pleased." His eyes went demonic black as quickly as ink bleeds through cloth.

Rachel shivered and drew back.

He grabbed her at the shoulders and mounted her. The scratchy blanket slid from her breasts. She whimpered as the pressure of his body on hers turned her soreness to sharp pain. His hand ready to rip the covering away, Rachel fought the urge to shrink away.

"Please." She violently drew up the woolen barrier, pressing it close.

The back of his hand thwacked her across the mouth, and she tasted coppery fluid on her tongue. "You forget I'm your *Master*," he said with a growl.

His eyes were so black. She got lost in the void where the guilt and shame of submitting festered. Her whole life had been a struggle to take her power back and now she had to give it away. "Yes, of course, M-master." The title stuck in her throat.

His inky eyes bored into hers, taking her deeper than before. She longed to look away, but didn't show weakness. So he stepped inside of her, making himself at home in her secret places, coaxing her shadow self to come out and play. Then he raised her invisible puppet strings and took hold of her will.

He flung his robe aside as he rose onto his knees. A musky scent of essential oil infiltrated the air. His gaze fell upon his readiness, and Rachel knew what he wanted. She sat up, took him in her mouth, and shut her eyes tight while he grunted in satisfaction.

When he finally tired and rolled over to sleep, Rachel got to her feet, wrapping the blanket around herself. The fires were dying in the caldrons, but a faint illumination remained.

She spun on her heels to survey the tent. In the far corner, propped against one of the beams was a gilded mirror, making the space seem double the size. She stepped closer. This was a newer version of the antique hanging in her office. The curves of the carvings were the same, yet the gold paint seemed fresher and there was less grit hiding in the grooves. No signs of tarnishing under the glass yet. For the briefest of moments, Rachel swore she saw the image of her mother, but when she examined the reflection, only the tent was behind her.

Putting her hand to the surface, it became liquid, like the rippling surface of a pool. When her body broke through the permeable barrier, she had no idea whether she was alive or dead, awake or dreaming. In this limbo, she transformed. Looking down, her skin lightened and her body slimmed. The water-like portal pulled her through and back into her office.

Standing on the area rug, she turned to the antique mirror at her back.

She patted her belly, grabbed at her breasts, and dug her nails into her wrist.

Her face in the reflection went white. She was in her red Calvin Klein dress and a black blazer, but didn't recall the last time she wore it. Her legs went rubbery.

At her desk, she lifted papers in search of her phone. Her hands trembled.

A knock sounded on the office door. "Doc, ya in there?"

She knew that voice.

Standing paralyzed, she considered ducking under the desk in case her door was unlocked. With her luck, he'd find her cowering under the furniture. That was a sure way to have to terminate the therapy, and to ruin her reputation.

Whenever a performer gets just enough mojo to go on stage,

even if deathly ill, that's what Rachel mustered. A little winded, she opened the door. "Mr. Wilcox. Come in."

"Call me Rick, will ya?" His voice rang forth cheerily, the smell of alcohol on his breath.

"We'll keep it Mr. Wilcox." All of her other clients were on a first name basis with her, a sign she was comfortable with *them*. She went to her seat, the pad of paper and folder already on the side table.

Her patient sat and palmed the side of his hair. He inhaled deeply, clenching his jaw and twisting his ring.

She swallowed, fighting off the memory of his dick in her mouth. The burn of guilt and regret filled her. It was the ultimate client-therapist violation.

"So tell me—m-more—about your childhood." The pencil shook in her hand, so she rested it in her lap.

"I was short, scrawny, wore glasses." His finger pushed the bridge of his frames. "Was bullied."

It was the classic victim turned bully scenario, if he spoke the truth.

"But I told you all of this *last week*. Don't you have your notes?" He pulled his sleeves down and crossed his arms.

Her heart galloped. She scrutinized the pad and flipped a few pages. Sure enough, the details were there. "I—I see. How did that make you feel?" Her body quivered.

"I didn't. Got into some drugs, *remember*?"

Rachel jotted this down, not sure what was noted and what wasn't. "So you self-medicated. That's fairly normal." She was befuddled, unprepared. Like she was under the influence herself. "Do those memories still surface?"

Darkness bled into his eyes. "I want to talk about how I feel *now*."

"Yes." Her stomach contracted. Rachel clamped her notepad

and the sweat dampened the yellow paper. "Okay, let's discuss what's on your mind."

"I'm overwhelmed by my thoughts. I'm not sure I can really say it out loud." His tone was laced with taunting.

"If you want to get *better*, we need to talk about it. It can't be that bad." But it could be *really* bad. And she couldn't detach herself from whatever was coming.

"I'm not sure I can."

Rachel squeezed the pencil. "How about this. You can write it down. I don't need to know. I can still help you." At the shelf, she obtained a blank composition notebook which was there for her clients to use as a journal.

Wilcox reached for the notebook. He licked his lips. Keeping steady eye contact with Rachel, he got up to help himself to a pen in the canister on her desk. Once returned to his chair, he began scribbling.

Periodically, his glare raked over her. She examined her calendar, searching for any stray notes or cancellations. Nothing amiss, appointments seemed status quo. She longed to scroll through her text messages and missed calls, but refrained. She had to keep a modicum of professionalism. Finally, the digital clock on her phone signaled the end of the hour.

After a subtle sigh of relief, Rachel said, "Well, our time is up. If you want to keep writing, you can take that with you." She folded her hands and squashed them together. Her fingers cracked.

"Why don't *you* keep it?" He got up and handed the book to her.

She followed him to the door and slid the notebook onto the shelf. "It will be here for your next visit."

He nodded. "Sounds good, doc."

And he was gone.

Rachel locked the door. Typically, reading through a patient's thoughts wasn't so pressing. She plucked the composition book off the shelf and flipped it open.

I just wanna get off the grid and shoot up heroin or oxycodone under the 42nd Street bridge. Hustling for cash on the corner. Shit, such freedom.

I'd hook up with my fav shorty. She thinks she's so in charge, wearing them suits. Hmmm... those get me hot. When she's sitting just a few feet away, I just wanna throw her down and rip her buttons off. I'd finally get a whiff of her panties. Mmmm...

She'd try her mumbo jumbo bullshit to stop me—but I'd make her do things she ain't done before. Things she ain't never do. Jesus, I can taste it—so sweet. I'd make her beg for it. Beg for me.

Can't you feel my hands, my cock inside you, Rachel? I've been dying to stick it to you since we first met. I know you want it. It's all over your face.

I can't wait till next time.

Yours forever, Rick.

Rachel smashed the book closed, and tottered to her chaise lounge. The fact was that they *had* been intimate—how many times, during how many past lives or dimensions, she didn't know. It couldn't have been just the one. What about that Xena the Warrior Princess dream?

She wished she had liquor stashed somewhere in the office, but it was probably better she didn't. A possible DUI lined up perfectly with the guilt and shame-ridden energy she was currently emitting, so it was fortunate this wasn't the case.

Her hands quaked, still holding the notebook. Wilcox's mere presence threatened her on so many levels. It frightened her that his words didn't entirely repulse her. Was she attracted to him? Did she want him? She pushed that from her mind.

She'd have to report his inappropriate inclinations, especially since he was so good at turning the tables. He expected her to invade his privacy, to want to dig deeper into his psyche, his soul. Pretending she didn't read the notebook was going to be a big test.

Just then, the mirror winked at her with a flash of light. The antique witnessed all of her fears, insecurities, and her anger at being so vulnerable. It was somehow alive with her emotions, seeming to know her better than she knew herself, magnifying the sensation of powerlessness to unbearable levels. Since she couldn't destroy herself, she had to get rid of *it*.

Rachel jerked the golden frame forward and lifted. The wire on the back wasn't unhooking, so she tugged upward until it snapped and the mirror plummeted into her hands.

She lugged the antique, her arms extended as wide as they could go. Angling and navigating the doorways and stairwell, Rachel staggered onto the pavement.

She rounded the corner to the Dumpster, heaped with bulging garbage bags. A sour smell blended with that of dead animals. Pizza covered in mold spilled from boxes. Chinese takeout containers leaked spoiled noodles. Padding burst from the ripped cushions of a chair. Rachel set the mirror on the concrete and wiped her temples. Then she picked it back up, hurling it with all her might onto the pile of refuse. It landed as if on a safety net, bouncing up and settling down.

The last thing Rachel wanted was for some other sucker to find this seemingly valuable treasure. So she scavenged through the neighboring vacant lot until she found a rock that she hurled at the mirror in the Dumpster, cracking the glass and sending shards to pierce the trash bags.

After dusting off her hands, Rachel climbed the stairs. Once inside her office, she gasped at the mirror back on the wall, which glowered at her like a defiant child.

She hauled ass into the hallway, practically tumbling down the stairs. Busting through the rear door, she rounded the bend to the Dumpster. Its open mouth was still crammed full of trash, but minus the mirror.

Rachel heard a thwacking and recoiled. Thankfully, it was just one of the awnings on the neighboring building flapping in the gust. She inhaled a lungful of fresh air.

The idea of Wilcox creeping around in the parking lot, in the bushes, around every corner of the building, leaked into her mind. Hearing a rustling in the shrubbery behind her, she jumped. Hand over her heart, she turned to observe a stray tabby cat scampering through the leaves and scurrying away.

The question of whether or not the mirror lay somewhere in the mountain of waste still pressed upon her. She stepped to the rim of Dumpster and reached for a two-by-four, using it to poke through the filthy contents. The antique was definitely not there.

Rachel kicked the side of the Dumpster.

Someone gripped her shoulder and she hopped. Her veins pulsed with adrenaline as she turned her head. To her relief, John stood there.

"Hey, I didn't mean to scare you. I saw your car and figured you had to be somewhere," he said, putting his hand effeminately to the front of his plaid button-down.

"Well, you scared me." Rachel's blood settled. "Congratulations."

"What are you doing out here with this junk? And why haven't you returned my calls?" John palmed the back of his neck, something he did when he was uncomfortable. "You look like you're wigging out."

"So sorry. I have a lot going on."

"Lemme buy you a drink."

"I need *more* than a drink."

"What's up?" His face looked worried, like he imagined this had something to do with *him*.

"This damn client Wilcox." Rachel noted John's insecurity and knew she wasn't making it any better. "He's got the hots for me."

"Why not? Good old Stockholm syndrome—plus, look at you." He raised a hesitant eyebrow. "What's the big deal?" His voice betrayed that it *was* a big deal.

Rachel had bigger things to worry about than John's jealousy and whatever other issues plagued him. "Things are getting weird."

"It's not the first nor the last time this'll happen. Confront it during your session. That usually works." There was a mixture of wounded puppy and a mustering of bad ass in his gaze.

"*Usually*, huh?" Rachel rolled her eyes. "Look, I need to finish some paperwork. Then I'm going home to crash." This standard therapist line was always the perfect excuse. He knew the plight firsthand.

"I thought we had plans. We still haven't talked." The hint of bass ass vanished.

"I'm so sorry. I can't."

"Look, I deserve some answers."

Rachel was impressed he was self-advocating. "I know. Just give me a little more time." Leaning in, she kissed him softly, hoping to appease him.

Her lips seemed to be a serum that gave him hope and patience. Nodding, a trace of a pout turning to a pucker, he fished his car keys from his pocket. It appeared he wanted to say more, to have the last word, but he grimaced and walked away.

Rachel entered the building, ascending the steps in slow motion. Pity and sadness were not the sensations she desired to experience with a romantic partner. Not that she wanted to be a rescued princess, either. That actually disgusted her. Where was the mate she could go head to head with? But other things cried out for Rachel's attention. When she opened the door at the top of the stairs, she half-expected to see Wilcox on the other side.

Thankfully, the hall was empty.

Back in her office, Rachel grabbed her purse from the desk. At the wall, she grasped the frame of the mirror with authority, heaving it from its place. She dragged the heirloom down to the backseat of her Toyota, planning to give the thing the same respect a serial killer gives his victim by leaving her abused and naked on the side of the road.

The next couple of days were like existing underwater. Rachel's thoughts were murky. She didn't want to move, much less to go in to work.

Once she left her condo, every strange man's face was Wilcox's. Had he been following her, she had no way of knowing. And, babies were suddenly everywhere. One good thing she focused on: the mirror stayed gone.

Driving to the office, she couldn't shrug the recent dreams. Sometimes she'd be giving birth, the agony so unbearable she'd awaken. Then there were the times that Master was sweating on top of her while she underwent the sharp pinch of conception, like her body rejected their union and the point of creation. She often cried uncontrollably upon waking, unable to erase the residual cellular memory.

Her phone rang.

"Hello?" Rachel said.

"Dr. Conrad, it's Ashley. I'm sorry, but I'm not going to make today."

"Oh? Everything alright?"

"I'm not well. I missed some of my anxiety meds." Her voice was unsteady. "On my way to pick up a refill now."

"Are you sure you don't want to come in?"

"Thanks, but I just want to stay home."

"You can tell me about it now if you want." Rachel hoped Ashley didn't hang up.

"It's nothing. It'll go away with the pills."

Rachel sensed it wasn't nothing, but knew it wasn't time to push. "Okay, call me if you want to come in earlier. And don't forget to tell the pharmacist about your condition." Meds and an unborn child were not the recipe for health. But Ashley had to get ahold of her mental faculties, as that was equally important for the fetus.

"Thanks. Sorry about today." Ashley hung up.

In her office, Rachel worried about her pregnant client. Maybe it was just the anxiety that troubled Ashley, but there was a chance she'd developed a severe coping mechanism. Rachel was going to have to ask a different line of questions and look for new evidence.

The outer door creaked. Rachel's palms moistened as she swung the office door open. "Come in, Mr. Wilcox."

He entered, carrying her mother's mirror. "Where'd ya want this?" he asked, propping the antique against his side.

Rachel blinked in rapid succession. "Where'd you get that?"

"In the hall. It's yours, isn't it?" He carried the mirror to the vacant wall where he looked up at the screw hole. "I'd put it up for you, but seems I'd need to bring some *tools*." Something about the way he spoke made the remark an innuendo.

Rachel cringed at his sleaziness, trying to forget his naked body pressing up to hers. It was so fresh and real, like he'd bedded her last night. "Just put it there."

He set it down. "Whatever you say." Then he took his chair, spinning his ring, a twinkle of crimson coming from his pinky.

After fetching the notebook from the shelf, Rachel sank into her seat. She tried to get a closer look at his ring, but he kept touching it. Firmly holding his gaze, she sat taller.

Wilcox eased back in his chair, his legs splayed. Uncapping the water she'd placed on the side table, his eyes softened, and he appeared to repress a smile. "What'd ya want to talk about today, doc?"

"I thought I'd leave that to you." She pressed her lips together, immediately regretting giving him control over the conversation.

He ran his hand through the side of his hair.

That always sent a chill through her. She clasped her hands and gripped them tight. Her palms continued to dampen. "How about—?"

Wilcox crossed his arms. "How 'bout whether or not ya read that." He eyed the book.

Rachel's insides were like soda and Pop Rocks fizzing. Perspiration dotted her upper lip. "Did you *want* me to?"

He grinned. "I'm interested in what *you* want."

"None of this is about *me*. You're here to work out *your* issues. Don't you want to see your kids?"

"I want lots of things."

She wasn't going to fall into that line of questioning. "We all want things. I think we need to get to the source of what makes you tick. Tell me about your mother." It was probably too early to press, but she wanted to push back on him, and hard.

"My mother?" His eyes shifted. "I didn't have a mother."

"Did she leave? Did she die? Where was she?" Rachel bent forward and intensely peered into his eyes.

"I dunno."

Her instinct told her he was lying. "What did your father tell you?"

"I went from foster home to foster home. There's nothing to tell."

"That's not in your file."

"Not everything's in the file, doc." He pulled at the hair at the nape of his neck.

"You're going to have to tell me about your past if any of this is going to work." Rachel resisted the urge to swing her crossed leg.

"That's not happening."

"How about you write about it?"

His eyebrow raised in a dramatic arch. "So ya can read it?"

"I'm not going to read it. If you want, you can take the notebook with you." Rachel got up and snatched a pencil from her desk, handing it and the book to him.

Needing the buffer between them, Rachel moved to her desk chair. Her fingers drummed on her thigh as she pretended to go through her notes.

While the clock ran out, Wilcox wrote quietly, radiating impure thoughts.

She refused to look at him directly, until the buzzer sounded.

Wilcox tried to pass her the book, but Rachel refused to take it. He wryly grinned.

"You keep it this time, remember? Until you trust me, you're in charge of it."

"Alrighty." He pursed his lips.

"Just make sure you bring it next time." She regretted not addressing his fixation on her. Avoidance. If only she could avoid her entire life, including her dreams.

He stepped nearer, bringing a whiff of cigarettes. "No hug goodbye?"

"No, Mr. Wilcox." Her attention on the door, she willed him to walk through it.

"You're no fun." He thumbed one of his pockets.

"If you keep this up, we'll need to terminate therapy." In her peripheral vision, he adjusted himself at his fly. It took all she had to keep her line of vision aboveboard.

"See ya, doc." He put a finger to his lips.

"G-goodbye, Mr. Wilcox."

A startling thwack of thunder boomed, followed by that of a downpour of rain. Rushing wind howled. Rachel glanced at the window. It was still light outside, the sun peeking through the wispy clouds. But ominous ones floated in the mirror.

Not noticing the sudden storm brewing, Wilcox went for the door. He turned to regard her one last time with an air of knowing the secrets they shared.

Rachel drilled her gaze into him, wondering how privy he was to their past together.

A strobe of lightning flashed from within the glass, wiping her thoughts away. She plodded to the mirror, watching sheets of rain falling in the reflection. A spray of water sprinkled her face. Her feet stuck to the floor, even though she had the urge to run.

Wilcox reached for the doorknob to leave.

Wind swirled around her, pushing her closer to the antique until she leapt through the liquid-like surface. She changed physically, filling out with womanly curves. Her short hair spilled out into thick, curly waves. Her skin darkened to soft mocha.

Rachel stood amid the cauldrons as the flames vaulted, generating long spectral shadows. Wind whistled outside and the pelting rain transitioned to the occasional drip on the hide of the tent.

A baby shrieked in the distance. Her heart hungered for the child not nursing at her milk-filled breast. She had never known such a painful separateness. It was worse than losing her mother. Worse than not knowing where her father was.

Following a cinching of the woolen blanket around her, she poured herself some red wine into a pewter cup, slugging the liquid courage.

Rachel pushed the flap of the tent open—nothing there, except darkness and the smell of rain. Bare feet touched the muddy earth. Gradually her vision sharpened. There was a smoldering campfire on the horizon, human silhouettes gathered around it. They piled kindling, fanning the embers back to life.

Rubbing the chill from her arms, Rachel walked toward the cluster of people. A droning vibration traveled on the breeze. The closer she got, the more it sounded like singing. She strained to listen for the fussing of a child. Was the crying she had heard only her imagination?

Rachel squinted into the night. Smoke spiraled into the air, and she whiffed frankincense and some unrecognizable herbs. An owl cooed nearby. She plastered herself against a massive rock.

Everyone in the crowd wore dark robes, fading into one another. Someone with long white hair spun around. Rachel locked with those maternal green eyes from her dream. The crone waved to the Master as Rachel contemplated her offspring's supposed *great destiny*. Would she ever know what that meant?

Rachel quickly slipped to the other side of the rock. Her fight or flight instinct prompted her to flee—but to where? Into one of the caves? Into the wilderness?

Just as she was about to run back to the tent, someone caught her by the arm. "I see you've changed your mind." His voice was calm, soothing.

Rachel peered into his familiar eyes, her knees buckling. "About what?"

He grinned, the pale moonlight highlighting his smooth face and the piece of upturned hair peeping from the hood of his cloak. "The tide of your soul is turning after all."

Rachel clutched the blanket tucked at her cleavage.

"You were *meant* to be here. Come." He motioned for her to follow. His congregation whispered amongst themselves, patiently waiting for a continuation of the ceremony.

"The gods smile upon us tonight." The low timber of his voice bellowed. The Master regarded Rachel with admiration and raised her hand into the air. After releasing his hold and she retreated, he signaled to his helpers.

Two hulking figures took their places at his side.

Rachel's legs wobbled and she closed her eyes. A sinister vibration enveloped her.

An infant wailed, shaking her back to awareness.

The Master took the bare baby and lifted it above his head. It squealed even louder.

The gathering sang words Rachel didn't understand.

"We offer this innocent life for your glory!" the Master proclaimed. Then he lowered the squirming newborn on the stone slab and waved his hands up.

The two other men closed in on the child. One man seized its arms, the other man snatched up the legs.

Rachel couldn't look away.

The baby yelled for loving arms.

Rachel fought the urge to run to the child—one that might

have been hers. Her heart broke thinking of the life never to be. Emptiness and grief consumed her.

She shut her eyes, not able to watch after all. The chanting masked any horrific sounds. But Rachel's imagination saw the animation in the blue eyes go out like waning flames surrendering to the darkness. She put her hands on her belly, a tear sliding down her cheek. Her stomach turned.

The crowd's droning rose up and then died.

Rachel finally opened her eyes. A red spattering covered each murderer, their black eyes vacant. No blade in sight, they had used their bare hands.

The Master's bloody palms painted his face crimson. He loosened the top of his robe to draw a symbol with two fingers on his chest. He shoved what looked like raw flesh into his mouth before putting his hands together in prayer and bowing to the altar.

Everything went dark as Rachel's legs finally gave way.

She lay in the Master's arms, his lips touching her forehead. He lightly snored while cradling her body in what seemed like a loving embrace, spiked with a sinister power.

Her awareness was foggy.

The memories of the horrors around the campfire blipped through her mind like a television shorting out. She pried herself from him and climbed off the bed.

The mirror loomed in the same place, this time covered with a black cloth. Time seemed to carry on without her on the other side. It must have been the same here.

Rachel went to unveil the antique, the material pooling on the ground. Her hand touched the surface. In the reflection, a dark shadow rose from the man on the mattress. Its ghastly shape swarmed to her and hovered above her head. Eyes like black marbles burned hot red for an instant. A wicked sneer faded as the figure disappeared through the mirror, taking ahold of Rachel's hand. It towed her through and everything whirled like a spinning kaleidoscope.

She sailed onto the carpet in her office, nearly floundering to the floor. The shadow rose up in front of her like a genie coming out of a bottle, before it evaporated.

Rachel scratched her head.

Someone knocked.

"One moment," she said, taking a look at her desk calendar. Then she realized she had no idea what day it was. Her hands covered her mouth. There wasn't time for her brain to process anything.

She took a swig from a half-consumed water bottle, hoping to ground herself.

After opening the door to the waiting room, Rachel sighed in relief. "Come in, Ashley."

The client sat, her back a bit straighter than the last session Rachel remembered.

Instead of noting the body language and commenting, Rachel searched the air, wondering where the shadow went—or what the hell could possibly happen next.

Rachel forced herself back into therapist mode, which was second nature. "Did the medication help you?"

"Yeah. The next day I was better." Ashley picked at her fingernails. "It's a lot less, but it still happens."

"What happens?" Rachel had to wrangle her attention. The blood. The innocent sacrifice. She repressed tears.

"I'll be like looking in a store window and there's a reflection —of something that's not there."

Rachel perked up and her eyes widened. "These could be important projections of your mind. What do you see?"

"There's no sense to it. Sometimes it looks like a pile of baby dolls. Other times—"

"Can you describe the dolls?" Rachel scratched her nose, her lip quivering behind her hand.

"They're naked. Some don't have eyes. Arms and legs are torn off. They're all scraped up." Ashley's eyes watered.

Rachel shuddered. "How does this make you feel?" The source of Ashley's vision could be her abandoned inner child, the abortions she had as a young woman, or a sign she didn't want to bring a child into the world. But it was the coincidence of what Rachel just experienced on the other side of the mirror that tormented her. Her heart broke again as she relived the slaughter in her mind.

"I'm so sad."

"It's okay. Allow yourself to feel. It's actually a strength. Honor it." But all Rachel wanted to do was make her own emotions stop.

Ashley wiped her eyes. "It doesn't feel like that."

Rachel's words sprang forth as if not her own. "Because you've been told not to feel, that your feelings didn't matter. But they *do*. They *do* matter. *You* matter. You're starting to realize that." If there was ever a time to face her own advice, it was now. She mattered. Emotions were power. However, it rang as psychobabble bullshit.

Ashley plucked a tissue from the box on the table and blew her nose.

There was more time in the session to kill before Rachel could wallow in her own problems. "Let's see if we can heal your inner child some more. We'll do another regression."

Ashley got up and reclined on the chaise.

Rachel led the client through some deep breaths and a descent down a spiral staircase. Meanwhile, there was a rewind of the Master telling Rachel he was pleased, that destiny brought her there. She literally stood by while it all happened. Her complicity was inescapable.

Rachel tapped her pencil on her chin to keep her present. "Once you get to the landing, what do you see?"

"It's dark. I don't see anything." Ashley's eyelids scrunched.

"It's okay. Just relax." She swung her leg back and forth.

Several seconds passed. Ashley's head rolled from side to side. "It's dark."

"Good. What else can you tell me?"

"I hear babies crying. So many babies. I can't see them, but I know they're there."

Rachel held her breath. "Trust what you're sensing. Do you see anyone? Do you see your inner child?" She bit her nail until she bled.

"There's a man. He's tall. I only see a shadow."

"That's okay. Does he seem familiar?" Uncrossing her leg, Rachel hunched forward.

"He tells me he's my father. But I'm scared."

Confronting father figures was always a good thing in therapy, but a strong apprehension paralyzed Rachel. "Is he someone you've known in this life?"

"No." Ashley's head lolled. "There is something wrong with his eyes."

Rachel jumped in her chair. "What do they look like?"

"They're black. They look like holes."

"He can't hurt you. I'm here." She bit her lip, attempting to believe the lie.

"Yes, you're my mom. You want me away from him."

"I'm *there* with you?"

"Yes."

"What do I look like?"

"Tan skin. Eyes so blue. Like they're now."

Rachel forced an inhale. "Do you know what you're doing in this place?"

"No. You won't tell me. You're crying and say to forget, to leave and never come back."

"Where is this place?"

Ashley paused, her head shaking. "I don't know. Carpathian something. Somewhere in the mountains. A long time ago."

The connection between their experiences became concrete as Rachel relived snippets of her cave abduction. The lines of subject and therapist blurred again. "Are you getting anything else?"

"No. You push me back to the stairs, telling me to leave."

"Why?"

"Because it's dangerous. The present can be altered." Ashley's forehead crinkled.

That was the point, to heal past and present, creating profound change. Rachel had done regressions many times. It wasn't dangerous at all. "That's okay. You are there to *release* the past."

"You're saying something about the mirror."

Rachel gripped her pencil tight. "Oh?"

"Something about not going through it?" Ashley thrashed her head back and forth, her body stiffening.

Nothing made sense, yet it all made sense. Was it a past life? Was it their alternate selves? Rachel had read that we all have counterparts existing in other realms at the same time. "Okay, it's time to climb the staircase. With every step you are more and more relaxed…"

After Ashley had gone, Rachel stood by the window, watching the clouds wander, hoping to calm down. They morphed, creating fluid shapes. A profile of a man with a beard became a stork. Then like an apocalyptic nightmare, she swore the entire sky washed with crimson. Blood. Motherhood. Birth. Life. Death.

Strangely, the portal hadn't been active today. As much as that was a relief, Rachel contemplated what was different. There had to be some catalyst that activated the phenomenon.

Glancing down at the courtyard, she noticed someone sitting on the bench. His legs spread apart and his arm stretched out along the top. That signature curl of the man's hair was just like Wilcox's. He peered up at her window. His dark eyes flashed in the sunlight while he puckered his lips, kissing the air.

Rachel's heart hammered. She wanted to duck out of view. Instead, she stared right at him. A blue jay landed on a nearby branch. When she turned her attention back to the bench, Wilcox had vanished. How she didn't detect his departure, she hadn't a clue. Was he even there at all?

She went to examine the mirror's age spots to clear her thoughts. The flecks of brown-gray splotches dotting the edges looked like eyes, and she wondered what they'd seen coming and going. Did her mother ever have any experiences?

Putting her hand flush against the surface, she studied the duplicate hand outlining hers. The surface didn't ripple. Nothing amiss caught her eye in the reflection. The horrific game being played with her soul, with her life, on the heirloom's terms, infuriated her. She longed to blame it all on Wilcox, but he wasn't pushing her through the portal.

And then there were the dreams. The memory of the latest one shot into her mind. Her gut wrenched with starvation as she stared at a bowl of raw meat. The cold glob of flesh was wet with blood. It dripped through her fingers when she slurped the last bits into her mouth. In the mirror's reflection, runnels of red dribbled from her lips and gore covered her teeth, the shrill cry of an infant ringing in her brain.

Standing in her office, sorrow made her want to shriek and drop to the floor. She had to find a way to end it all. Rachel grabbed her purse from the drawer and pocketed her phone, glimpsing the mirror glinting at her in the late afternoon light. That bottle of prosecco called to her from inside the refrigerator door at home. Passing out on the couch was the only way to forget.

When outer door squeaked, she braced herself for it to be Wilcox. Digging her hand in her purse, she gripped the gun she had started carrying, her finger searching for the trigger.

Rachel let out her breath and loosened her hold on the gun as a man in a brown uniform strolled into the room.

He held an electronic device and punched in some information. "Good afternoon."

Too stunned to speak, she set her purse down and signed the digital screen.

"Have a great one." He handed her the delivery and left.

The return address was "Katz and Associates, LLC." She ripped the paper and pulled out the letter and a small envelope marked "For Rachel."

The attorney stated he'd come across the document in her mother's safe deposit box. She admired the familiar rendition of her name before opening the note.

Rachel skimmed the words and zeroed in on the crux of the message.

Perhaps you will understand this reoccurring dream.

A dark shadow flies to me, flaunting a silver ring with a ruby or garnet and symbols marked on the sides. I have no such ring, nor have I seen it, but the shadow always whispers your name. Whenever I stared into that old mirror, I thought about how that ring must have some kind of power. I know it sounds silly, but I've always thought the mirror was alive—it's made me wonder who in our family acquired it and where it came from.

Anyway, I can rest, knowing I have told you. I wish you a long happy life and hope to see you again, my dearest. Love always, Mom.

Rachel sat on top of her desk, her hands crunching the letter in her lap. Her thoughts raced about Wilcox and the ring. A terrible idea popped into her head, but her mind was made up. It was the only way to put an end to her madness.

A row of pregnant women slumped on a dirt floor, manacles cinching their arms and legs, darkness shrouding them. The cave emanated the most profound despair. Rachel couldn't look away. One of the women clawed her own face, her cheeks shredding as she scraped, chunks of flesh dropping onto her chest. Her breasts were already gouged, blood dripping from gaping wounds. Milk dribbled from her nipples. The white and crimson streams ran down her nakedness, rolling along her swollen belly. The mother next to her ripped out fistfuls of hair as she wailed in unimaginable anguish.

Infants screeched like prehistoric birds. Amid it all, a man finished thrusting into one of the women he pinned to the wall.

Her head hung, her face wet with tears. He pushed off her, letting her fall to the ground.

His black eyes found Rachel's. She looked away, noticing a teenage boy, his back pressed against the wall. His eyelids were shut tight and his mouth twisted and puckered, just like John did when flustered. "Some protégé," Master barked.

She'd woken herself up with her own snores before, but had never screamed herself awake. Gasping for air, Rachel dashed from the bed and gripped the toilet seat, dry heaving into the bowl.

Rachel's mind was numb as she drove to her office.

Turning the key in the door, she noted the scraps of gel polish clinging to her nails. One of her jagged fingernails snagged her dress as she teetered into the room. She caught a glimpse of her make-up free face in the mirror as she passed. Her hair was only a slightly neater version of bed head. Rubbing her tongue across her teeth, she realized she'd forgotten to brush. She swished a swig of water and swallowed. After spraying herself with perfume, she set the bottle of Zephyrhills on the side table.

Tapping her foot, she watched the digital clock on the wall.

He'd arrive any minute.

Once the outer door sounded, she rushed to let him in.

"Mr. Wilcox, thanks for coming in." She waved him across the threshold.

"Any excuse to see you." He winked. "I like your new look, by the way. Sexy."

"Have a seat." She fumbled through the papers on her desk. "It's here somewhere."

"A little unprepared today, huh?"

Pulling the desk drawers open, she rummaged through the folders. "I just had it."

He studied her every move.

"Here it is." After whipping the form from the file, she passed it to him.

"Pretty sure I signed this one already." He tilted his head while taking the pen from her.

"If you did, it's not in your file." Lying was not one of her talents. "Your caseworker is going to be checking in. I'd hate for all the ducks not to be in a row."

Smacking his lips, he autographed the form.

Rachel glimpsed the bottle on the table. He'd usually have opened it by now. "This might be a good time to address your flirtations."

He laughed. "Who, me?"

"You know exactly what I'm talking about."

Leaning back, he patted his hands on his thighs. "Does it bother you?"

"That's not the issue here, Mr. Wilcox. The issue is that I'm here to help you as your *therapist*. I'm calling this to your attention so we can continue a professional relationship. It also gives you the opportunity to correct your behavior."

"And if I don't?"

The lack of sleep and her shot nerves were wearing away her filter. She wanted desperately to swear at him. "You know the answer to that."

"Okay, I'll behave, doc." He smirked as if they just had sex. All the vivid positions of their intertwined bodies probably reeled through his mind.

She tightened her teeth, fanning herself with the file folder. There was a flash of him getting up, seizing her by the arms, and kissing her passionately. Her body surrendered as if it was happening in real time.

He uncapped the Zephyrhills and drank, watching her cheeks flush.

Discovering some gum from her desk drawer, she popped a piece in her mouth. Soon she was chewing it like she was Olivia Newton John in her hot pants, a shred of her feminine power emerging.

"Well…I-I t-think I-I-I'll be going, d-doc."

She pushed back in her chair, mentally thanking one of her addict clients for mentioning where he met his dealer. It had come in pretty handy last night when she scored the GHB. She was half-ashamed of herself for stooping so low and half-proud of the balls she had mustered.

Wilcox's eyes lost their bad boy fierceness. His head bobbed as he struggled to stay conscious. He jerked to alertness. "What the f-f-fuck have y-y-yo-o-ou done?"

Rachel rose and approached him. "Who, *me*?" she asked in a mocking tone.

He tried to get to his feet, but he plopped back into his chair. His lips moved, but no words came out. After swaying back and forth, he collapsed, arms dangling to the floor and drool pooling at the corners of his mouth.

Rachel picked up his hand and regarded the ring. She had to twist and finagle it from his finger. All the while she watched his face to make sure he didn't wake.

Once the ring was in her palm, she breathed easier. Slipping the silver piece on her forefinger, she was surprised at how perfectly it sat there. Admiring the red stone glimmering in the lamplight, it seemed as if the jewelry had always been hers.

Her vulnerability faded, and an intense determination replaced it. As she kicked off her heels and confronted the mirror, she sensed it bending to her will. The surface stirred as if a finger dipped into the liquid glass. Her reflection rippled, her blue eyes turning the color of the deep ocean, almost black. Not waiting for an unseen hand, Rachel boldly stepped through the pervious barrier leading to the other side.

In the tent's glow, he slept peacefully on the mattress. Rachel gingerly slipped the ring from his finger as he stirred.

His eyelids opened, revealing a gentleness there. Although still familiar, his eyes were a light hazel. While climbing onto him, she put the ring on, smiling to herself.

He appeared startled, but didn't protest as Rachel bent down to kiss him. His lips were eager for hers as he grabbed ahold of her hips. The bond between them, whatever it was, coursed within her. For a moment they seemed as equals—finally, it was happening. She allowed herself to embrace the sensation as her body awakened, so alive, so aroused, like never before.

Any residual guilt and shame melted away. The victim energy disintegrated. She had come back here to end the nightmares, to end the infanticide. She was terminating the suffering of all the breeders and the life they spawned. Then she'd be healed, and maybe by proxy, so would Ashley and Wilcox. No more powerlessness. Her soul independent and whole—her own inner child safe at long last.

These noble ideas ebbed and flowed. She rolled onto her side, drawing her lover to her. The dark shadow she'd encountered awhile before had materialized in the center of the tent, suspended above them, its eyes burning like flames. The face was a black skull. Its talons unfurled in wisps, one pointing to the mirror.

You can end it all. Kill him. It's the only way.

That was like murdering herself. As she continued to kiss the man in her arms, she no longer feared him. But she knew not to trust the shadow. She closed her eyes, ignoring its urging.

A gust of air blew against her face. The skull's flaming glare was only inches from her as it floated at her lover's back.

Wilcox has woken. He knows what you've done.

She didn't care what happened on the other side of the mirror. The ring was here. It was on *her* finger. What did it matter what took place in the present? She was righting the wrongs in the here and now.

Ah, but if this one goes back there. That'll change everything.

What did that even mean? Suddenly fear prickled in her belly as the shadow dissolved into the body of the man with her on the bed. His eyes turned black. A frightening anger roused in him as he shoved her aside. The force sent her tumbling from the mattress and onto the ground.

He went for the mirror, the glass twinkling with warm candlelight.

She scrambled to her feet and searched for a heavy object—any heavy object.

Closer and closer to the portal he marched, his hand beckoning to the reflection. His intent expression was accented by the slightest grin—one that indicated a plan.

Rachel lunged for the pewter cup next to the wine. With all the force she could muster, she launched it at the mirror. The image of the man surrounded by the golden light shattered as the shards of glass clinked to the floor. While the shadow left her lover's body and dissipated amid the broken fragments, he toppled lifelessly to the ground.

She sank to her knees. Putting her hands to her face, she knew there was no going back.

A servant boy held a silver bowl. Rachel's thick chestnut tresses pooled over her shoulders. Eyes black as midnight looked back at her from the surface of the water as she wet a cloth and cleaned her face and neck.

Any recollection of her life as a therapist or a man named Wilcox somewhere in another time and place was erased.

"Bring him to me," she said forcefully, beaming with expectancy.

The boy bowed. After a few minutes, he tugged the leash of a collared man. The captive's hazel eyes studied the floor as he obediently trudged along.

Rachel loosened her ebony robe while sauntering to the mattress that lay between them. "Look at me," she barked.

He hesitated, so she reached for his chin and lifted it.

"I said look at *me*."

He finally did as she commanded. "Yes, Master."

They had taken her purse, her hat and gloves, and made her surrender her jewelry.

"It's for your safety, Ms. Rachel," the nurse with emerald-colored eyes said. "You follow the rules, and you might just get out of here—just in time to fulfill a *great destiny*." She plopped a few pills into a tiny paper cup.

Rachel considered the consequences of telling the woman to fuck off. That's what she really wanted to do, but she was in enough trouble already.

"We all have one, you know." The nurse adjusted the pins on her cap.

Rachel chased the pills down with water, studying the linoleum.

"A destiny," she said, as if Rachel cared.

"Oh." Rachel's face was devoid of expression.

Smacking her gum, the nurse regarded Rachel's face. "Weird. Something about you is so familiar."

Rachel dispatched a look of irritation, rolling her eyes.

In a daze Rachel followed a waddling orderly, who puffed on a cigarette, down a sterile white hallway and through the communal room. A female patient swayed to Jo Stafford's "You Belong to Me" crooning from the radio. *Maybe you'll be lonesome too...and blue...Just remember until you're home again...* The same song had played when Rachel and Johnny were in her basement. His lips contorted nervously as she, wearing only her Bobby socks, shoved him back on the couch, pinning him by the wrists. Although his eyelids widened in surprise, she felt him through his pants. Having grown bored of his submission, this time she had raised the stakes, wanting to hurt him.

In one of the rooms down the next hallway, a young woman hugged her knees, rocking herself on the bed. Beyond another window, a girl knocked her forehead on the glass, her eyes crossed and her sweaty hair clinging to her scarred cheeks.

Rachel refused to examine the other rooms as they went by. The orderly almost disappeared into the walls in his white smock and pants. Stopping in front of a metal door with a rectangular strip of glass, he handed her a cotton gown and pair of slippers. "Leave your clothes on the bed. I'll be back to take you to your session with the doctor."

Rachel tripped into the cell, the door clanking at her back. She harvested the ring from her bra, admiring the blood red stone sparkling in the sunlight from the tiny window above. Rubbing the silver with her thumb, she swiftly tucked it away again before anyone caught her with it.

Then she changed into the gown, folding her pink floral dress at the edge of the bed. Her lividness at being in here riled under waves of giddy euphoria.

She hummed as the orderly returned and led her to an office at the end of the hall.

The doctor behind the desk wasn't the ordinary-looking nerd she'd expected. His short brown hair curled up just above his forehead, and she wondered if it was a cowlick or if he intentionally styled it that way. His kind hazel eyes hid behind horned rimmed glasses.

She stood in front of the desk, pulling her gown tight against her womanly figure with one hand. With the other hand, she traced a line from her neck to her décolleté. An eyebrow raised, she projected a feigned innocence.

He averted his eyes. "Please, have a seat."

Wetting her lips, she lowered herself into the chair. "Only since you asked me so *nicely*," she purred.

"Do you know why you are here?" he asked.

She twirled a dirty blonde lock around her finger. "I'm sure you'll remind me."

His brow wrinkled while he jotted something down. Perspiration dotted his temples. "Tell me about the neighbor boy—about the restraints."

She bit her lip, remembering Johnny writhing beneath her, not asking her to stop. She examined the therapist's mouth, wondering what he'd taste like. Chuckling deviously, the lock of hair wound even tighter on her finger. "Oh, that?"

"Yes *that*. That has your father in a very serious pickle. Do you understand the gravity of this?" He pushed the bridge of his glasses and ran his hand through the side of his hair.

"I understand *lots* of things, doc." Rachel leaned forward, the V-necked gown revealing her ample cleavage.

The therapist didn't peek, but she knew he took in the sight in his peripheral vision.

"I see." He adjusted his glasses. "Like that you could be pregnant?"

"Why—because we're all just baby machines, is that it?" She bit her lip, the drugs stripping away her filter.

"It's not that simple."

"Isn't it? My mother cooks and cleans in a dress and high heels. That's not what *I* want. Can you understand that, doc?" She ran her fingers up her thigh, gradually peeling back the gown.

He got up to open the window.

"It *is* getting hot in here." Turning to the gilded mirror to her right, she admired his ass in the reflection. The daylight beamed around him, making him angel-like. She grinned devilishly to herself, fishing the ring from her bra and enclosing it in her palm.

A deep sigh exhaled from his lungs. "We must work on redirecting the tide of your soul. You're on a slippery slope—but it *can* be corrected." He spun around in a daze, watching something in the mirror.

The ring now on Rachel's finger, she played with it.

Seemingly in a trance, the therapist paced toward his reflection, his hand outstretched…

ABOUT THE AUTHOR

Theresa Braun was born in St. Paul, Minnesota and has carried some of that hardiness with her to South Florida where she currently resides. An English teacher and adjunct college professor for over twenty years, she continues to share her enthusiasm for literary arts with her students. She earned a Masters in English literature with a thesis on Shakespeare's *Twelfth Night*. In her spare time, she enjoys delving into her own creative writing, painting, photography and even ghost hunting. Spending time with her family and traveling as often possible are two of her passions. In fact, her world meanderings are often backdrops for her work. Striving to make the world a better place is something dear to her heart. When she's not writing, she can be found looking for romance or shopping for antiques.

For more information and to stay up to date with Theresa's latest, check out her social media!

www.theresabraun.com

facebook.com/theresa.anne.braun

twitter.com/tbraun_author

instagram.com/theresa.anne.braun

tiktok.com/@tbraun_author

amazon.com/Theresa-Braun/e/B007YTA6C2

ALSO BY THERESA BRAUN

Standalones

Fountain Dead

Dead Over Heels

Dying for an Invitation

The Celestial Assignment

Anthologies

Double-Barrel Horror

Best Indie Speculative Fiction

Strange Behaviors

Monsters Exist

Society of Misfits Stories

Hardened Hearts

The Horror Zine

Schlock Webzine

Emporium of Superstition